THE VAMPIRE DOESN'T LIVE HERE ANYMORE

Eric Robespierre

Library of Congress Control Number:
ISBN: 978-1-7365781-3-1
Published by Eric Robespierre
www.ericrobespierre.com

ALSO BY
ERIC ROBESPIERRE

The Yummy Hunter's Guide
The Best-Tasting, Low-Calorie Foods and Where to Shop for Them
(With Helen Brand)

Cracking the Walnut
How Being a Little Nuts Helped Me to Beat Prostate Cancer

Living Large in America
The Life and Times of the Family Ginsburg (pronounced Du Pont)

Lighten Up and Log In For Love
How Humor Helps Baby Boomers Survive Online Dating

We Gave Them Life, Now They're Trying To Take Ours
How To Successfully Communicate
With Adult Children Before It's Too Late

Sex, Meds, Livin' The Covid Life

Sex, Meds, Reincarnation, Livin' The Covid Life

The Muse Who Served Me Breakfast

ACKNOWLEDGMENTS

I owe a debt of gratitude to Robert Leung, my former agency art director, who again showed his brilliance when I asked him to create this cover. To Audrey Winograde for her diligent and superlative copyediting. To the multi-talented, Richellb, who again designed my book's interior and cover and formatted the e-book.

"Feeling a bit batty?
Just wing it and
write a book about vampires!"

— THE AUTHOR

*"The two most important days
in your life are the day you are born
and the day you find out why."*

— MARK TWAIN

DOWN BY CONTACT

Life was going so well for me. I believed I was a two hundred and fifty-nine-five-year-old Hollywood handsome vampire, never suffering from the *ennui* of so many of my bloodsucking pals and living the life of Reily or *viviendo la vida* if he spoke Spanish, when I stumble over a stupid subway grating on East Thirty-Fifth steps away from Madison Avenue and my apartment, like some clumsy old fogey who doesn't have an immortal trip advisor installed, and hit my supposedly impenetrable headset silly and lose all memory of who I am. And that changed everything.

Holies of Molies, I know the God of the Old Testament divided light from darkness, but first turning me into *El Supremo Vampire* and giving me a taste of life everlasting and then pulling my feet from under me and turning me back to *Inferioroso Humano* is one mortal coil too many and not something to give one a funny face.

I'm not bitter, mind you. Okay, I may be a little. And, all righty, perhaps the world is a safer place with one less vampire sucking the blood out of some innocent woman. That's right. I'm straight and proud of it, although back in 1765—we'll leave my last *tête te neck* with Napoleon for the yet-to-be-written chapter in my tell-all biography,

"Famous Necks I Have Known." (I am writing something else, but more on that later.)

Let's get back in a hurry, Murray, to my anger issues. Oh, what? Do you think vampires are above it all? No, no, and no. Just like real folks, we get pissed-silly when we lose our baby fangs and don't find any money under our pillow.

And boy, was I perturbed when I finally found out how fucked I was when I became a monster without being a myth.

I love that word, don't you? No, not *fucked*, although I love that word too. *Perturbed.* It sounds like something Shakespeare would say when being messed about.

It's been eleven years since I took up residence in Murray Hill under the name Nick Cummings. Ten years in one place without showing a wrinkle is usually the limit before people get suspicious. In this case and with several other residencies, I've stretched it out by hinting that I've had a touch of cosmetic beautification. It's remarkable how a lovely lid lift to get the orbs to glow like keg lights will make the neighboring Gossip Girls believe you're 'younger than springtime,' which, at a perennial thirty-something, is the standard definition of 'someone getting pulled out of your normal life by a mysterious call.'

In truth, I was just seventeen and known as Bernard Bertrand when I was so rudely transformed. It was wartime (wasn't it always back then?), and the ravages of battle aged me twenty years and made me appear as I do today and will forever more.

Hold on, everyone, to the edges of your books, Kindles, or whatever miniature electronic devices you're ruining your eyes on—I'm jumping around too much and probably have you saying to yourself, what the fuck? So, let me provide a little backstory.

One month ago, give or take, I lost my footing in my favorite tan Alan Edmonds slip-ons and did a face-plant on the pavement, the force of which landed me in La-La Land for two days, or so they tell me.

When I woke up, I was in a hospital bed and had absolutely *no* memory of how I got there or who I was, which is a good thing because if they found out who I was, I'd be the first one they blamed for a shortage of O negative.

The doctors kept me for observation for a third day and then released me onto the sidewalk of First Avenue and 31st Street—talk about a rush! The neuro guys wanted to keep me longer and do a boatload of brainwave tests that would either make for a Nobel Prize or a Netflix series. That was not to be as the business office, holding hands with the insurance companies, did some digging high and, lo and behold, discovered my plan wouldn't cover the extra tests.

It also didn't help the neuro guys that, despite going face down on the pavement, I hadn't suffered a scratch (another vampire benny), giving the pointy-heads in accounting further reason to set me free to be me, whoever that was.

Why *moi*, a forevermore kinda guy, had any health insurance in the first place is paradoxical. Ah, the trials and tribulations of keeping up the appearances of mortality with the Kardashians, *n'est pas*?

On my last day, Dr. Rosamund Mickeltee came into my room (with no view), a visit that was going to set in motion a series of events that would threaten to almost certainly put an end to my life.

Dr. Rosamond Mickeltee is a mousey woman who proudly wears little makeup and does absolutely nothing to hide the strands of ugly, unruly grey that age her beyond her fifty-plus years. However, Dr. Rosamund Mickeltee makes amends for these deficiencies. As members of my tribe would say, "So fine was the neck he knew he could have spanned it about with the fingers of one hand."

It is this 'so fine was the neck he knew' that gets me in the suck. Naturally, your honor, I plead. I do not remember why I became fixated on this exposed flesh. All I know is that my eyeballing throws open the doctor's nasal pharynx, and her face contorts in a perfect imitation of Edvard Munch's *Silent Scream;* pretty scary response to my unwanted admiration, but a lot better than a Marie Callas ear-splitting high C that would break glass everywhere on the seventeenth floor.

I get wise and force a smile through tight lips that gives me a sudden migraine. Living forever isn't for sissies, but as Coach Lombardi used to say, "When things get tough, the tough get going."

The man was my God, but more about playing football for the Packers in another of my yet-to-be-written chapters: "Yes, Vampires Can Tackle."

Dr. Mickeltee carefully explains my situation as if I haven't read Homer and don't know amnesia, which comes from the ancient Greek word *forgetfulness*.

Fortunately, I don't make things worse and show off by quoting Demosthenes' First Phillippic (calling on Athenians to recognize the threat Bernard II presented to the autonomy of Athens), thus permitting Dr. Mickeltee to inform me with as sweet a smile as someone who could pass for a warden in a woman's prison can muster that she is a psychoanalyst who has vast experience with cases of confusion resulting from a concussion like mine and offers to help me get my memory back.

Not being in my two hundred and fifty-nine-year-old right of mind, I don't see any way out of my unwelcomed slumber land, so I foolishly leap out of the bedpan into the fiery, mad red eyes of Dr. M and say, "*Sure, I'll give it a go.*"

Dr. Mickeltee signs me out and, to show me how much she really cares, has her associate (and probably girl toy), the innocent young Dr. Betty Furness, usher me home.

Had my memory not been in the freezer section of my two-century-plus brain, else I would have immediately remembered the glamorous TV star of the same name in the Fifties who swept into the kitchen and theatrically opened a refrigerator, selling every Suckersapien Homemaker in the US on the benefits of having a Westinghouse fridge; and would have giggled when the first thing her namesake did was open my fridge and throw out the spoiled food. Coincidence, I think not!

Oops, I just spilled the beans; no pun intended. Did you catch it? The reference to a refrigerator and the food that's in it. I could lie and say it was for show. Keep up the pretense that vampires only survive on blood; however, if I am to bare my soul to you in these pages, I will need to blow my cover and reveal what we self-proclaimed frequent night flyers can and cannot do, i.e., only dine on blood, sleep in coffins during the day, or unable to see our reflections in a mirror to name a few of our so-called peccadilloes.

Oh, I know what you're thinking. Who's this guy hosing? He can't be legit. Sorry, Bela Lugosi fanboys and fangirls. All those comics, books, movies, and TV series you grew up on—know what—it was all made up so you would all feed from the same hyped-up propaganda trough and shit in your pants if you ever came across one of us at a cocktail party.

Firstly, we eat processed foods. Besides the obvious blood sausages, do we not enjoy steak tartare? And how's this for a news flash? For decades here and there, I have said *nada* to anything, not pretending to be farm-fed, and even for a while, to impress Maria Tallchief, I went full vegan. Wrap that homegrown Mary Jane in your Zig-Zag and smoke it, Bud.

Apart from the bloodletting, which at first bite may not seem romantic, but seen against today's sexual asphyxiation rage, is, to my mind, more appealing and transmogrifying into an appalling bat (we all have our bad side), all other attributed behaviors carefully orchestrated to be passed down through social media, have nothing whatsoever to do with how we vampires actually live, love, sleep, piss, or occasionally call the *Home Shopping Network* at three in the morning to order bathroom tiles.

While we are coming clean, let's debunk the mirror, mirror— why can't you see me on the wall? myth. Vampires can—you heard me correctly there, Archie—see our reflections, and believe me, that ordinary action once caused me almost to lose my lunch. Talk about bat-shitting moments; it occurred at a masked ball on the night I decided to mock myself and dress as a Vampire Bat.

Forgive me if I'm once again jumping around and springing too much information at you all at once. I've got a century and a half of good stuff to tell you, and sometimes, I confuse even myself in the retelling.

The best thing to do is share with you the oral history of We Who Love De Blood (*na zeis or,* as our Greek Brothers jokingly nickname us*),* which has been painstakingly passed down from the Ancients to me throughout my lifetime.

ONE

SMALL TALK

"How are you feeling today, Nick? Any residual effects of the fall, headaches, dizziness, for instance," asks Dr. Mickeltee.

"No. None."

"I know the hospital gave you a prescription for Extra Strength Tylenol, but I can give you something stronger if you need it."

"No, I'm fine."

"No nausea or vomiting, either?"

"I don't have much appetite, although I had a pretty good breakfast today."

"That's good. What did you have?"

"Two eggs over with rye toast and a side of tomatoes." I laugh.

"What's so funny?"

"I wasn't really hungry for breakfast, so after I had a cup of coffee and read some of the Times, I went for a walk in the neighborhood. I wasn't going anywhere in particular, but when I turned the corner of Thirty-Third and Third and saw this diner, I went in."

"That happens to me, but usually at Zara's," smiles Dr. Mickeltee. Nick smiles.

"Was the diner familiar? Have you remembered you've been there before?"

"No, nothing like that, but the way the lady at the register greeted me was obvious I had. Several servers said hi, and one in particular said it was good to see me and wondered if I had gone on vacation."

"So, it appears you dine there often," says Dr. Mickeltee

Nick laughs "I didn't even have to look at the menu before the server who asked if I had gone on vacation sets a cup of coffee down and says, 'Same as always?'"

"So, you are a regular."

"Seems so."

"Would you mind if I examine you before we start? You don't have to undress. Just stay where you are."

"No, go ahead and do your thing."

Dr. Mickeltee comes around from behind her desk, takes out a pencil light, and examines Nick's eyes.

"No vision or balance problems?"

"None."

"Any sensitivity to light or noise?"

"No."

"Any neck pains?"

"A little stiffness when I wake up. But it goes away when I start moving around."

Dr. Mickeltee finishes her exam and returns to her seat.

"Apart from my memory loss, I'm feeling pretty good."

"I'm glad to hear that. Oftentimes, after suffering a concussion days later, one can have physical side effects."

"I'm good."

"What about behavioral side effects?"

"What do you mean?"

"Some people experience mood changes. They withdraw from friends. Others go in the opposite direction, even cry more than usual, and seek more comfort than usual?"

"Nope"

"What about your sleeping habits? Any changes in sleeping patterns?"

She holds up her hand. "I realize you can't remember anything before the accident, but since the accident."

"No, I'm getting my eight hours."

"How about not wanting to engage in usual activities or inappropriate emotional responses?"

"Absolutely not!"

"I'm sorry, but I have to ask."

"Nah, it's okay. So, tell me, Dr. Mickeltee, how will this work?"

"I'm going to hypnotize you and then ask you if there is anything you want to talk about. This open-ended, give-and-take is the most comfortable way to bring back memories. I've had patients talk about the first time they rode on an airplane or their first high school basketball game. Whatever subject pops into your mind, Nick."

"I bet you've heard some crazy shit—sorry, I mean, stuff?"

She laughs, "I've been doing this a long time. I've heard it all, and nothing surprises me."

TWO

WTFK

Transcription #1: (From French & High German)

The Vampire: When the first of our tribe discovered the deal, a little blood-taking for immortality, they wisely recognized they had the opportunity for idolization as living Gods who rule the world or hide in cold, wet, and darkened caves to escape the inevitability of being stoned, burned or quarter by jealous people with wrinkled skin. Both choices are fraught with peril, and it took a decade to convince those who saw ruling the world had no downside except a constant shortage of blood to accept a third, alternative lifestyle. Who precisely came up with the solution? I don't want to brag, but I'm probably one of my fellow Libras exhibiting our splendid reasoning style of blending spirituality with logic. And here is what the Balanced Ones proposed. Our tribe would roam the world forever in plain sight, but should their immortality be discovered, they would pretend to take on the guise of a loathsome fiend no sane person believes exists. Okay, perhaps not precisely hiding in plain sight, but close enough to be accepted, not outed. As anyone familiar with the process knows, the first order of such a transmogrification is creating a legend that will resonate fear and loathing with the great unwashed. During this period in man's early history, the most frightening creature was the mythological dragon. Our elders, channeling the coming of Stephen King, decided a loathsome living thing was far more horrifying, and voilà, they ingeniously came up with the Camazotz, later known to all of us who have one in the Belfy. As with the dragon, the bat's most frightening feature is its razor-sharp incisors and canines. While the dragon's teeth tore you to pieces, the bat used them to puncture holes into its prey to satisfy its unquenchable thirst for blood. How's that for a coincidence? I think not. What makes this choice additionally brilliant is that, like the fictional dragon, the bat can fly, furnishing our metamorphosis into another terrifying dimension and our eventual obsession with skydiving. But what to call this being: Leech Lovers, Plasma People, The Bloodsucker Boys? For another example of how good things happen to good people, our oral history just so happens to dovetail with the roots of the word 'vampire,' which arises in the Slavonic Magyar from vam, meaning blood, and pir or monster. Vampire—It does have an certain, *joie de vivre, n'est pas?* Our imaginative elders knew how to embellish and added several idiosyncrasies to our vampire profile. Exposure to the sun will turn our skin to dust; therefore, we can only go out at night. This night prowling concept works hand in hand with our bat transmogrification. Let's be real here: seeing a bat flying around at noon is undoubtedly less frightening than one coming for your jugular at midnight. How about the idea that vampires can't see their image in a mirror and, therefore, should avoid it at all costs or, ironically, be spotted? And, of course, this Crazy Horse of vampire propaganda—to catch up on our sleep, the only fitting Posturepedic for such vile creatures was a dirt coffin. How can vampires always appear so well turned out if we can't check our look in the mirror? *C'est impossible!* And to lie down in our finery on a dirt bed, imagine the dry-cleaning bills! *C'est incroyable.* But, like other *bubbe meises,* Lady Godiva never got chapped thighs; it's better to take these inconsistencies with a grain of salt and never examine them too literally, and to that end, I can provide some insider info. Our founding fathers, who were real clotheshorses, as well as more than a skosh narcissistic, devilishly improvised, proclaimed that if we were to be roaming around at all hours of the night, we must dress in formal eveningwear, a black tux, gloves, and a cape. And as far as having no reflection in the mirror, pish posh! No vampire can nor should resist falling in love with their image in every storefront window while strolling along Fifth Avenue or any fashionable street on planet Earth.

THREE

FOUND IN TRANSLATION

I can only take so many translated recordings of this vampire character before switching them off and wondering who is crazier, the voice on the recording or me, in believing all this lunacy.

I must confess that after listening to these forty-five-minute sessions, they affected my psyche, particularly in my nighttime reverie. In one such dreamscape, slowly, I turned, step-by-step, inch-by-inch, bringing back memories of William Powell nipping at Myra Loy's neck as they stood at the railing of Niagara Falls.

Whether fact, fiction, or just delusional, after binge-watching *Thin Man* movies on TCM, it was painfully apparent that my sanity was in jeopardy. I soon discovered that it was so with my good doctor, Mickeltee.

Mickeltee 's new understanding of my real identity becomes apparent when I come out of my trance during what turns out to be my last session and ask if I am into vampire movies.

Now, is that a trick question? Is she trying to bait me into confessing that the patient sitting just feet away from her is the second coming of Bela Lugosi?

"You're asking me, someone who can't even remember his name?" Now, how is that for a quick and witty retort?

It works because, for a moment, we have a good laugh about it. Then the laughing stops when Dr Mickeltee says, "Nick, I don't want to shock you, but each time I put you in a trance, you relate fantastic stories of being a one hundred and fifty-nine-year-old vampire."

I want to ask her if I mentioned the *Thin Man* movies, but I think better of it. Naturally, I want to appear shocked and not let on that I've heard the tapes, and I'm as wound up in self-doubt as she is.

So, as calmly as I can muster, I say, "You're kidding. A vampire? That's crazy. What do I say exactly?"

Dr. Mickeltee carefully explains how, when I'm under hypnosis, I provide a history of my life as a vampire from when I transformed to the present day. I name names, dates, and places in such an intimate and detailed way that they convince her I must have been there.

However, what shocked her the most was that the tales were recounted in various modern languages, like German, Italian, and French, but when I go back in time, I speak Latin, ancient Greek, and Egyptian.

She recoils when I tell her I haven't bitten anyone in the last hour. I mean, I had to make another witty retort. Otherwise, I would have had to face the fact that, in the worst-case scenario, I'm not William Powell.

I swear, with all the sincerity I can muster without laughing at the farfetchery of it all, that I have absolutely no memory of being a vampire, and sure as hell can't speak any foreign languages, but don't go into details and mention my dust up at the Chinese.

I tell her with a little more conviction that it's a disgusting suggestion that I have the slightest taste for blood. I even went so far as to prove my point by recounting the chopping carrots-cutting finger incident when I didn't even suck the wound; instead, to stop the bleeding, I quickly wrapped my finger in a paper towel. Why I made up that ludicrous story is beyond me. I mean, anyone who knows me knows I only buy pre-cut carrots at Trader Joe's.

For a moment, I believed these explanations would do the trick and calm her disturbed psyche. Still, when she informed me that she was going to stop treating me for amnesia temporarily and instead contact her mentor, Dr. Frederick Sebastian Hangmenn, to thoroughly examine the tapes in an attempt to determine the origins of these imaginings, I hesitated but finally said, "Go for it."

When I return home, I first look this Hangmenn fellow up on Wikipedia, and my worst fears are confirmed. Dr. Frederick Sebastian Hangmenn is the chief bottle washer and nutcracker at the East Meadow Shock Therapy Center, specializing in long-term patient care.

Before I continue, let me provide you with additional information about how I obtained these recordings. At the start of our first session, Dr. Mickeltee told me it was necessary that she record them so she could review the session at a later date. When I ask if I might have a copy, her eyebrows twitch, her eyes squint up attractively, and she replies that it was against policy.

This jerking of my chain is unacceptable. However, instead of arguing and putting a kibosh on the entire process, I was inspired in a flash to use my iPhone to secretly provide me with my copy.

When I returned home from my first session and listened to the recording, I couldn't understand a word. The voice on the tape was speaking foreign languages; two I recognized as French and German, but the others were an unintelligible mystery.

I shut the damn thing off and tried to forget about them until that evening when a voice inside me (I wonder who that could be, huh?) told me to use Google Translate and transcribe the recording.

Okay, so let's fast-forward to when I'm listening to my last session and the moments before she takes me out of my trance. Thinking I'll never hear the conversation, Mickeltee calls her shock jock, puts him on speaker and explains my situation. Hangmenn listens, then, goes on to diagnose me as extremely delusional and someone exhibiting a dissociative personality that definitely requires immediate institutionalization at Electricity Central before I go off into the night and bite some woman's neck off, or worse.

When Dr. Mickeltee calls me to confirm tomorrow's visit with Dr. Hangmenn, I'm Ready Teddy. I tell her I'm as anxious as she is to meet the Hangmenn and get to the bottom of this crazy idea that I'm a vampire, but unfortunately, my mom's dying.

I have to fly off tomorrow morning to New Castle to care for her, but I'll call her when I return and reschedule. Before she can respond, I will thank her for all her help and hang the hell up.

New Castle, why did I say New Castle? Then I remembered one of the recordings.

The Vampire: New Castle—it was one of my overnight haunts in London. It was a bit of a distance as the bat flies, but the longer I stayed in London, the farther out I had to go if I wasn't going to draw suspicion. Remember, you don't drink blood at a blood bank. That meant I had to abide by the rules of the Vampire Life and couldn't hunt within twenty miles *of* another vampire. I was fortunate during those years because the south of France and Monaco were all the rage, and there weren't more than one or two other bloodsuckers in England, so it was easy to relax the rules a little and still stay out of each other's way. As an aside. If Starbucks can be less than ten blocks away from each other in a big city like New York, why can't we?

I have to laugh; my vampire can spin a yarn, can't he?

FOUR

VAMPIRES UNDER THE INFLUENCE

Transcription #2. (From French & High German)

Dr. Mickeltee: The Ancients you speak of sound like wise men who understand the true nature of human beings in all their varying degrees."

The Vampire: I was in advertising, don't you know. Now, that's where you have to have a handle on what makes people tick if you want to sell the great unwashed what they don't want or need. My journey began back in the day when I was called, among other things, a proselytizer, snake oil salesman, and pitchman—differences without a distinction. Along the way, I never forgot what the Ancients taught, my study and learn—study and learn, my dear.

Dr. Mickeltee: Study and learn; that's excellent advice, Nick.

The Vampire: You know what else I learned, Dr. Mickeltee?

Dr Mickeltee: Tell me.

The Vampire: People were all the same. They desperately wanted to buy what you were selling; all you had to do was permit them.

Dr. Mickeltee: Do you think that's why you became a vampire?

The Vampire: That's very good, Dr. Mickeltee. You should think about becoming a psychiatrist.

Dr. Mickeltee: Study and learn, isn't that what you told me?

The Vampire: So, you believe I wanted to be a vampire so desperately, I bought what they were selling? Went out looking for one? Put an ad in the paper. Must have my blood sucked out of my body, call this number anytime.

Dr. Mickeltee: It happens, you said so yourself.

The Vampire: Not to me, it didn't.

Dr. Mickeltee: Tell me about it then. Tell me how you became a vampire. Can you do that, Nick?

The Vampire: It all began on April 1, 1542. I was minding my own business, that is, doing what any other hot-blooded seventeen-year-old boy does, eyeing a pretty mademoiselle across the avenue when I was waylaid, shanghaied right off the *Promenade Plantée* in broad daylight, and overnight, I became a French conscript soon to be caught up in the Italian War of 1542. If I thought my life ended then, I was in for a rude awakening because the end of life, as I knew it, came twenty-four days later during the Battle of Bonchurch on the Isle of Wight off the coast of England. Our beloved, I 'll-follow-you-anywhere-commander, was a Le Seigneur de Tais, whom I never had the opportunity to make his acquaintance on the battlefield, and was said to be always at the head of his troops. Since I made it my business to keep to the rear, with my head down, and when possible, come out of the safety of a trench unless a gung-ho officer prodded me with his sword, I cannot possibly comment on who led us all into battle. By the way, I run into this same Le Seigneur de Tais, again as if life isn't full of little coincidences—I think not; years later, when I get an invite to the wedding of his sister, Jeanne to Louis Brossin, lord of Méré and Sepmes, where I feasted on four plates of soup, a whole pheasant, a partridge, a large plate of salad, two slices of ham, mutton au jus with garlic, a plate of pastry, all followed by fruit and hard-boiled eggs and the neck of Eleanor of Austria that first night and Anne de Pisseleu d'Heilly, two nights later. I must say one thing: Le Seigneur de Tais knew how to throw a party.

Dr. Mickeltee: That was quite an entertaining story, Nick, but...

The Vampire: Oh, don't worry, I haven't forgotten the son of a neck-buggerer who set me down the Path of The Bloodsucker. Nope, I will address it in another yet-to-be-written chapter, "When You Come to a Neck in the Road, Become A Turtle."

Dr. Mickeltee: Is that the person who attacked you on April 24, Nick?

The Vampire: April 24?

Dr. Mickeltee: Twenty-four days later, you said something happened to you?

The Vampire: I'm dazed and confused from the shelling, and suddenly, a soldier I've never seen before jumps into my hole and lands right on top of me. He moves off me and then lifts my head; his eyes blaze with a paralyzing glow. I haven't the energy to resist and cannot prevent him from pulling down my collar and sinking his sharp teeth into my flesh. I must have passed out because when I awake, he's gone, and it's nighttime, the shelling's stopped, and it's eerily quiet. Before I can make sense of what's happened to me, I experience an unexpected surge of energy you might get from a double shot of espresso; instead of staying safely put in my hole until I know what's what, I crawl up out and begin moving toward the front. During this walk, I feel remarkably relaxed, as it's a sunny Sunday Parisian morning, and I am strolling down the *Promenade Plantée* in Paris on my way to my favorite patisserie. Do you think I could have a glass of water?

Dr. Mickeltee: Of course.

(The sound of water pouring. Sound of drinking water.)

The Vampire: Thank you.

Dr. Mickeltee: You never saw this soldier before?

The Vampire: Max the Magyar? No.

Dr. Mickeltee: Max the Magyar—did you know his name?

The Vampire: (Laughing) It's the name I gave him. You have to understand half the army was made up of conscripts from all over Europe: Frenchmen, Poles, Magyars—what a bunch of rag-tail misfits we were.

Dr. Mickeltee: And you never saw him again?

The Vampire: And that's a fact. Hard to believe, right? You would think that of all the thousands of people I've met in the last century and a half, Max and I would have crossed paths, *n'est pas*? You know, for instance, at a reunion of Vampires Vets who fought for France against the Holy Roman Empire, hosted by the Friends of Charles V, Henry VIII of England, and old Suleiman I of the Ottoman Empire.

Dr. Mickeltee: What would you do if you ran into him tomorrow, Nick? What would you say to him?

The Vampire: I thought these sessions were a fact-finding mission to help Nick get his mojo working again. If you want me to get in touch with my inner feelings, manage my anger, and do all that other good stuff, Dr. Mickeltee, I suggest we both get naked and maybe roll around on the carpet.

(A moment of silence)

The Vampire: (Laughing) I'm only pulling your chain. (Pause) So, Dr. Mickeltee, have you ever strolled down the *Promenade Plantée* in Paris?

FIVE

MY TURN AT THE WHEEL

It is at this moment that I stop the recording. I go to my computer, log onto Google, and search for *Promenade Plantée*. I don't recognize the street or any of the shops, even on Google Earth, and then I understand what a fool's errand it is to think *Promenade Plantée* looks anything like it did back in the mid-Fourteenth Century.

I typed in 'French historical museums' and discovered *The Musée des Archives Nationales*, but I was all out of luck because their archives are unavailable online.

I need quiet time, so I make myself a cup of coffee, half regular and half decaf, and read today's New York Times, which appears at my door each morning. I'm drinking coffee in this proportion because why else would bags of each blend sit up in the cupboard?

When I open the Times, I automatically go to the obituaries. Why am I doing that? What possible motive could I have? If I'm to believe the recordings, I'm one hundred and fifty-nine years young and still going strong—okay, maybe with a touch of I-can't-remember-the-last-time-I-bit-into-someone's-neck-for-a tasty-taste-of life-giving blood—nevertheless, it's a sure bet I don't need these listings to know if I'm alive, ha, ha, ha; so why pour over these obits so diligently?

Am I some sick sadist, lauding it over these poor departed souls, smirking, thinking—you're dead, but I'm not and never will be? Am I looking for a friend? I've found a contact list on my phone. Some of the names must be pals. I don't see why I can't have amigos and have friendships as long as I don't outlast my stay, and they don't become jealous over my forever-30s look.

Recipients—could they be on the list? There is nothing like having someone take a bite out of your neck to say, Sir, could I have another?

Lovers? Why not? I have urges—no, besides the need for blood, fool! And I've certainly got the looks. Me, myself, and Robert Redford's look-alikes, we're talking catnip, my brother, cat-freakin'-nip!

FYI, Recipients—I hate that dog tag. It sounds so insipid. How about 'the mark'? While the recipient sounds a tad willing, the mark is so much more colorful; it puts a bull's eye on you as the poor, unsuspecting, and unwilling target of my fangs that will sooner than later puncture your flesh and suck the precious blood out of your body, don't you think?

In the meantime, I want to get a better handle on what I've been up to while living in Murray Hill. My wallet has offered the most information. First among the clues is my current New York State driver's license. In addition to providing my name, Nick Cummings, which I hear from a recovery room nurse for the first time, and my Murray Hill address, it displays a photo of me taken in 2014 when the license was issued.

That jives with the ten years I've stayed in one place—in this case, New York City. I wonder how many out-of-state driver's licenses have that same ten-year expiration date. If I can locate them, it would give me an idea of where I've been in the States. There could even be international driver's licenses that could—hold on—what about passports? Boy, finding them would provide a treasure trove of information.

My elation is short-lived. If I were a vampire, I would want clean skin every ten years so that I would bet dollars to donuts; my vampire doesn't leave any incriminating evidence that provides clues to his ageless past.

In the photo, I'm wearing dark blue, plastic-rimmed glasses that immediately draw attention away from my features. My blond hair is cut short, and I sport a wispy, thin mustache, which is so slight. Is it intentional, or did I just forget to shave? No, my vampire does nothing that isn't well thought out and thoroughly planned to the last detail. He's had enough practice, right?

When I wake up in the hospital, no glasses are in my possession, and I discover I don't need them. My hair is now a lighter brown and slightly under my ears. I don't have any facial hair except for the growth of stubble, which I decided to shave off as soon as I returned home.

The wallet is chock-full of credit cards and a New York City Library card. I locate two years of credit card receipts in a spare bedroom's metal cabinet. These pages hold a treasure trove of information. I glean from the charges almost all of my daily moves. Where I shop for food: Trader Joe's. Order in: Frank's Trattoria, China Bowl East, The Santa Fe. Where I dine out: China Bowl East, The Santa Fe, Hanne, and The Oyster Bar, to name a few.

The totals suggest that I usually eat alone, although there are spurts when entertaining a guest. When I do a cursory check of the dates, I see that the more significant total occurs on the weekends, hinting that this is when I'm not dining alone.

There are no photos in my wallet, which is a disappointment. Not that I think I will find a picture of me taken in 1826 by the French scientist Joseph Nicéphore Niépce at his family's country home, *Le Gras,* another pal mentioned on the recordings of my vampire. This is the subject of my yet-to-be-written chapter, "Yes, Vampires Love Selfies," which debunks the myth that vampires can't be photographed.

For your information again, I looked up Monsieur Joseph Nicéphore Niépce on Wikipedia. I discovered that, as my vampire recalls, he was "a French inventor and one of the earliest pioneers of photography."

This famous guy popping up doesn't surprise me because I'm beginning to get the feeling either my guy is the biggest name-dropping bull shitter the world has ever known, or more astounding, if you're a vampire, you're always on the A list. There's no red carpet that doesn't bear your footprint or two tiny bite marks on the neck of any famous femme you desire

I discovered more treasure in the filing cabinet, but the most important was a sheet of paper under my computer. Yes, indeed, for all you people who can't remember how to access your Spotify, Boot Barn, or Chase Manhattan Bank accounts, you get four hundred dollars, and you can pass Go twice if you guess correctly—the paper is my vampire's password cheat sheet!

I'm disappointed that my vampire, with all his gifts, doesn't have a highly superior autobiographical memory and requires such a prop.

I'm suddenly interrupted by a text prompting me to open my Zoom app. These messages, signed W, have been popping up daily for the last week, and I have refused to obey them for no other reason than pure obstinacy. However, at this very moment, I'm thinking, why the hell not?

The Zoom directions are so simple that a child can follow them, but I haven't been a child for two centuries, so I can be forgiven for messing up the sound volume. In the first minute or two, I tried reading the guys' lips and realized I was not Helen Keller.

The man is about fifty, nice looking, and extremely friendly, judging by the I-slept-with-a-hanger-in-my-mouth-smile that never leaves his face.

"Nick, where have you been? I've been trying to contact you for the last week. I know you like to go out of town, but when you do, you always leave a forwarding address; he inquires with the earnestness of a priest about to give you the *Ordo Ministrandi Sacramentum Extremae Unctionis.*"

For the life of me, I don't recognize the man's face or the voice, and I certainly don't remember someone named W. I figure the truth, at least in this case, works best.

"I had an accident. I fell on the street, knocked myself out, and ended up in the hospital, but I'm okay now. So, what's up, W?"

W lowers his voice. "Around here, they call me Mr. W."

"Well, you can call me Mister Tibbs. Ha, ha, ha."

"Very good, get with the *Heat of the Night* quote," Mr. Nick."

Don't ask me how I remember the movie when I can't remember my name. Ah, another sweet mystery of life once removed by amnesia.

"Seriously, Nick, you're the third client with an accident this month. You're lucky: Guy Hartley broke his right wrist in two places, and Emily Ann Francis fractured her hip and had to go in for a replacement at HSS. These city streets are treacherous."

This W guy is trying to imitate an evening news anchor who is giving viewers the weather report. I nod, pretending to recognize those names, but I don't.

"Well, I'm glad you're okay, Nick. I've reviewed your outline, and something didn't sit right."

"No?"

"Oh, don't get me wrong. It was fantastic, but something was bothering me. After several nights of tossing and turning, I decided to give it to Clair Cowens, my reader, for her thoughts, and she saw what I should have immediately seen."

"And, what's that, W?"

"Your outline contains two major storylines! Both are exciting, action-packed, and terrific."

Boy, this guy knows how to rub your body parts better than a masseuse at *The Happy Ending Massage Parlor*, doesn't he? I wonder if this smooth-talking Agent-man snows my vampire as well? How else would he have gotten him to sign onto his agency?

"That's so nice of you to say, *W*," I finally reply, throwing him a grin that would make even The Joker jealous.

Since I have no idea what he's talking about, I have to play along.

"Think about it, Nick. One protagonist, but he's telling two stories. First, he's an *epicurean bon vivant* who takes the reader on a once-in-a-lifetime trip to all the tables of the Kings and Queens in 19th-century Europe. It's an intimate look at these royals in a setting that reveals their true nature and provides the reader with those royal recipes they can create, turning their kitchens into a five-star Michelin destination. The second story is about a cloak-and-dagger rollicking romp through the bed-chambers of those royals, as told by the same gentleman, now a notorious lothario equal to Casanova. 'Both stories are so thrillingly authentic it's as if your protagonist has lived the combined lives of Porfirio Rubirosa and Aly Khan.' "I'm quoting Clair now," says W.

I'm unsure how I missed discovering this outline on the computer, never mind any clues as to my vampire's desire to be a published author who has already set the wheels in motion by making contact with a literary agent.

"So, Nick, how does that sound? I don't want to push you until you fully recover, but if you agree that you have two books here, let's discuss the next steps."

"W, could you give me a day to think about it? I don't want to make any promises I can't keep."

"*Absolutement, mon ami,*" grins W.

"*C'est très gentil de votre part,*" smiles Nick.

"Nick, when did you learn French? You're not one of those people I read about in Oliver Sacks' book, *The Man Who Mistook His Wife for a Hat,* are you? You know, people who can't speak a foreign language or play a musical instrument, and then, bam, they suffer a brain injury. Suddenly, they quote Dante in the original Italian or play the violin like Itzhak Perlman."

Hold on there, Big Fella; I told you I couldn't speak a foreign language just a minute ago, but now it seems I can. And this Oliver Sacks fellow, why does his name ring a distant tinkle? A member of the tribe?

"Are you all right, Nick? You're shaking your head and looking very strange. You're not going to faint, are you? Can I call someone for you?"

A tiny square at the bottom right-hand corner of the computer screen catches my eye. Without consciously thinking about it, I can now direct my ocular nerve center to magnify the image tenfold, filling the screen.

Unfortunately, the image is alarming. You would also be unnerved to see your head bobbing uncontrollably from side to side, inviting my cheek muscles to come floating loose from their musculature moorings, twisting and shouting in locomotion with my head bobbing in the most unattractive and unsettling way.

"Not to worry, I'm okay, W. No problemo," I manage to say.

"I'm glad to hear that, Nick. I'll hear from you in a day or two."

"No problemo," I repeat.

We sign off.

I stare at the black screen. What if I can't pull this off? What if I'm not a vampire? What the hell am I supposed to do with all my formal evening wear?

SIX

PUBLISH AND PERISH

Thinking about this book deal is causing me to reflect upon my situation. All I actually know about my so-called two hundred-plus years of debauchery of the neck comes from the recorded tales spun by some French cat called Bernard, whose voice appears on Dr. Mickeltee's recording made while under hypnotherapy as part of my treatment before she ditched the motto, 'do no harm,' and planned to help turn my psyche into Tostitos.

Of course, this unsettling vampire pedigree fills me with 'fuck, why me' like those celebrities on *Finding Your Roots* who discovered their forbearer believed they revolved around the moon. Look on the bright side, if there is one; that's better than believing The Man In The Moon is your Daddy, which explains your unexplainable and insatiable desire for Blue Cheese.

I know, I know if I hadn't been a Nosy Rosie and made copies and then used Google Translate to decipher some multi-lingual psycho-babbler who swears he's an old-as-the-hills-fanged-up-night-flyer, I wouldn't be in the fine mess I'm in now, would I, Ollie?

Speaking of using Google Translate, I researched this Oliver Sacks fella online after my sudden burst of French with Senior W. What do you think I learned? I think doing a facial on the concrete may have played whack-a-mo with my noggin and rewired my brain to the point that maybe, just maybe, one day, I will be able to speak the *Lingua Franca* so well that I can listen to my vampire's tapes in the original.

Okay, this may be a load of bullshit because up until that moment with W, besides ordering a *cerveza* at the corner bodega and impressing a server at my local French Bistro when ordering *les pommes de terre frites*, otherwise, no foreign languages, have bubbled forth out of the blue, nor my mouth; nor am I able to understand Cantonese or Mandarin when the servers at the nearby Chinese mocked my pronunciation of *Tsing Tao* beer. I dream of wasting them all, a la Chow Yun-fat in *The Killers*.

Okay, okay, I'm losing the big picture. So, who the hell is this *non-grata person* at a blood bank who lives on those recordings? For a New York City Heartbeat, I think that ain't my voice, no way, no how, no siree bobcat.

Come on, be honest; how many of you have listened to an iPhone recording you've made of yourself while having phone sex with someone, not your partner, and reached the same conclusion?

Then I came up with this brilliant construct—my concussion sent me flying head-on into *The Matrix*, and I'm the poster child for one of those companies that promise to teach you a language when you're sleeping, or in my case, swimming in the Ocean of Forgetfulness—*voilà*, my drifting way of tongues.

One thing is truer than true. Since regaining consciousness, no matter how alluring the neck is in sight, I haven't bit, nipped, scratched, or yearned for one single, solitary, softer-than-soft nape.

However, listening to my vampire recall his escapades, I have to admit I get a chubby or two and wonder what it would be like to sink my teeth into the softer-than-soft flesh of some hottie and get away with it without being listed on the MeToo website.

Talking about getting listed on the MeToo website or any other social media platform, the fastest way to do that is with a successful book deal. If you're a vampire on the down low, the last thing you want to do is call attention to yourself. Am I right, or am I talking to a stupid? And to tentatively title it: *The Handsome Blood and his Tasty Queens?* Are you f'in insane?

And don't give me this shit Mister Neck Man about how readers love this vampire crap, as seen by the public gobbling up the Anne Rice books and subsequent movies with heartthrobs like Tom Cruise and Brad Pitt playing Hollywood Handsome vampires,

So, what—you ask yourself, why shouldn't you, who lived the life, grab your share of fame and fortune? The only trouble is, you, Handsome Blood—you're a real rootin'-tootin' vampire who, should you be outed, will be hunted down and shish kabobed in living color on TikTok.

SEVEN

AFTER ACTION REPORT

Before I listen to the recordings, I turn on the movie theater-size TV screen. I'm still getting used to all the channels, but what interests me more are the shows the vampire recorded before the accident.

Scanning the list, I look for additional clues and patterns that might provide insight into Bernard's mind. Will I discover blood-curdling vampire films or ones less obvious, like *Batman* and *Batwoman* movies?

What about historical films featuring the guillotine? Name another scene that better features such an alluring neck as Merry Marie Antoinette's in the last minutes of her life.

I become momentarily excited when I see the title, *The Way We Were,* but other than my resemblance to the lead actor, I can't see why it was on the list.

For some reason, the 1939's *The Adventures of Sherlock Holmes,* starring Basil Rathbone as the famous Victorian detective, catches my eye. I quickly find myself totally transfixed by the sets, especially the foggy street scenes, but like the super sleuth, I'm searching for the tiniest misstep, the wrong kind of bulb in the gas lampposts illuminating the shadowy, East London neighborhood, or the correct number of horses pulling the Hansom Cabs ferrying Holmes and

Watson in a mad dash over the cobblestone back to 21B Baker Street to meet their nemesis, Dr. Moriarty.

As I stare at the screen—bam— it's happening again, but I haven't had any lactose this morning! A tiny square at the bottom right-hand corner of the TV screen catches my eye, and there I go again, ordering my ocular nerve center to magnify the image tenfold.

Come on, how weird is this? Doesn't this make me feel special? You bet it does.

Fortunately, there is no head-bopping or floating cheek this time; instead, I'm pulled into a particular 24-per-second moving image that instantaneously commands the screen and viscerally makes me one with every pixel. This mind meld lasts only seconds (or maybe an hour, how the fuck should I know), but it's enough weirdness to undergo the sensation of bodily transportation without distracting from the flow of imagery to my brain—of course, it is.

Can you see where I'm going with this new-fangled head-trip? If you correctly guess, the cumulative effect of all these sanctum cranial transfers will eventually make me the star of my own movie; you are the second coming of Carnac the Magnificent.

There is no transmogrification on the menu, so I'm not feeling Sherlock, Watson, or, thank God, one of the nags pulling the Hansom Cab. So, what am I, a bat on the wall?

I have to ha-ha at that equivalence, but it's no laughing matter when you're undergoing a disorientating out-da-bod trinity trip, even if you're rubbing elbows with the great Sherlock Holmes and his flunky pal, Dr. Watson. Damn my eyes, I can even smell the aroma from his pipe tobacco. Is this *moi* being the vampire?

(For the record, I toy with the idea of calling my vampire by his name, Nick, but then I'm Nick, so you can see why that won't work. So, it's 'my vampire' or 'Bernard.' Got it?)

The landline rings electrify my synapses like phone lines snapping in an electrical storm, and it doesn't take more than a few eyes jolting blinkity blinks to jolt me back into reality if reality is simply the brain telling you you're in danger of having your head explode. Can you feel me, bro?

When I get to the phone, all I hear on the other end is static. I'm not surprised. Periodically, I receive these electrically charged signals, figuring it must be a fax machine misdialing my number, ET calling home, or perhaps it's all romping around in my head. What a place to be, huh, bro?

This me-inside-the-picture phenomenon is new and, as of yet, rare. Thankfully, every image that crosses my eyeballs doesn't spontaneously enlarge or whisk me into the computer, iPhone, or Samsung innards.

That wouldn't be a vampire meld. That would be a *Me* Meltdown and so disorientating to render me malfunctioning. That's the good news. The bad news is I never know when my vampire decides to put me in the picture.

I hop onto Google and ask how I can find a file on my computer, and the answer is so apparent that I turn red and look away from the screen so the computer camera doesn't capture my embarrassment, and Google fingers me for a total moron.

You think I'm kidding, don't you? Perhaps my amnesia has made me stupid. Well, you're right. So, what if it has? Sue me. But, beware, at any moment, I might be coming to suck your blood.

It takes me seconds to locate what I'm looking for. I don't know if it's my present state, but I find printing out the pages easier than reading them. I'm quickly impressed. It's a breezy, clever, and witty read. The story about food is mouthwatering; the Smart Set will eat it up; the tales of the heroic lothario are so erotic, it will wet pants and give chubbies to all. I can understand how W's reader glaumed the two books instead of one.

I completely understand the impulse to write and to share those gifts with the world. I want to give Bernard a Bronx Cheers and tell him I'm so sorry I questioned his motives.

So, what's my next move? Obviously, it's to discover if Bernard has written anything beyond the outlines. If so, how much? If not, well...

In either case, let's be real. I can't possibly write the books without fully regaining my complete memory. However, I do have access to my vampire's voice.

What prevents me from reviewing the audio files for relevant recollections and reminiscences? If I find enough material, it will be a simple cut-and-paste job, and there you have it, two books! I will have to change the title. I mean, what the fuck was Bernard thinking he was doing, writing tag lines for Frito Lays or Beaver Hunt?

I have to once more digress for the moment and talk about the state of my memory, or lack thereof. Actually, it's more about my awareness of the simple things, which I imagine are the same things, for example, choosing what to wear each day. When I first arrive home from the hospital, I spend the day pulling out shirts and pants randomly; I quickly discover Bernard to be a fella who separates his clothes seasonally, putting the flavors of the month in the bedroom closet and drawers and the others in the second bedroom. (And color coordinated, that, to my mind, takes him out of the neat-freak section and puts him on the autistic spectrum.)

I have to hand it to my vampire and say his tidiness makes choosing clothes a no-brainer. I easily pull out a pair of jeans off the first hanger and the pullover sweater from the top pile in the sweater drawer, and that's all she wrote. Shoes, boots, and sneakers take a little longer, but I usually wear the same Nike shoes. Outerwear is easy because Bernard has a favorite lightweight down jacket that happens to be the one I wore when I fell and happily never damaged, kissing the concrete. Come to think of it, I was also wearing these same Nikes. Coincidence, I think not.

Over the last few days, I have considered what to wear based on how the clothes make me look and feel. Consequently, I'm looking in the mirror when I dress, something I've unconsciously avoided since my accident.

Going one-on-one with my face is unnerving because it compels me to look for signs of recognition. The mouth and the nose, but it's always the eyes that I dare not linger on.

What's the saying, the eyes are the windows to the soul? That's some scary shit if you're unlucky enough to have my scary-as-shit magical magnifier that could transport me on a terrifying *über alles Night on Bald Mountain* ride into the vampire's orbs and get an eyeful of the ghastly machinations of a living, breathing, blood-sucking monster. Can you feel me, bro?

Returning to the state of my memory or lack thereof, I believe this amnesia business is bizarre and unnerving. Movies, TV shows, and books teach us that the amnesiac will remember nothing, *nada, rien*. A total brain wipe, clean cranium slate, *n'est pas*?

No, no, Nanette! Case in point: the Sherlock Holmes movie. I instantly know who he is. I immediately recognized the actors, Basil Rathbone and Nigel Bruce. And I know who created the character in books, Sir Arthur Conan Doyle.

Another more relevant example is how I function day to day. No one has to be by my elbow to show me how to make coffee without it tasting like mud or toast without burning it to a crispy critter. This fact is *muy importante*: I also check for the correct wattage before I change a light bulb because blowing a fuse is a bitch.

I automatically know how to shave without so much as a nick or a skin cut, apply deodorant and avoid odoriferous armpits, and use the right amount of cologne so I don't *eau de* too much and smell like a cinnamon bun.

While these tasks appear baked into my brain, my memory bank lacks remembrance of things vampire. In bloodletting terms, all my yesterdays are gone.

If you've been paying attention, you'll say, Not so fast, Sugar Bear. You talk about being transported back into the London of Sherlock Holmes. Isn't that an obvious vampire memory?

That is fair enough, and a question that I should ask. My answer is: why are blueberries called blueberries when they're purple? In other words, WTFK!!!

Suppose I do appear to be *blasé*, perhaps even jocular. In that case, I can only assume it's the vampire-in-me-attitude I come by naturally, so I'm going with it, not that I have a choice, nor do I enjoy the lack of control if the powers inside me want to take me into the fourth dimension.

EIGHT

GOING DOWN

My brain keeps warning me that there is a place where, at any moment, I risk being whisked into this space-time continuum to a destination even more perilous than the threats posed by Professor Moriarty. That place is the elevator in my building!

What's the big deal, you say? It's a bit tight, there's no wiggle room, and you're belly-to-belly with overly friendly neighbors.

The devil child also comes to taunt you during the holidays. Squirmy, nose-running demons visiting grandparents cling to your pant leg in such an unnervingly unsanitary skin-crawling way that if you don't want them driving you up a wall, you better stick to the stairs during those festive occasions.

So, what's really the trouble here? I confess it's the gentler sex, those not-so-innocent provocateurs whose self-serving smiles always initiate Gestapo-like tactics when cornering me between floors.

The weather is the most common line of interrogation. However, recently, the closing of the rooftop garden due to the ongoing façade work has become the only issue that requires a reply.

Naturally, I don't want to draw attention to myself by being rudely nonresponsive, so I gaze into those alluring faces, and perhaps, my eyes flicker momentarily. There is a tantalizing, roving, lip-smacking lingering on a tempting, tasty bit of exposed neckity neck-neck, just begging for my canines to take an incy wincy bite of their yum-yum, fleshy-fresh flesh.

Does not a man have needs? You don't have to be a vampire to admire a neck, do you, and possibly risk your own flesh, flame broiled by Bunsen Burner-wielding villagers? (Okay, maybe that's just *moi* projecting a tiny bite, I mean bit.)

My plan of action in dealing with these anxious minutes is equal to Patton's defeat of Rommel's tanks in Tunisia. Let me explain.

Whenever I encounter a hussy-like honey in the elevator, I muster up my inner spiritual self and beg my muscles to smile, consummate the briefest of brief eye contact, and then, in a saving Beau Geste gesture, cast my eyes downward and concentrate on the wavy geometric art deco design of the floor rug; otherwise, I'm simply tempting the gods to turn me into a rabbit but take away my love of carrots.

Ironically, I have a third-dimensional bite wish to hell and damnation, poor, pitiful me.

Instead of limiting myself to taking the elevator when I have a legitimate reason to leave the building or, better still, taking the stairs, I'm drawn to my pal, Otis, and get a thrill out of riding it up and down, breathing in the rich wood paneling and admiring the elegantly appointed bronze fixtures, earmarks of the premier elevator company of the early 19th century.

My apartment building was built in the 1930s as a hotel, with a small number of rental apartments on each floor. The Otis Elevator Company is the first choice when installing an elevator in any property over six stories.

Was I part of the rich history of a company that began operations in 1894? Am I residing in New York City at the turn of the Nineteenth Century? Is that why my vampire desires me to ride these elevators, to pull me back to that time and place?

Time marches on, and I'm in the elevator now. One of my lady neighbors, thankfully a nonagenarian who applies her makeup with the back of her hand and would scare even a vampire into choosing another elevator, gets on.

Immediately, she begins to rail about the lack of service, mainly blaming one particular porter who never emptied the garbage bins on her floor in a timely fashion.

Suddenly, her voice disappears, and I hear Bernard on tape recalling a time at the turn of the century in America when his name was Stove Coleman and how humorous but eventually boring it was that friends and acquaintances insisted on believing Stove was the only son and heir of the recently departed German Ice Cream Schlotbaron, Stove Coleman Hagen-Dazenlimburg, thereby seeking favors and ingratiating themselves by giving him the unrestricted use of a Rolls Royce, a luxury Fifth Avenue Penthouse, a boat-load of senior positions at the most prestigious international banking firms and even a Russian Sable for his lady friend or multiple furs should he require; wink, wink.

"Nick, are you all right? You look a little peaked. Still recovering from your accident, are you? June Champion, in 15 J, fell on that same block. Do you know where the subway grating takes up half the street?" Inquire Carly Ford as seriously as Walter Cronkite when he announced JFK's death?

I snap back into reality. The most delectably delicious neck is in the elevator. Bite or take flight. Maybe ramble until I say, be gone with you.

"I'm fine, thanks for asking."

Now, before you throw the book down in disgust, listen up. There's nothing odd, necessarily perverted, or prurient when drawn to a particular part of a person's anatomy.

Chubby chasers, for example. The affectionate *nom de plume* for lovers of plumpness in extremes, who cream in their tighty-whities when following those joyous jellyrolls of fat waddling down the street of sin.

I believe voluptuous, Rubenesque chest bubbles provoke the obscenest vocalize, mawkish grins, gawks, and glares, while word on the Freud side of the couch has it that men never suckled by their moms have the greatest need for the snuggle pups.

Meanwhile, J. Lo has driven man's love of the butt cheek maddeningly over the edge of decency, even threatening to overtake the love melons in the need to squeeze 'em silly hierarchy.

The sobriquet, Leg Man, applies to fans of the muscular, gyrating Tina Turner, the cross-uncross limber wickedness of Sharon Stone, and to the older generation, pin-me-up to-the-wall-and-rub-against-me, long-tall, Betty Grable; and to all who fetish the fleshy thickness of thighs, bonerisms of knees and shins, the promise of the curvaceous calves or the enticement of the tiny ankle, walk on, walk on.

Last but certainly not least, how 'bout that luculent part of a woman's anatomy lusty men lust after—yep, you guessed it—the lush, full lips of a Scarlet Johansen, Angelina Jolie, or any lady nature's naturally endowed with the pillow *soft labium superius oris* and *labium inferius oris*, or those artificially blessed with blissfully bloated fillers or the wonders of Botox injected into their vermilion and cutaneous surfaces all of which promise divine boner intervention.

So, ladies, can you tell me why femmes get so all riled up when you catch us staring lasciviously (is there any other way) at their neck, our cheeks flushing with anticipation (hey, we can't control your blood pressure, can we?) when instead, you should be gleefully recalling the love bites you so get and greedily give when in the grip of unrestrained passion.

Señoras and *señoritas*, I have another idea. From now on, don't turn away in shame and horror, your lips forming the word *pervert*, as if we caught you in your birthday suit and were lasciviously (is there any other way) eying your most magical place, but instead realize we are simply admiring the start of their spinal column and spinal cord as Leonardo or any artist admiring a thing of beauty, might. Pish, posh!

"Nick, are you still getting headaches? Your neighbor, Joe, told me you were still experiencing headaches," declares Eloise Charles, doing her best Dr. Meredith Grey impersonation, who I realize has gotten on the elevator with Carly Ford.

Eloise Charles is wearing a high-neck blouse, but for me to respond, I must tear my eyes away from Carly Ford's glowing pink, gooseneck-badass nakedness.

"Thankfully, no headaches or dizziness. I was a little concerned about losing my balance and falling again, but my doctors said that usually isn't a residual effect of being concussed."

"My friend, Audrey Hastings, in 7E, has the most terrific acupuncturist. She swears she got rid of her migraines after just one one-hour session. Can you imagine," intones Carly Ford, as if she's just seen Jesus weep in a cloud formation?

I love the term, *concussed*. It's one of Dr. Mickeltee's favorites. Dare I call her again and get lit up with a thousand watts of electricity? Actually, it's the lovely young Dr. Betty Furness I wouldn't mind again seeing bending over my open refrigerator door.

"You're lucky you didn't injure your face, Nick. My husband, Ben, you met him at the Christmas party last year. He said he had a lovely time talking to you about Formula One race cars years ago, fell on the Squash Court at the Yale Club, and no matter how Dr. Howard, who is an absolute Michelangelo with the scalpel, worked on it, his left cheek is just so out of proportion with the rest of his body. Isn't that right, Carly?"

"Nick, Eloise is so, so right, and we wouldn't want anything to happen to your face now that Kirsten Hayward has moved into the building," wink-a-dinks, Carly Ford as if she has read the tea leaves, and I'm about to win the Mega Millions Jackpot.

Questions about my face not being affected by the fall make me squirrely. I had to brush them aside when the ER doctors and nurses kept talking about how, aside from a few superficial scratches that healed amazingly quickly, my face wasn't damaged, a miracle, they said, considering I fell face-first onto the concrete. On the other hand, as I mentioned, it didn't help the Neuro guys who wanted to keep me for more tests when the pointy heads in the accounting told them it was further proof, I was ready to be discharged.

We're leaving the elevator, moving toward the lobby, and onto Thirty-Fifth Street, when Carly and Eloise Charles lay their hands on me. I'm again caught up in a magical, mystical Pentecostal Sunday when I'm not the only one speaking in tongues and throwing my limbs out of joint.

"Did you know that Kirsten Hayward is Hildegard Hayward's granddaughter, the founder of Nefertiti, and its CFO?" Chirps, Eloise, as if announcing the coming of spring after being snow-bound for five months.

"So, Nick, I'm having a little *soirée* this Saturday at 3 p.m., and I want you there. It will be good for you to meet Kirsten, who, I might add, is anxious to meet you after I told her a little about our mysterious Robert Redford look-alike," continues Carly Ford, her giggle turning into the gurgling of someone giving head while living up to a prenup.

Even as my temples pulsate and my brain continues to slowly Humpty Dumpty itself and digests my memory of recording #2, Bernard's message to me is loud and clear. I have to meet Kirsten Hayward.

NINE

THE HIGH JINX
OF HIEROGLYPHICS

Transcription #2. (From French and a bit of Egyptian Slang)

Dr. Mickeltee: Nick, I'd like to take you back to the end of yesterday's session when you were about to tell me about Fathima Fakhr-un-Nisa.

The Vampire: I didn't have the slightest clue that when I devoured the lovely and delicious Meketaten, I was ingesting the blood of Nefertiti through the daughter of Akhenaten, Amenhotep IV Tut's father, buried in the King Valley 55, 18th Dynasty, Amarna, and Nefertiti, 18th Dynasty, Thebes. I can be forgiven for not realizing all history is in the ichor, but remember, I was a relative newbie and didn't have enough days gone by flowing in my veins at the time I found myself supervising a band of French workmen helping to raise her husband's artillery and arsenal to the levels upon which he could defeat the rebellion within his territories, and then do the same to the forces of Wellington when he decided to invade the Kingdom of Mysore in southern India. It was in the winter of 1782 when I was still in the French Army, this time under Napoleon's command, whom I was to meet face to face when he was first Consul. He moved into the Tuileries Palace on February 19, 1800, when I first met dear, sweet, tasty Fathima, the wife of Hyder Ali, who was a real nasty piece of work, although nothing to compare to his son Tippoo Sahib, 'Tiger of Mysore,' who, because of his smallish limbs, is someone Napoleon gazes down upon with some relish. When I finally had the opportunity to sit down across from Napoleon and drink an entire bottle of Gevrey-Chambertin, he admitted to me his lost vision of a new empire, patterned after that of Alexander the Great and centered in Alexandria. This vision had driven him and his men toward India and me to discover the Rosetta Stone, but that bit of history is lost in translation.

Dr. Mickeltee: Nick.

The Vampire: Yes?

Dr. Mickeltee: These stories...

The Vampire: Yes?

Dr. Mickeltee: Did you ever see the movie *Zelig*, starring Woody Allen?

The Vampire: You think I'm pretending to be a Zelig?

Dr. Mickeltee: You can see the similarities, can't you, Nick?

The Vampire: No, I can't, Dr. Mickeltee. Zelig is nothing like me. He's a fictional character who Woody Allen imagines becoming famous by using a talent for mimicry to gain access to people like Hitler and other historical figures.

Dr. Mickeltee: But you can see how one would make the comparison after you say you discovered the Rosetta stone?

The Vampire: Do you want the long or short version, Dr. Mickeltee?

Dr. Mickeltee: Nick, please, I don't mean to question your truthfulness or put you on the defensive.

The Vampire: You're doing a good job of it.

Dr. Mickeltee: Please, tell me then.

The Vampire: All right then. It's a year earlier. I'm in a battalion commanded by Pierre-Francois Bouchard and on July 15, was ordered to dig additional fortifications onto the fort near the town of Rashid, located in the Nile Delta. Rashid, for your information, translates to Rosette.

Dr. Mickeltee: I see, go on.

The Vampire: Ah, huh. Okay, so we're digging against an ancient wall for most of the day, and it's hot, and there are mosquitoes the size of your fist, and we're tired as hell when one of the soldiers yells out that he's found something. I'm second in command, so I go over and see a stone that appears to be a broken part of a bigger slab. Strange letters and symbols cover the stone. Nobody can decipher it. Don't ask me why; as soon as I see it, I recognize that it has three types of writing, and it's a message carved into the stone. By this time, Captain Bouchard comes over. He tells everyone but me to get back to work. He can see I'm reading the stone and asks me what it is. I show him the three kinds of writing. The first I recognized was a hieroglyph used by priests for messages. The second, written in Demotic, is the cursive Egyptian script used for daily purposes, and the third, I know, is Ancient Greek, the language of the administration; in other words, the rulers of Egypt who, at the time of the writing, were Greco-Macedonian after Alexander the Great's conquest.

Dr. Mickeltee: But how could you recognize it?

The Vampire: That's the 64-dollar question, isn't it?

Dr. Mickeltee: Didn't your commander, what's his name? Didn't he want to know?

The Vampire: Captain Bouchard? Because I was an officer, Bouchard assumed, like him, trained at the *École Militaire*, where we studied Latin and Greek, and believed I must have come by the other languages as well. He was too interested in taking the stone to Napoleon and claiming credit for himself, which he successfully did. It's his name in the history books, not mine.

Dr. Mickeltee: And your abilities to read those mysterious Hieroglyphs and the other two languages?

The Vampire: I couldn't make a big deal of it, or else Captain Bouchard would have become suspicious. Besides, I had already understood that being a vampire brought with it specific changes in me.

Dr. Mickeltee: Changes? That's what you call them?

The Vampire: Look, Doc—you must realize I was a poor, simple, uneducated French teenager, so I accepted these changes without too much introspection. Had I not been so, I believe my transmogrification would have driven me crazy.

Dr. Mickeltee: And now?

The Vampire: And now?

Dr. Mickeltee: And now that you are no longer a poor, simple, uneducated French teenager, are you crazy?

The Vampire: Tue es le psy tu me dis—you're the shrink, you tell me!

TEN

SPEAKING IN TONGUES

Tue es le psy tu me dis— you're the shrink, you tell me*!*"

Don't you just love it!

After listening to Bernard talk about his language skills, I wanted to revisit the original tapes. Just as I hoped, my vampire now had the uncanny facility to translate each and every word into English.

I'm so caught up in the experience that I automatically repeat his words aloud. I even stand in front of a full-size mirror at the back of a bedroom closet just to see how my mouth forms the same word in, say, Greek, then Latin, and for the hell of it, Yiddish.

Kish mir in tukhes—kiss my ass, is one I find myself repeating that is always good for a laugh or two.

Naturally, I'm safely alone while doing my Babel experiments, but then I fantasize about what I would do if this sudden expertise got the better of me.

How would it play out if I'm reaching for the Mandarin Chicken in the frozen foods section at Trader Joe's when the memory of things deliciously past takes total control of my mind and the vampire in you blurts out in Mandarin how "it felt like an explosion of your most precious bodily fluids into a pillow of cottony cotton," when I consumed Lady Lu in her golden bedchambers in the Forbidden City, that snowy, February evening in 1760, hours after the four-foot three cutie pie with chinaware nakedness set against a blood-red magical place is elevated to 'Consort Qing' by the Qianlong Emperor, Yinzhen, the fourth emperor of the Qing dynasty; and the third Qing emperor to rule over Chine Proper and a great ballroom dancer in his naughty way when he gets dolled-up like one of his concubines."

Those are nights to remember, but not at your local supermarket.

"And now that you are no longer a poor, simple, uneducated French teenager, are you crazy?"

I whirl away from the mirror, but Dr. Mickeltee is nowhere to be seen.

Fuck me—seven ways to Sunday, do The Ancients ever divide! I'm fluent in a laundry basket full of languages (alive and dead), but with that gift of gab, I get Mickeltee, the She Wolf of the psycho ward, ping-ponging in my cranium.

"Thou must be gone, wench, thou must be gone!"

I whirl around. No one. I try to control the breathing that threatens to leap out of my heaving chest, hopefully, before it cracks my sternum. I listen. Nothing! Mickeltee is no more.

It appears I can bring up the quote from *Troilus and Cressida*, Act IV, and I bet if I try, any quip from Shakespeare appropriate to that moment. I must remember that today.

Speaking of today, let's give a think on that for a moment. Will this afternoon's *soirée* at Carly Ford's apartment be as memorable as my assignation with Lady Lu?

Will the joy and delightful frolic be mine, alone, or must I share each living, breathing moment twining with my Janus, Bernard in my head?

I spend an hour choosing my party clothes, finally opting for the very first selection I flung onto the bed sixty minutes ago: Tom Ford slim black jeans, a black Ralph Lauren turtleneck, Alan Edmonds black loafers, and Lorenzo Uomo red socks, living up to the Vampire

Motto; a little dab will do ya! (I only go sock-commander in the heat of the summer.)

Back to the mirror, I go. I look damn good for a vampire my age, don't I?

"Put yourself first. Self-love, my liege, is not so vile a sin as self-neglecting." The Bard got it right again, didn't he?

I return to the bedroom and take in the stack of clothes on the bed.

Is my vampire as indecisive? I have listened to almost all of the recordings and, so far, haven't detected vacillation in any aspect of the vampire in me's behavior, except, perhaps, when selecting his next Recipient. His encounter with one's new companion' in particular, Miss Nellie Bye, demonstrated the vampire's first noticeable change of heart. (FYI, I preferred 'new companion' to the Recipient or the Mark.)

ELEVEN

SUEZ SCHMOOZER

Recording #3. (In English, some French, and Egyptian Slang)

Dr. Mickeltee: Yesterday, you mentioned Nellie Bly, and then you became tired. I'd like you to tell me more about her.

The Vampire: I ran into Nellie Bly in 1889 at the Suez Hotel when she attempted to beat Jules Verne's record of traveling solo around the world in less than 80 days. By the time she reached the Canal, she had crossed the English Channel. She traveled by train from Calais to Paris, stopping in Amiens, where she met Jules Verne himself, who, I read in Hickey's Bengal Gazette papers, told her, Miss, if you are capable of doing it in 79 days, I will congratulate you publicly. She then continued through Brindisi in Italy, crossing the Mediterranean and reaching me in the Suez Canal. From what I also read in Hickey's, she would then be on her way to the Red Sea, the Arabian Sea, Colombo in Sri Lanka, Malaysia, Singapore, Hong Kong, and Yokohama, crossing the Pacific and finally ending her journey by arriving in San Francisco. I could have told her that on a whim two years ago, I, too, decided to break the record, and I did by an entire *five* days. Naturally, I had the advantage of flying when others had to take a train or a ship; however, over long distances—the Arabian Sea is a bitch for a bat, and don't let anyone tell you otherwise, I chose a steamer with a captain who couldn't do enough for me when I told him it was my recently departed mother who lay inside the coffin that accompanied me during that journey. He had only just lost his dear Papa and found in me a kindred soul to whom he could unload his grief buried these last months that made him take to drink and nearly sink his vessel off the strait of Hormuz that, thanks to my companionship would keep him sober and sail unharmed until his mother passed. He would run aground off the coast of Madagascar and lose his captain's license five years down the road. There were no women aboard, so true to myself, it was a dry run.

Dr. Mickeltee: Excuse me for interrupting, but I thought you said vampires didn't sleep in coffins.

The Vampire: (Laughing) Good catch, Dr. Mickeltee. The coffin was empty and only for show, as dictated by the Code, to keep our Vampire legend alive should our movements ever be discovered. For your information, I slept comfortably in my cabin.

Dr. Mickeltee: Again, excuse me for interrupting. Please continue, Nick.

The Vampire: Ahh, Miss Nellie Bly. I've met some ladies who love the grape over the last five hundred years, but my wild Nellie B topped 'em all when it suited her. While she could drink any ten men, including me, under the table, Nellie could then get up on a table, leaving most of us reeling and delivering a Shakespeare soliloquy with the artistry of Ellen Terry. Of course, I knew all about Nellie, who changed her name from Elizabeth Cochran, taking the *nom de plume* Nellie Bly from a popular Stephen Foster song of the same name when she decided to become a journalist. Nellie was a pretty petite thing with the marvelous ability to charm the skin of a snake when it suited her and the guile and tenacity Nellie needed for the scoop of a lifetime that allowed her to commit herself to an asylum at Blackwell Island in New York to expose the conditions there, and eventually wrote the best-selling exposé, *Ten Days in a Mad House*. To beat the record of Phileas Fogg, hero of Jules Verne's romance Around the World in Eighty Days, Nellie had to lay off the vino, so when we met up at the hotel bar, she was nursing a sweet tea. I ordered a Sazerac, a drink that I knew would attract her immediate attention, having read Nellie's articles on the history of the Mardi Gras. I quickly had her in stitches, regaling her with racy tales of past carnival balls without revealing my true nature or the intimate details of my recent journey to The Big Easy, a tasting always limited by the rules of the Code, for as one would expect since the start of this festival in 1699, New Orleans was the numero uno destination for every thirsty vampire who loved coming out of the prerequisite coffin and riding on a float in a Dracula costume. I looked especially dashing in my army uniform, proudly displaying the rank of colonel in *Le Compagnie Universelle du canal maritime de Suez*, known snappily on the canal as *Le Suez*. Every woman grows weak in the knees for a man in uniform, and Nellie was no exception. She was on a tight timetable and had only an hour for lovemaking before she had to set sail for the Red Sea. The temptation to take just a tiny-weensy nip nearly overwhelmed me, but knowing any loss of blood might slow Ellie down and cause her to miss breaking the record she so cherished made my choice for me. While she almost ruined it by giving me a love bite ten seconds after I took off my uniform, no precious liquid drawn on my part, and fifty-seven minutes of joy, I sent Ellie Bly on her way, a little wobbly and her circulatory system flowing a little faster, otherwise, full to the brim and unsucked.

Dr. Mickeltee: Nick, I think that's enough for you today, so when I count to three, you will remember nothing of these memories. One, two, three.

TWELVE

PARTY TIME

It's a pity Dr. Mickeltee let her fears get the better of her, and she jumped the gun and attempted to have my brain fried. Otherwise, I'm sure she enjoys hearing about my meeting with Nefertiti's real-life kin, which turns out to be one heck of a trip down memory lane.

I step over the threshold, into what appears to be a cavernous apartment, and use every bit of mental fortitude to prevent my saliva glands from going Drool-City.

Kristen Hayward, as Billy-Bob of the Double X, where Bernard broke horses back in 1905, said of any woman he had to look up to, "is one tall drink of water."

I slowly push through the crowd to the middle of the living room; head and shoulders above the rest with an attenuated neck that could make Pontormo jealous, Modigliani absolutely bonkers, and every vampire weak in the knees, stands the living, breathing reincarnation of Nefertiti.

Hold your horses! I know that back in the day, Egyptians weren't tall people. Of course, I saw 5'6" Joan Collins in *Land Of The Pharaohs* but that's Hollywood; and boy, if ever a bitch deserved to be buried alive, it was Joanie's character in that film. (It's too bad Joanie's didn't career end there as well, sparing us from watching her in that dreadful *Empire of the Ants* movie.)

Let's put the growth patterns of ancient Egyptian history aside for a moment and consider that with improved nutrition, the magic of pharmacology, and, of course, natural selection (the tiny die young, look it up), if the average basketball player in the NBA has grown over six inches in the last decade, it's a sure bet Egyptian princesses can grow a foot since the 14 century BC.

My CFO goddess has to crane her neck downward to exchange air kisses with Carly Ford, whose blushing cheeks swell making me believe had it been lippy to lippy, our Ms. Carly Ford would have wet her Pucci silk trousers. Was it my admiration for a woman's designer threads that made me lose my concentration and have me play a Red Skelton "Guzzler's Gin" routine and trip over a subway grating on Thirty-Fifth Street?

A woman whose face I can't quite place greets me by name in a lilting Spanish accent and offers me a flute of champagne, winks, and murmurs. "I will see you this Wednesday at 9 a.m."

My confusion doesn't last more than one bubbly sip when Eloise Charles grabs my arm and turns me around. Her delicious gooseneck neck is adorned with a set of egg-shaped pearls that sent an entire South Seas village of divers to their deaths from the bends.

"Isn't Gloria the best housekeeper ever? You know, Nick, she never missed a day during the pandemic. And the places she gets to, you'd think she's double-jointed or a member of *Cirque du Soleil*," glistens Eloise Charles' cheeks as if learning she has enough sky miles to fly free to Antibes.

I'm glad that I'm just a tad over six-one, no, I have no info on a vampire's growth patterns, when I feel a delicate touch graze my right shoulder blade, turn and find myself eyeball to eyeball with Kirsten Hayward who, I'm delighted to report on her choice of footwear, selects a pair of Christian Louboutin Mimiflirt Leather Red Sole Ballerina Mules, instead of his Suede Red Sole Platform Sandals that would add another 5.25 inches and have me staring up at her dimpled chinny-chin-chin I will gleefully wipe clean with tongue, later that evening.

"Hello, Nick. I'm Kirsten, and you're the mysterious gentleman from 6J who has the misfortune of knocking himself out while crossing Madison Avenue. Not paying attention and following some attractive damsel, I take it,"

Right away I catch her smile secretly suggesting she knows I'm hearing her voice through Nefertiti through Meketaten, making the dog in 'His Master's Voice' stand the fuck up, and realize RCA isn't the first one in the history of mankind to transcribe a voice.

I don't want to correct her and tell her I tripped over the subway grating on 35th and not while I was crossing Madison Avenue. Still, as far as disabusing her of the idea I was eye-balling a pretty young thing, well, I thought I'd just grin and let her think I'm a cool kiddy from the city.

I instinctively take the hand that isn't holding a flute of champagne and gently hold it a moment longer, allowing my self-driving vampire–in-me vibe to Kelvin-up Kirsten's palm.

The immediate results of my touchy-touch-touch are, for her cheeks to flush-rush in anticipation of the open road of ecstasy awaiting us on our journey to a ravishing *dénouement*. (That verbose description is short for 'I know, she knows, I know, we're going to get it on.')

"Joe tells me you're in advertising."

Joe—Joe, right, June Champion's partner and the one who took her to the ER after she fell in almost the same spot I did on Thirty-fifth Street. I wait for more from Kristen, but there isn't any, so to avoid any rude silence, I have to respond.

"Freelance copywriter," I quickly chinwag. I can be so cunningly humble if I say so myself.

"Oh, don't be modest. Joe said you're the creative genius responsible for the slogan: 1-10, the best beer is Westvleteren 12. The taste that's off the charts!"

Snappy, not bad if I say so myself, says my grinny grin grin as I take the win for the home team.

"I showed your ad to my advertising team as an example of the kind of catchy headline and tag I'd like to have for my new fragrance, which is yet to be named. Do your creative gifts lend themselves to naming products as well, Nick?"

You kidding, lady! I'm the one who came up with the name 'Animal Crackers' and put Standard Bakery's biscuits in every kid's lunch box back in 1871. Naturally, I don't say that. Do you think I'm an idiot?

"I enjoy naming products; it's always a challenge." You can never pretend to eat enough humble pie when you know you're The Man.

"Nick, I don't want to put you on the spot, but could you name one or two slogans I might recognize?"

"*Restless Love.* Why don't you call your new fragrance *Restless Love?*" I respond with all the self-assurance of a man who doubles down on a Royal Flush.

"*Restless Love?*" Kristen's ready to do a Jeté out of her Ballerina Mules.

"A fragrance that is abundant, overflowing, without measure, and most of all, never cautious," I continue. Over-flowering, sure, but in truth, the description I would give of my vampire and not some dab-a-do, *eau de cologne.*

I have to blink. It's Nefertiti through Meketaten through how many other women bundling up centuries-in-the-making photons now ganging up on me and gangling onto my centuries-old electromagnetic microwaves. Are you ready to rumble?

"Let me talk to my team, but I simply love it."

"I'm glad."

"Of course, I'll pay you."

"No need, my gift to you."

"Nonsense, and let's not argue."

She takes in the room. "You're lucky to live here. I think this is an amazing building. Built first as a hotel to serve the department store across the street, and then turned into a co-op for discerning tenants who know how desirable it is to live in Murray Hill. The history of New York is filled with fascinating histories, don't you think, Nick?"

Before I can respond, Kirsten turns and accepts another glass of champagne from Gloria, whose laughing eyes slyly throw me an approving sparkle, indicating that she expects to find Kirsten between the sheets when she arrives at my apartment at nine, next Wednesday.

"Are you not a lover of history, Nick? I could swear you are."

Her eyes, which are equestrian brown, flicker playfully now that she's lowered their Kelvin intensity from flame broil to simmering. Thankfully, this relieves me of my throbbing headache, snaps my sleeping synapses back into Electric Avenue activity in time to control my drooling, and allows me to say, "Sure," so damn cleverly.

Tell me, I don't have a way with words.

"Is your apartment as charming as this and so full of secret passageways that one could just lose oneself in?"

She takes a slow mo sip of champagne, and all atoms are one: glass and muscle. Hi-de-ho, my Insane Love Serpent awakens, unfurls full length, hi-de-ho; and Kirsten's eyes once more flame broils as I cleverly respond, "*Sure.*"

It's worth repeating- do I have a way wid words, or not!

THIRTEEN

I LEFT MY BLOOD
IN SAN FRANCISCO

Recording #3. (In English, no translation needed)

Dr. Mickeltee: You told me about living on the West Coast and your connection to the Egyptian Pharaohs.

The Vampire: I was thrilled and delighted when I recognized my new neighbor at 710 Steiner Street, the French artist BH, to be the living incarnation of Meketaten the moment she showed me her sculpture, Behold the Aten. Aside from the fact that Meketaten, in Egyptian, translates to 'Behold the Aten', standing beside her statue, BH, and the second of six daughters born to the Egyptian Pharaoh Akhenaten and his Great Royal Wife Nefertiti, is unmistakably two peas in an eternal pod. I had taken up residence two months earlier at 710 Steiner Street, known around San Francisco as one of the 'Painted Ladies' for the row of Victorian houses at 710–720 Steiner Street, across from Alamo Square Park. These distinguishing houses were built between 1892 and 1896 by developer Matthew Kavanaugh, who lived next door in the 1892 mansion at 722 Steiner Street. According to the latest gossip supplied by my landlady, Sister Terry Bachman, she, of enormous girth, unshakably believes he is a direct descendant of the emperor, Julius Caesar. Still, when I met Mr. Kavanaugh, I instinctively marveled at his resemblance, not to Caesar, but to Marcus Claudius Marcellus, a Roman consul whose reincarnate, Agostino Crispi, I dined with at his home, Villa Trastevere, in June of 1901, and to the bedroom ten days later, when Agostino was away in Palermo. I had the opportunity to have my way with his wife, Giuditta Tavani, a Neapolitan of extraordinary beauty and a neck to equal Maria Salviati, whose portrait by Pontormo in the Walters Art Museum in the Mount Vernon Section of Baltimore is one I never tire of viewing whenever I fly into the neighborhood. I have to confess I am inexplicitly attracted to women of a particular historical lineage. The drawing of their precious fluids brings unexplainable flashes of a past existence I had never experienced otherwise. Even in my dream state, when a jigsaw puzzle of jumbled misadventures bombards me, sometimes frightening me because of their realistic weirdness, they never transport me beyond five hundred years, whereas, when I consume the ichor of these women of a particular lineage, I'm instantly whisked millenniums, to a time when I walk amongst the Pharaohs, dare I admit, as one of them, even more alarming, more than one of them. The only constant is that my tripping will last forty-eight hours, and as their vital fluid mixes with mine, I never know how many bodies I will inhabit or for how long. During these hours, as our intermingled blood travels through my circulatory system, I experience my heart rate remaining steady, my senses sharpening, but my conscious brain separating into two, one containing my thoughts and the other of the body I inhabit. Yet, this separation doesn't interfere with or disrupt my behavior. Nor is it like a fever dream, where one can have the out-of-body experience of looking down at oneself. I never leave my body. I continue to be who I am while being someone else. The first time I experienced this phenomenon; I thought it to be a hallucination. How can my consciousness be split into two yet work seamlessly together? After two more encounters, one with the Duchess of Amalfi and the other with a Persian Belly dancer, I saw a shrink, actually two shrinks. The first, a Freudian, tried unsuccessfully to hypnotize me and, believing he had put me under, declared my problems were due to the fact my mother never breastfed me. The second, a Reichian, blending somatic and cognitive awareness, shook me up until my teeth rattled and I came clean about my double-life traumas; he acknowledged he experienced the same phenomenon when he smoked the opium pipe. That afternoon, as I left his office after saying no to joining him at a local opium den, the Vampire Code strictly prohibits drugs for obvious reasons of public safety, I looked up at the sky and said, fuck it, and now I just go with it.

Dr. Mickeltee: You wouldn't be talking about Dr. Gregory Von Verklempt, by any chance, would you? He wrote the groundbreaking book *Narcolepsies and Me: How I Will Never Go To Sleep Again, and Neither Should You.*

The Vampire: You know, he was a great ballroom dancer.

Dr. Mickeltee: I did not know that. I always wanted to be a tap dancer. I'm a fool for all those Fred and Ginger movies.

Dr. Mickeltee begins singing:

"I'm in heaven. And my heart beats so that I can hardly speak.
And I seem to find the happiness I seek.
When we're out together dancing cheek to cheek."

FOURTEEN

WALK LIKE AN EGYPTIAN, DANCE LIKE FRED ASTAIRE

You heard him, right, didn't you? I walk amongst the Pharaohs, dare I admit, as one of them, even more alarming, more than one of them.

Turn me into a parakeet and pull my voice box out! How much can a guy take before he throws himself off the nearest bridge?

Isn't it enough to want to blow the top of your head off to discover you're a vampire, not even a millennial or even a baby boomer vampire, but one that is a two hundred and fifty-nine years old French country bumpkin?

And now, and now and fucking NOW—to learn, white boy, you're a lot older—like 5,174 years older, give or take, a few thousand leap years!

The only way to handle that without scoring enough animal tranquilizers to knock out a rhino is to turn the recording off and immediately go onto YouTube, locate the 'I'm in heaven' scene from *Top Hat,* and play it repeatedly while singing and dancing around the room until I lose my voice. (I have a terrible singing voice, which is odd because on another of the recordings, my vampire brags about how he seduced the young wife of an octogenarian Swedish ambassador by singing, "One Enchanted Evening.")

I collapse on the sofa. Actually, I'm feeling giddy. Being a vampire only has grim implications, even though I'm really not the monster of the myth, only a creation of an ancient tribe of immortals who wanted to live forever without being hunted down like—well—vampires.

Nevertheless, we are a PR nightmare, but to be an Egyptian Pharaoh is a new set of golden threads and one worth strutting your stuff in.

Who isn't a fan of movie spectacles like *The Egyptian*, *Cleopatra*, *The Prince of Egypt,* and *Land of the Pharaohs*? Let's forget *The Ten Commandments;* the boss man in that saga was a bad motorcycle.

Or maybe not! Maybe, if I listen to more of the recordings, I'll find out my Pharaoh helped Moses and really did 'let his people go!'

You don't think so? What about his relationship with the artist BH in San Fran? He was a good guy there and left her alone, right? He stuck to the rules. Rule Number Five, or wasn't it Six? Don't drink blood out of a blood bank.

In other words, never choose your next mark as someone you see regularly: neighbors, co-workers, building employees, your local cleaner, and certainly not your barber.

Kirsten's relationship with my neighbor, Carly Ford, is a perfect example and puts a kibosh on Kristen and our mixing of de blood. However, as with every rule, there are extenuating circumstances.

Hold on! What could ever allow a vampire to break Rule Number Five or Rule Number Six of the Vampire Code?

Well, also according to the Code, except for discovering the two tiny puncture wounds in their neck—on occasion, they miss even this telltale sign—' A Friend of the Family'—another innocuous euphemism the Ancients used to minimize the horror—will not immediately remember a single detail of the encounter; so, should you come face-to-face with them the next day in the elevator, on the bus, at work, or serving coffee at your local eatery, it will be business as usual.

Here's the rub! Sometime during this grace period, your 'Friend of the Family' will begin to experience a recurring nightmare that slowly but surely brings bits of the bite to the surface of their conscious memory until the entire suckling event wakes them, and their ghastly screams bring the house down in abject terror.

The lesson all vampires must take from this information is always to cover your face when you go for the gold and make sure there are no identifying marks like bat, fangs, blood drippings, or Bella Lugosi tattoos that could finger you in a police lineup or even worse, to a mob of your fellow villagers, out for blood, no pun intended, and ready to plunge a stake through your heart.

By the way, any place on your torso would do the trick, but we like to keep that under wraps lest it spoil the legend.

Yes, yes, I understand these inconsistencies make following my story confusing, but how do I feel each time I listen to a recording, receive new information, and hear stories that don't jibe with other previous versions? Vampire/Pharaoh—Pharaoh/Vampire, this unspooling makes *Rashomon look* like a skit from Sesame Street.

I suppose I'm contributing to the confusion. Had I begun listening to the recordings linearly instead of haphazardly skipping around, perhaps that straightforward approach would have solved the problem. Unfortunately, I'm not a linear guy but more of a hop, skip, and jump kind of boy, lest you step on a crack and break your vampire's back. The upshot: We have to go with the flow and hope it all gets fixed in the mix.

However, I don't intend to bite and run with the lovely Kirstin. No, I have another plan. I'm going to leave her blood supply intact, but instead, 'have my way with her.'

Don't you just love that phrase—*have my way with her*? I mean, it is so much more grown-up and gentlemanly than 'I'm going to get me some.'

What makes me believe vampires can even have sex? All the words I associate with 'having my way', like devour or ravage, that come from the recordings appear to relate to the act of filling up to the brim with hemoglobin.

Moreover, my vampire's only physical moves are one-on-one with the neck. There is no whole-body lovemaking, throwing one's sacroiliac out in tumbling and twisting embraces that even the Kamasutra doesn't include for sound orthopedic reasons.

So, again, you ask, what makes me think vampires can have sex?

I'll let you in on a little secret, but you must promise not to tell anyone. I may have memory loss but buried deep in my hypothalamus; I have an unexplainable cranial E-ZPass to being a Smooth-Moving Dude who enjoys taking his sweet, gentle time with a woman, slowly, carefully, caressing, exploring every exposed, and not so exposed, nook and cranny of flesh and sweetness and can feel in his loins the tightening of her muscles and the increasingly rapid jerking and thrusting until he experiences the powerful jet-like explosion of his precious bodily fluids flooding her pulsating G-spot. Can you feel me, Bro?

FIFTEEN

ALWAYS THE BRIDESMAID, NEVER THE BRIDE

Recording #3. (In English, no translation needed)

Dr. Mickeltee: Do you resent being a vampire, Nick?

The Vampire: Resent being a vampire? What makes you say that?

Dr. Mickeltee: I detect a tone of bitterness when you speak about the famous people you've come in contact with over the centuries.

The Vampire: You're reading the smoke signals incorrectly. I'm not bitter. I've come to terms with who I am. I accept my fate, and I understand my destiny.

Dr. Mickeltee: You're not at all jealous of these individuals in some manner?

The Vampire: Why do you think that just because I might have mentioned that others have gotten credit for what I did—Edmond Haley, for instance?

Dr. Mickeltee: Edmond Haley?

The Vampire: As in Haley's Comet.

Dr. Mickeltee: Oh, I saw it in 1986, I think! It was so exciting!

The Vampire: It was February 9, 1986, to be exact. It was when Halley's Comet came closest to Earth on its way out of the solar system at a distance of 39 million miles. Where were you?

Dr. Mickeltee: Marfa Texas. It's a small town near Big Bend National Park in West Texas, that's where I grew up. My parents and cousins still live there.

The Vampire: I was also in Texas, at the Dallas Planetarium, at the director's invitation. Naturally, I never told him I met Edmond in 1761, when he was first carrying out his observations of objects in the sky.

Dr. Mickeltee: Of course you did.

The Vampire: At the time, I was going under the assumed name of the Italian-born astronomer Giovanni Domenico Cassini.

Dr. Mickeltee: You were impersonating someone?

The Vampire: Don't look so shocked, doctor. I should have mentioned this before, but I would assume another person's identity multiple times. I suppose it's another one of the Gifts of the Vampire or something I took to and was certainly good at.

Dr. Mickeltee: You don't know?

The Vampire: There's no mention of Identity Theft in the Code, and as I don't attend the yearly Vampire Convention in Transylvania, get the Vampire News Letter, chainmail, or have an account on Tic Toc or Instagram where I can see Vampires doing ramp and grab tricks on a skateboard, I'm out of the blood group, so to speak. (The vampire laughs)

Dr. Mickeltee: You don't appear to take your actions very seriously.

The Vampire: Oh, but I do. Becoming Dr. Cassini allowed me to join Dr. Haley in the spring of 1681. It allowed me to explain to him my theory of comets and identify them as objects in space, heretofore known as unexplainable objects.

Dr. Mickeltee: My god, you were also an astronomer!

The Vampire: It was my observations that were the basis of A Synopsis of the Astronomy of Comets, which Edmond Halley published in 1705, in which he described the parabolic orbits of 24 comets that I had observed from 1337 to 1698. (The vampire laughs)

Dr. Mickeltee: What's so funny, Nick?

The Vampire: I couldn't even get the credit when posing as someone else.

Dr. Mickeltee: I don't understand.

The Vampire: Here I am, one of the greatest astronomers in Europe known for his work in determining the rotation periods of Mars and Jupiter and discovering the four satellites of Saturn, but does Edmund Haley acknowledge the great Dr. Giovanni Domenico Cassini when he publishes his synopsis, not one word, not one thank you. Talk about being pissed off. I was ready to turn the stuck-up English prig into a vampire when I realized that would be too good for him.

Dr. Mickeltee: Where was the real Dr. Cassini during this time?

The Vampire: Oh! That's the beauty of it. You see, my friend Cassini —I really did admire the guy— was a real man about town. If he hadn't been helping Pope Clement IX with fortifications, river management, and the flooding of the Po River, he would have been in Paris, creating a topographic map of France. His constant traveling made it so easy for me to assume his identity. I knew we'd never be in the same place or country if I planned my trips accordingly. Of course, with cell phones and all kinds of tracking equipment, it can get tricky today, but if I wanted to, I could still pull it off if I were careful.

Dr. Mickeltee: When did you have the time to... (Mickeltee laughs) When did you study astronomy, Nick?

The Vampire: 1761 to 65, Trinity College, Cambridge. The best four years of my life. Where else could I meet the man who influenced me more than any other, at least until then?

Dr. Mickeltee: Will you tell me who that person was, or just sit there grinning?

The Vampire: Do you have any apples, Dr. Mickeltee?

SIXTEEN

I NEED TO BE PUT UNDER

I don't need the money (more on my money situation later in my yet-to-be-written chapter, "Blood Money").

I already discussed 'no attention, please,' so that's not why I want to complete my vampire book and make it to the New York Times Bestseller List.

Do I owe it to Bernard to finish what he started? Is that it? I have no fucking clue, Boyo.

I do know one thing for sure: I will figure out how to include Sir Isaac Newton in the story.

"Do you have any apples, Dr. Mickeltee?" I would have loved to see her face when my vampire went to the open window and dropped the Red Delicious down those fifteen stories to its smashing finish.

So, what's my plan of attack? I will re-listen to all the tapes and make notes, but I'm pretty sure I don't have enough material for one, let alone two, of the concepts. There is only one thing for it. I have to go under again.

For about a millisecond, I toy with the idea of calling Dr. Rosamund Mickeltee. No kidding, Sherlock, that's a non-starter. The minute I hang up, she's on the horn ratting me out to the coppers, informing them that she's got a patient who thinks he's a vampire (Imagine that?).

She'll go on to say she's afraid that Nick is so loony tunes, not only is he a danger to himself, but to the community at large, which, by the way, is the wealthy Murray Hill section of our fair city and, therefore, must be hospitalized ASAP, so her pal at Electric City can shock the shit out of him and turn him into a drooling zombie who won't hurt a fly.

The last thing I need in life is two muscle-bound men from Shutter Island fitting me into a ready-to-wear, straight jacket, and duck-walking me out the front door for all the daytime doormen to see. Do you have any idea what that will do to my maintenance?

But wait! Suddenly, the image of Dr. Mickeltee's associate's shapely and substantial ass bending over to put food in my fridge lights up the wattage in my eyeballs, fifty volts.

I guarantee the pretty young Betty Furness won't immediately dime me out if I call her for a cup of coffee. It's times like this when stress overwhelms me that I need to seduce a lovely woman, and by seduce, I do not mean put two holes in her neck and suck some blood.

But can I take the chance? Suppose her phone's tapped, and when pretty young Betty knocks on my door, her bitch boss, Dr. Mickeltee pushes her aside, and those same brutes in their summer whites barge in with tranquilizer guns and put me down like a defenseless antelope?

Somewhere in the back of my mind, a tiny bell rings. No, it's not a signal that another angel has gotten their wings (thank you very much, Frank Capra). I quickly go to my contact list. Down the list, my fingers fly! A's, B's, H's—there it is—M's! Madame Lumière: Magic, Mysticism and Masseuse.

Magic, Mysticism, and Masseuse! Shit ho—if the 3 M's aren't enough of a good omen, what do you know, Little Big Man! Madame Lumière is a Murray Hill neighbor living just down the street, between Park and Lex.

Hot damn! I hop onto YouTube, type in "When You're Hot, You're Hot," slip off my Alan Edmonds, hit play, and begin dancing and singing to Jimmy Nick's throaty, twanging tune. Whoopee and whoop-de-do!

Madame Lumière's address is an elegant, four-story limestone townhouse. When I looked it up on the Internet, I discovered it is also the home of *Magasin d'antiquités* 35, whose proprietor is S.J. Shelby. I wonder if they could be the same person.

More hot damns! I must become a shamus. A what? A shamus, a private eye, a detective!

Okay, I confess, I just saw *Lady In The Lake*, and maybe I let myself be carried away. (You think?)

For the three days, feeling less vampire and more Phillip Marlow, I park my Mazda 3 across the street from her place (more on my car in the yet-to-be-written chapter, "And The Vampire Went Vroom"), and to keep me company, I'm watching *Farewell My Lovely* on my iPhone for the umpteenth time and like the fictionalized detective, I'm pretending to be, I'm scoping out a villain's lair, or in this case, Madame Lumière domicile.

I play with the idea of pretending to be a shopper (again, out of that movie), but the fancy placard in the window declares 'to the trade only.' I take that as a sign warning me to play it straight, so I call for an appointment.

The recorded voice, which has a distinct and very inviting South Carolina accent (how my subconscious recognizes that only the vampire in me knows) informs me that Madame Lumière only sees clients on the weekends (coincidentally when the shop's closed) and only between 11:00 a.m. and 1:00 p.m., and kindly requests that I leave my number. Madame Lumière will get back to me.

That evening, I received a text informing me that Madame Lumière could see me this coming Sunday at 1:00 p.m., if that is suitable, to reply with a 'Y' if yes and an 'N' if no.

I immediately responded with the 'Y,' recognizing her 21st-century communication skills as a tad anachronistic, considering she's a mystic. I would be expecting something more—well, mystical— say, like a ghostly message on a mirror that disappears as soon as I read it.

Naturally, I'm at sixes and sevens. How much of myself should I reveal before Madame Lumière née Miss North Carolina of a certain age puts me under?

Let's be real here; if she's halfway decent at this hypnosis business, she will quickly discover the awful truth. Then what? While I'm in La-La Land, does she stick to the script and put a stake through my heart, or will she take the road more traveled and turn rat fink; that way, when I come to, I'm alive but twisted up like a pretzel in my summer whites, cocooned in a padded cell on the familiar Shutter Island, doing the Chlorpromazine shuffle, thinking I'm Eric Carmen and singing "All By Myself."

Risk vs. reward—how much do I want to be an author? Again, let's be real here. I can call W and tell him my face-painted-sidewalk- slam has forever changed me. Instead of spending the next months cooped up in my apartment, writing novels about my past lives, I will look to the future, live life to the max, and travel the world.

On the other hand (there is always another hand when you're telling a Vampire Story), if I do want to complete the books, one way I can ensure that Madame Lumière doesn't turn me over is to tell her right off the bat (no pun intended) if I don't call a certain number five minutes after I come out of my trance, a very disturbed person will come a calling and burn the house down, but not before he will slowly saw off her limbs and then cut out her tongue because that's what they do with stoolies.

I feel so good about this second scenario that my anxiety about completing the book totally disappears, and I feel incredibly confident that my meeting with Madame Lumière will go over swimmingly. It's good to be a vampire or someone thinking he's one.

SEVENTEEN

LADY CHANEL

In the end, I confess all. Madame Lumière is nonplus.

After listening to my vampire's lineage, this sweet, charming, sixty-something lady from South Carolina (decked out from neck to foot in Chanel—more about Chanel and how I met Coco in the yet-t0-be-written chapter, "I Can Sew With The Best of Them"), who is either on heavy tranqs or indeed is the Universe's E-ZPass, gently reaches across the table, gently takes my hand in hers and asks if I have a preference for cheesecake over mousse au chocolate.

Nothing calms a nutter like me more than meeting a nuttier nutter. When I reply that it's like asking me to choose between a pair of Gucci or Ferragamo velvet soft loafers (Don't get me wrong, I love Alan Edmonds, but nothing beats the Italians for softness), she releases my hand and playfully slaps me on the shoulder, directing me to stare straight into the giant crystal ball between us.

Something tells me I should do as she instructs, or she'll turn me into a walnut tree. A string of bright connecting crystal balls, signifying what I suspect are the planets in our solar system, float inside the orb.

"Nick, on each of those distant worlds, live our reincarnates. When the Universe so dictates, these souls are then granted the opportunity to reach out to their reincarnate and once more live in a corporeal body."

I nod agreeably. That's what you do with someone who can raise the dead.

"In the Universe's infinite wisdom, I have been granted the gift of facilitating these reincarnations. This past year, I am happy to say that Cleopatra, Richard the Lion-Hearted, Leonardo da Vinci, and Peggy Lee lived again through my auspices. However, I must tell you, Nick, that past life entries are not simple."

"No kidding," I say with real excitement because that's what you do when you hear that Peggy Lee probably sat in this very chair.

"Recently, one of my reincarnates thought himself the reincarnation of Humpty-Dumpty. Still, after a two-hour-long regression, it became apparent that Spanky from the Our Gang Comedies required re-entry. While I don't think your situation will be anything like that, I am concerned that your desire to ask your reincarnate a set of questions and treat him like a material witness or, worse, an unaccredited ghostwriter may cause him not to re-enter this world."

The last thing I want to do is throw Madame Lumière back on her Chanel heels and make her believe that I'm acting like the Grand Inquisitor.

"So, Madame Lumière, I need your wise counsel. What questions should I ask Bernard when I'm put under?"

"Well, Nick, after listening to the recordings, is there anything about your reincarnation that piques your curiosity other than discovering his meals before he seduced the cook, the maid, and all the ladies at the table?"

I didn't have to think twice. "I'm constantly thrilled by Bernard's accomplishment and curious as yellow as to what other talents my vampire may possess."

"Well then, let's see if we can bring him out, shall we?"

EIGHTEEN

THE ASYLUM SEEKER

Recording #1/mp (English, no translation needed)

Madame Lumière: Good afternoon. I want to introduce myself. I'm Madame Lumière. To whom do I have the pleasure of speaking?

The Vampire: (French accent) Madame Lumière. *Bon après-midi. J'ai eu beaucoup de noms.*

Madame Lumière. I'm afraid my high school French won't do. Too rusty, you know. Could we continue in English?

The Vampire: *Bien sur.* (He drops the French accent.) Of course, of course. As to my name. I've had many. If I knew what questions you have for me and could provide answers in a suitable time frame, I could provide an equally suitable name.

Madame Lumière: I understand you have many accomplishments. You speak multiple languages. What other talents do you possess?

The Vampire: I accompanied Beethoven on the violin.

Madame Lumière: Thee Beethoven?

The Vampire: I was known then as Julius Otto Graham from Warsaw, so that you may address me as Otto.

Madame Lumière: And when was this, Otto?

The Vampire: It was during his Violin Concerto #5 performance, opus 24.

Madame Lumière: Oh, go on! I just listened to it on a recording by Yehudi and his sister, Hephzibah Menuhin, on WQXR.

The Vampire: It was December 23, 1806, and I remember that evening as if it were yesterday. Do you know the Theater an der Wien in Vienna?

Madame Lumière: No, I don't. Please continue, Otto.

The Vampire: Ah, that's a shame. It's gone now, of course. Destroyed. But, back in the day—magnifique. The building was designed by the most famous architect of the time, Franz Jäger, naturally in the Empire style. It was marvelously adorned, lavishly equipped, and enormous—one of the largest theaters of its kind in all the world.

Madam De Lumière: I'm sorry I never had the opportunity to see it, but now I'm seeing it through your eyes, aren't I, Otto?

The Vampire: The night in question was a benefit concert for Franz Clement, who, as you probably are aware, was the leading violinist of the day. And, such a good friend to Ludwig. (Whispering) I happen to know that Franz helped him sort out some problems when Ludwig was writing *Fidelio*.

Madame Lumière: I know, of course, the famous violinist Franz Clement, but I never knew of his part in helping Ludwig—I mean Von Beethoven, finish that wonderful opera. It's a pity he never wrote another opera.

The Vampire: (Regular voice) That's a story for another time. What I tell you now—it's not for publication—*N'est pas*.

Madame Lumière: *Bien entendu*. (Giggling) I can't believe my French is coming back.

The Vampire: You feel like a schoolgirl again, don't you?

Madame Lumière: Oh, Otto, you're a devil.

The Vampire: So, some have said.

Madame Lumière: No, no, it was just an expression, Nick—I mean, Otto.

The Vampire. Pish, pish. Anyway, Ludwig finishes the solo part so late that when he arrives at the Theater and hands it to Franz, Franz has only one choice: he must sight-read his part of the performance. Unfortunately, it became too much for poor old Franz, so with the lights aimed at Ludwig and just before the *Ma Mon Troppo,* I slipped in during the Allegro and replaced Franz until the beginning of the Rondo, at which time, with the lights again directed on Ludwig; we once more switched places. Happily, Franz and I were of similar height and weight, and since we were both dressed in formal wear, the audience was never aware that Franz hadn't accompanied Ludwig throughout the entire performance.

Madame Lumière: When did you begin to play the violin? Were you encouraged to play by your family? Were they also musically gifted?

The Vampire: Gifts, you say? Let me tell you about gifts. When a human turns into a vampire, specific childhood memories are stored temporarily until the new entity can, sometime in the future, handle their past. How's that for a gift, or is it a curse, or is it neither, but what is? I understand the question, and if you must know, I have no idea where my musical abilities come from, nor do I question any of them.

Madame Lumière: Them? Do you have more?

The Vampire: (Laughing) You can also say that the gifts keep coming when one becomes a vampire. You know my facility with languages. *Bonjour, Ciao, Hallo, Geiá sou, Kon'nichiwa, Nǐ hǎo, salve, Tashi Delek* is just a few off the tip of my tongue and the tip of the iceberg. Not only do I play the violin beautifully, but I also have a beautiful operatic singing voice. Back in the day, I successfully auditioned at Covent Garden as a *heldentenor* for the role of Siegfried in Götterdämmerung.

Madame Lumière: Have you performed in the States, Otto? Perhaps I've seen you at the Met, or did I hear you on WQXR from the Lyric?

The Vampire: In 1954, I was on a talent show on the radio here in the States, billed as the next Perry Como. Or was it Vic Damon? Then along came Bill Haley and the Comets, and I certainly had no desire to sing "Rock Around The Clock." I did like Doo Wop. Because I could change my operatic range, I could also perform as a countertenor and sing falsetto, if not better than The Flamingos' lead singer. Alas, it wasn't meant to be because I left for the Motor City to design automobiles. Remember the Pontiac Chieftain with the Indian hood ornament that lit up when you started the car? That was one of my inventions.

Madame Lumière: I certainly do. I had a sorority sister at Clemson with a bright red one and a white top. I believe it had air conditioning and power windows.

The Vampire: There was a certain young lady, the heir to one of the Big Three, with whom I became involved to the point where I had to choose between love and personal survival.

Madame Lumière: You intended to make her a vampire?

The Vampire: Ah, the best intentions of mice and men. What I desired and what I had to do were two different kettles of fish. The Vampire Code has stringent rules regarding that. Rules that one must stick to, like Gorilla Glue. The penalty for not obeying is absolute. Removed and banished for all eternity to where who knows? I can assure you that the location makes The Hotel California a better choice.

Madame Lumière: So, you left the lady and went where?

The Vampire: First to a private girls' school outside Toledo. Then, an advertising agency in Parsippany, New Jersey, a dairy farm in Pauling, New York, and finally to the sound stages of MGM at the corner of Jefferson Boulevard and Overland Avenue in downtown Tinsel Town. It was my 'Feel Good Century'. Don't get me wrong,

Europe, the Middle East, all those magical lands; I will never forget those encounters, and I look forward to returning, but there is something about America that allows you to be yourself. To let loose and be fancy-free. I think it is the open spaces. Just get in a car and go. In Europe, there are borders and inspections; one cannot pick up and go willy-nilly. Indeed, I can choose to fly and avoid the hassle, and in emergencies, I have done just that, but that creates its own set of problems: new papers, passports, vehicles, and clothing. And there is always the competition. Oh, I was clever and always found a clear path, but the stress can get to you. Vampires may be immortal, but we're not immune to the pressure of constantly looking over our shoulder to see if someone else is going to fly in and bite the neck that feeds us, or worse, knock us off our mark. Oh, I'm aware of the Hundred Kilometers Rule and the penalties for infringing on someone else's territory, but until we're all forced to wear body cams, it's 'he said, he said'. I'm using 'he' to mean both genders. More on female vampires in the yet-to-be-written chapter, "Lipstick on Your Collar, Blood on My Lips."

Madame Lumière: So, you have been here, in the States, ever since, Otto? Or shall I call you Nick now that you're living here?

The Vampire: Nick will be fine. He'll feel better about that, won't he? Ah, yes, I am a permanent resident at 31 East 35th Street, so it reads my New York State driver's license. Oh, but Madame Lumière, understand me. I'm still a Frequent Flyer. (Laughing) *Frequent Flyer*, I love saying that. Anywho, I get *shpilkes* staying in one place for too long, so every month or so, I take a trip.

Madame Lumière: *Shpilkes?* Is that a disease that strikes vampires?

The Vampire: (Laughing) It's Yiddish, another language I speak fluently. How long have you lived in New York, Madame Lumière?

Madame Lumière: Over thirty years.

The Vampire: *Oy vey!*

Madame Lumière: *Oy vey!* (Laughing) I get it!

The Vampire: Still haven't lost your South Carolina accent? Colombia, I bet.

Madame Lumière: Why yes, how did you know?

The Vampire: Another of my gifts. Mimicking any accent or dialect I choose. (Southern Accent). Why, honey child, I do declare tomorrow is another day.

(They both laugh)

The Vampire: So, *nu*?

Madame Lumière: *Nu*?

The Vampire: (Laughing) Go on. What else?

Madame Lumière: Ah, more Yiddish. Of course.

The Vampire: You got it!

Madame Lumière: You're a fascinating subject, Otto. Oh, I forgot, Nick.

The Vampire: Otto was such a long time ago.

Madame Lumière: Nick, I don't believe I have ever met a...

The Vampire: Person with such a unique...

Madame Lumière: Profile.

The Vampire: I was going to say DNA.

Madame Lumière: That, too.

The Vampire: I can imagine how confusing this may seem, Madame Lumière. After all, it's not every day you get to meet a monster that's not a myth. Oh, don't worry, I'm not going to leap up from this table and take a bite out of your neck, lovely, generous, and tempting as it is; render you a little light-headed, dizzy, perhaps, depending on your blood sugar levels; other than that, my bit is not an altogether unpleasant experience, I can personally attest to that. However, unlike what you have seen in the movies, I can assure you that if I did take a nip, you would not turn into a zombie, slave, or indeed a vampire. That last transformation takes place under exceptional circumstances; I can also attest to that, most assuredly, I can.

Madame Lumière: I'm happy to hear that. Now, Nick, you know that you lost your memory some time ago, aren't you?

The Vampire: A most unfortunate and unforeseen situation, but one I'm confident that you, with my help, of course, will soon rectify. (In an exaggerated Southern Accent) *N'est pas*, Madame Lumière?

Madame Lumière: (Equally exaggerated Southern Accent) *Bien sur.* (Giggling)

The Vampire: (Regular voice) So, let's get on with it, shall we?

Madame Lumière: (Regular voice) What would you like to discuss?

The Vampire: I think Nick would like to hear how I ate and loved my way through the great houses of Europe. I understand; my agent wants to see a manuscript. What about all those other yet-to-be-written chapters I've been discussing, you ask? I'm saving those for My Life Story and keeping that plan on the down low—even from Nick— until I'm ready to publish. *N'est pas*

Madame Lumière: *Bien sur.* (Giggling)

NINETEEN

IT'S GOOD TO BE ALIVE!

Goddamn it, I'll say it loud and proud—it's good to be alive!

Whoop-de-freakin'-doo, I only had to get up and pee once during the night, and if that doesn't call for a shout-out, I don't know what does.

What, you think, a centuries-old vampire doesn't have trouble with his bladder? Think again, *mein mann*. I may be timeless immemorial on the outside, but on the inside, all that glitters on the MRI may be old.

Before I discuss the intricacies of a Vampire's organ's life and times, let me explain how we Ageless Ones know how many candles to put on our birthday cake.

According to The Elders, back in the day, there may have been one too many calendars, so Pope Gregory XIII issued the papal bull *Inter gravissimas* in 1582, introducing the Gregorian calendar as a modification of and replacement for the Julian calendar. Greg does this because (as rumor whispers it) good old XIII is, in fact, a vampire, and like any obedient vampire who knows what's good for them, when The Boss Man orders him to make it easier for subsequent generations of Gregorians and Julian (i.e. vampires), he gets with the program, pronto.

The Hillels, Amirs, and Zichens of the world have their timetable, but when we Western Cats hear the Gregorians chant Neil Sedaka's "Calendar Girl," vamps from the world over come back at yah, singing and dancing to Bob Segar's "Still the Same."

So, what's with the organs, huh? I can only respond by saying that strange things are happening to vampires these days, and you can't blame it all on Global Warming, or you can.

Damn, Hurricane Sandy did see me peeing in my pants. The Pandemic also did a number on me. One never knows if the next plague will wipe Wee Willie Vampires off the pages of *The Enquirer.*

For sure, I had my COVID vaccinations; five so far, so says the health card I keep in my wallet (better be safe than sorry, and I had to get into restaurants, didn't I).

Still, who knows if there isn't a deadly variant coming to a vampire near you that's going to make their blood curdle, and toesy-wozzies curl up like a deader than a doornail marble statue of an unshod Egyptian pharaoh.

Now that I think back on it, I've always had an overactive bladder (probably genetic), and turning into a vampire didn't do anything to mitigate the symptoms except, over the centuries, offer more insight (reduce alcohol, coffee, no H2O less than an hour before you go to sleep and take doctor prescribed anticholinergics as needed). As far as my bladder is concerned, I've become philosophical. Why Worry? Be happy, the stream is strong.

It's truly bizarre that this medical history appears embedded in my consciousness, whereas so much of my past remains hidden until I hear it on my vampire's recordings.

No harm, no foul. I discover I'm not a vampire in a hurry. Nor am I prone to anxiety and sweating the small stuff, or, as my fellow Lucky Latin Speakers say, *Tardus et stabilis vincit genus.*

I say Lucky Latin Speakers because you guys are ahead of the Top 100 Language Curve. (Keep this on the down low, but once you-know-who comes out with her next album, where she sings three tunes in the old vulgate, every millennial and Gen-Xer on Planet Swifties will be like lemmings going off the cliff to sign up for Latin lessons on Babel.)

As another saying goes, "Slow and steady wins the race" (no Latin translation necessary), which is precisely why I can wait another week to pay my second visit to Madame Lumière.

While I have no urgency to see her sooner or more often, the only wrinkle to that is my agent, who demands a manuscript ASAP. Either he doesn't have another deal in the pipeline, or he sees a giant payday to end all giant paydays when he takes my tell-all to market.

I read about book deals, bidding wars, and six-figure advances. I can't figure out how this pertains to me unless W's thinking of outing me. Nah! How could he know my true identity?

I must set up a face-to-face; that way, I can look W in the eye, and then I'll know the truth. No one can keep the fear out of the orbs when they lock eyes with a vampire.

Wait, the fucker's a literary agent. When I stare into his eyeballs, is it possible that all I'll see are dollar signs? I'll admire his neck, that's what I'll do! I'll even find an excuse to touch it. So, what if he thinks I'm light in the loafers?

"It's good to be alive! Say it loud, and say it proud! And say it again, Sam. It's good to be alive! It's good to be alive!"

So, with a good night's sleep under my belt, I'm ready to rock and roll. Ah, you picked up on that, right? Another similarity between you and a vampire. We bloodsuckers need our eight hours, too.

Here's another fun fact we vamps have in common with you mortals: We dream. Yes, indeed, we do. And we dream in color and with sound. Dreams allow us to live in a parallel time and space. That's a laugh-riot of irony, for the last thing I need in my half-ass state of memory is to be split into thirds.

Hold on, a sec. Have I been missing something? Every evening, more or less, since regaining consciousness, I've been dreaming,

dreaming, dreaming, and in the following morning, upon opening my baby blues, I remember a good portion of my unconscious reverie.

It's true—it's true; most of those memories fade minutes after I wake, but on occasion, an event stays with me for a day or two at the most. I bring up my dream life because perhaps those nocturnal visions contain an actual event from my past.

If that is on the money, these trips into the land of Morpheus would provide an additional way for me to access my lost memory. Damn, I need to put paper and pen next to my bed, and as soon as I regain semi-consciousness, I scribble down every last detail of the adventure. Didn't I tell you it's good to be alive!

I haven't felt this much vim and vigor since I don't know when. Could it be that Madame Lumière put something in the tea she served me before she put me in a trance? Obviously, I can't remember what it's like to be drugged, but I have a gut feeling vampires are the ones who do all the drugging.

What about post-hypnotic suggestions? That may be the reason for my energy. I listened to the recordings, and there was nothing like that on the tape. Of course, Madame Lumière could have doctored the recording.

Stop the music! I want to get off this carousel of what-ifs! I feel good! Stop questioning the whys and what-ifs! Ride the wave! Put on your glad rags and smile, smile, smile.

All is good. It's going to be a bright, sunshiny day. Why, today, I might even have a taste for blood.

TWENTY

EYEBALL TO EYEBALL, BELLY TO BELLY

"Well, Nick, I hope the accommodations suit you."

"Very clubby. Very old world."

That's one of the reasons I picked The Martin Van Buren. Of course, the steaks here are amongst the best in the city, and I know you're a steak man. You often mention in your synopsis how you delight in having them, the rarest of bloody rare."

"How are their mashed potatoes?" I want to avoid any mention of blood if you get my drift.

Ah, Henry. You're always at my elbow when I need a drink. Henry—Nick Cummings. Henry's, here's my favorite waiter. I catch the winking and imagine the handful of bills slyly greasing palms."

"Please to meet you, Mr. Cummings."

"You as well, Henry."

"Henry's constantly dropping off bits of gossip, aren't you, Henry? Especially about seeing one of my clients in here with another literary agent? And for that, I'm eternally grateful."

Henry stands at Buckingham guard duty, attention. At well over six feet is one tall drink of water, as they say in West Texas.

"Nick's a new client, but his name will be on everyone's lips next year. You can bet we're celebrating right here, at The Martin Van Buren, with a bottle of your Louis Roederer, Cristal, 2008."

"We'll be looking forward to that, Mr. W."

Henry throws us both his time-honored and honed-to-perfection 1,000-megawatt servile smile, and I want to vomit in my mouth.

"Mr. W., the usual?"

"Yes, Henry, but tell Anthony to make it with three olives instead of two in honor of Mr. Cummings."

"Of course, Mr. W., Mr. Cummings, what is your pleasure?"

A 100 millimeters of your sister's ichor. "I'll have a ginger ale with ice on the side," I smile.

"Not drinking, my boy? Oh, you must have something a bit more majestic for the toast, you see."

A 100 millimeters of your sister's ichor? Where the fuck, where did that come from? "Bourbon, straight," I mutter.

"Would Woodford Reserve Kentucky Derby be your choice? Mr. Cummings?"

"Indeed, it would, Henry."

Fuck me again! How do I know I'm a Bourbon Boy?

Nick looks around the room. *I know you're here, and you've come out to drink, right?*

"Right away," smiles Henry from the heavenly perch. "Henry's been here since I've been coming, what, fifteen years now? Has it been that long? Jesus, Nick, it seems like I joined Neff and Keys yesterday."

"What's the saying, time flies when you're having fun," grins W, but underneath the smile, he's probably thinking, Is it time for an eye tuck or more filler?

He's gotta be in the room; he has to be. Nick looks around. *Do you feel me, Brother Vampire?*

"Speaking of fun, Nick, I was re-reading your synopsis this morning, and I have to tell you, if I already failed to mention it, your portrayal of historical characters is the most brilliant piece of fiction

I've read since Katherine Neville's "The Eight." The way you weave them into your story is simply enthralling."

I swear, I haven't the slightest desire to bite Henry's sister's neck if, in fact, he has a sister, and certainly not suck 100 millimeters of her blood into my mouth. I'm becoming nauseous just thinking about it.

"Have you read it?"

"Huh? What?" Goddamnit, Nick, pay fuckin' attention.

"'The Eight' by Katherine Neville."

"Yes-no-I can't remember."

"Nick, are you one of those writers who don't read other people's work? Helen Brandywine is also like that. She believes it pollutes her creativity and says her mind must be pure of the literary noise for her to write what she writes. Do you know her work, Nick?"

"Helen Brandywine? No literary noise, you say? What does she write, poetry in iambic pentameter?"

My attempt at humor flies right over W's head, or he's ignoring it.

"Science Fiction Porn! She writes Rub Books about aliens getting it off. Can you imagine," he giggles as if pushing a copy of "Beaver Hunt" down his pants and feeling the pussy juice print soaking his belly as he sneaks out the door of his local bodega without paying?"

I have no Dorothy Parker quip, Robert Benchley rejoinder, nothing saved from looking stupid when Henry returns with our order and expertly places them down before us.

"Thank you, Henry," grins W. "Could you perhaps bring out some of your delicious appetizers, the cheese tray, and the calamari? Nick, I hope you've brought your appetite with you."

As Henry laid out the drinks, his bony, bleached wrists peeked out from under his starched white cuffs, and a sudden flood of memories washed across the shores of Nick's memory banks.

It's the winter of 1921 and my last year at Marienbad. I'm there as the secret emissary of the Mayerling Mineral Water Company. It's all part of a scheme to convince the spa to allow Mayerling to bottle and distribute the healing waters of the mineral springs beyond the sanatorium walls. I'm doing this dirty work for a considerable sum of money that I don't need, but more to put a bit of adventure back into my life. In my timeless existence, I'm in Prague posing as Viscount Ernest Worthington, a distant cousin of George Nathaniel Curzon, 1st Marquess Curzon of Kedleston. Because of my title and being a frequent visitor to the spas of Marienbad, one of my social acquaintances, Jacub Smetana, who happens to own Mayerling, believes I would be the perfect person to carry out his devious plans. It's a windy winter's morning, and I'm returning from scouting out the springs when I meet the trio of sisters, Jolanda, Mafalda, and Giovanna of Italy, the elder daughters of King Vittorio Emanuele III. The sisters are there for a rest cure as none suffer from the more serious ailments of the day, like kidney disease or tuberculosis, but the less general fatigue due to the war in Europe. Peeking out between their fur parkers and velvet fur-trimmed gloves are the plumpest pink wrists imaginable, and at the moment, I'm into biting wrists.

"Cheers! Nick—Nick, are you amongst the living?" asks W when I appear not to be paying attention.

Now, that's funny, and funny always trumps daydreaming! "Sorry! *Salute!*"

We clink glasses. The bourbon turns into Vesuvius' finest, roaring down my throat and threatening to melt my larynx.

"Nick, can you believe her next book is about alien vampires? Alien vampires, can you just," smiles W, thinking another bestseller and serious money in my coffers.

I stifle a gag and feel the sweat pouring out of my armpits. Do not vampires sweat? Are we not made of flesh and blood and need a non-aluminum deodorant?

"Where she comes up with these subjects, I can't imagine, says W. "She won't let me even know the title, she's so goddamn secretive. I told her, Helen, I could be doing a little pre-pub hype that will do wonders for sales, but no, not a word, or she will tear up our contract and go to that little worm, Val Cannon, Literary."

W drains the last of his martini as if suffering from the bends, turning and squinting; "Where the fuck is that big swinging dick when you need another drinkie winky?"

"Bloodsuckers in Space," "The Planet of the Vampires" ... I'm much better with titles than my vampire, don't you know?"

"What are you saying, Nick, 'The Planet of the Vampires?"

"In space, no one hears the sound of sucking blood," I smile. If you think that sounds familiar, it's stolen from the movie *Alien*. It's time for me to giggle as if I've stolen a jizz rag.

"I say that's a pretty catchy, Nick, pretty catchy. Ah, Henry, there you are! You read my mind."

I scoop up the bourbon before the glass has time to say howdy to the linen and giggle, "Over the gums and through the lips, look out, stomach, here we go."

Man alive, when you swallow the whole thing in one gulp, it's as if it's a flamethrower's on full whoosh, lighting up your windpipe until belching out your asshole and setting fire to your chair.

"Nick, if you were to meet Helen, you'd never expect that under that serene, calm exterior seethes a randy lady. I can give you a signed copy of her last book, "The Naughty Nymphs of The Universe of Cum." I can assure you, Nick, it's pretty imaginative. All the creatures in the universe have multiple sexual organs with orifices that never close. The story revolves around the naughtiest of the nymphs, Nasty Nadine, who, according to the 'Myth Of The Magical Vagina', will lose the ability to orgasm when the only virgin in the universe claims her throne."

Goddamn my eyes, why didn't I think of that storyline instead of some also-ran vampire posing as a letch Lothario eating, sleeping, and biting his pathetic self through the halls of the castles with leaky roofs?

"The heroine is an intergalactic personal trainer and acupuncturist who, upon the death of her parents, is found wandering in the wild and raised by a family of Forest Murmurs who teach her the joys of self-gratification. Hence, Onina, her name, grows into a woman, a virgin, and..."

"W, stop! Don't be a spoiler; give away the entire plot, and take the joy out of my reading pleasure."

"Bien sur, mon ami." He gleefully gleams as his hand goes up, sweeping the air into hot currents. He's raising two fingers only this time, and I can only assume he's asking Henry for a double.

As if out of thin air, Henry materializes, already anticipating his master's call, and expertly sets down before W a martini glass, brimming to the lip with clear, motionless liquid. Two swollen, skewered olives emerge, looking like a stoplight stuck at the green.

"Thank you, Henry, and menus, *s'il te plait,*" grins W.

Henry, who must be a carnival juggler to survive in this gig economy, raises his free hand to produce two humongous menus.

"Why do I always ask for a menu, Henry, when I always get the same thing?"

"Caesar salad with extra dressing, New York Strip, *au jus,* baked potato, no chives, and a bottle of Chianti Classico Riserva," responds Mr. Servile with a two-mile, oil-slick smile, which I don't imagine would be as cheery if he knew what I wanted to do to his sister.

The bourbon makes my head spin because drinking on an empty stomach always makes me dizzy. Consequently, I can't decipher the menu even though I can read Greek.

"I'll have the same, only I'll have chives and extra sour cream with my baked potato," I preen, learning centuries ago to order what the person paying the bill orders. It makes them feel better for it.

"Ah, Jerry, the calamari! Wunderbar!" W salutes the fish with a martini gulp.

Jerry is Henry's sidekick and, if I failed to mention it when he first appeared, is as ramrod stiff and about four inches taller, and like

Henry for such an extra-long fella, moves with the agility of a guy half his size; dare I say, as equally shadowy, graceful as a vampire. Coincidence is to be determined.

The calamari looks tempting, but I pluck a piece of cheese along with a miniature dinner roll that appears with the appetizers, hoping this will settle my stomach, which is starting to roil and rumble. Do we vampires not suffer from acid reflux? Alas, poor belly! I know thy intestines well: a tummy of infinite upset, of most excellent indigestion.

"More sauce for the calamari, Jerry!"

I have never seen a voice carry so well when the mouth is awash in alcohol. It must be the vodka's unique properties that transmit sound and amplify it.

"Yes, sir, Mr. W," replies Jerry, whose wider-than-wide wild eyes flicker over from W to rest upon me with a frightened look that silently screams; *I gave blood with nothing to do in Denver while I was hanging out in an airport lounge.*

TWENTY-ONE

FAMILY MONEY

Recording #2/mp (English, no translation needed)

The Vampire: "What would I like to talk about today before you ask me questions about my book? Let me think on that for a moment. (Pausing) For me, the most challenging part of living the life of a vampire and never growing old was, and still is, overcoming my bourgeois upbringing.

Madame Lumière: Bourgeois upbringing? You mean, your childhood?

The Vampire: I thought that you'd find it surprising. I bet you thought all I wanted to talk about was, why the fuck me? (Raising voice) Why me, out of the blue for no f'in reason and certainly not because you were a bad Catholic boy who didn't believe in God and refused to go with his family every Sunday to church....

Madame Lumière: Calm down, Nick; I want you to relax during these sessions.

The Vampire: So, you may have committed a few sins. What kid doesn't abuse himself, right, Madame Lumière?

Madame Lumière: Nick, you don't have to...

The Vampire: We're all adults here, and you want answers, right?

Madame Lumière. There's some water on the table. Would you like some?

The Vampire: (Whispering) I was no Blaise Pascal.

Madame Lumière: I'm sorry I didn't hear that.

The Vampire: (Whispering) Richard Dawkins is another one. (Drifting off)

Madame Lumière: Nick, Nick...

The Vampire: (Suddenly aware and awake) Wham, bam, thank you, Mamma, you're no longer who you are, but a monster without being a myth. That's some heavy shit to deal with, Madame Lumière. Come on, I'd rather be tied to a railroad track with a speeding locomotive heading my way. At least then, I'd have a few minutes to see my poor, pitiful life flash before me.

Madame Lumière: Drink the water, Nick.

The Vampire: Okay, I'll drink the water. Are you happy now, Madame Lumière? Damn, you're as strict at the Code.

Madame Lumière: Ah, the Code. In your recordings with Dr. Mickeltee, you mentioned such a Code. Could you explain precisely what this Code is and how you learned about it?

The Vampire: You really did listen to the recordings?

Madame Lumière: I told you I would. I explained that it would help provide context for our sessions.

The Vampire: It's a voice, sometimes a few voices laying it all out.

Madame Lumière: Excuse me.

The Vampire: The Code—that's how you know what's what. Voices come to you and tell you what you have to do, how to do it, and when to do it.

Madame Lumière: Voices? Are you hearing them now, Nick?

The Vampire: (Laughing) No, it's nothing like that. You get a signal when they're coming, and when that moment arrives, you're told to be alone and in a quiet place to receive the transmission.

Madame Lumière: Do they come through a radio?

The Vampire: (Laughing). I wish. They come through your head.

Madame Lumière: Tell me about these transmissions, Nick. Do you remember what they said the first time you called the Voice or Voices made contact? The Vampire: It wasn't so much what they said. It was the feeling of well-being I got from hearing the words. Do you know what I mean?

Madame Lumière: I think so. So, what does the Voice say to do?

The Vampire: Say? I don't remember. I crawled out of the trench and started walking as if it were an ordinary stroll down the *Promenade Plantée* in Paris on my way to my favorite patisserie. (Pausing) It was a bell.

Madame Lumière: A bell?

The Vampire: More like a chime. Somehow, I knew it was a signal for me to get out of the trench and go to a safer location. So, I started walking.

Madame Lumière: This was in the middle of the battle?

The Vampire: Ah, that's the thing—they knew the fighting had stopped, and it was okay to leave the trench. The battlefield was empty, except, of course, for the bodies.

Madame Lumière: Oh, my god.

The Vampire: They were all over. Some are stacked on top of each other. The shelling had been intense. My comrades were hit and thrown into the air, and body parts flew all over the place. I dove into the nearest foxhole and clamped my hands over my ears; the sound of the bombs was ear-splitting, and the screams, you never forget the screams.

Madame Lumière: Nick, do you want a glass of water?

The Vampire: My name is Bernard Bertrand. I live at 10 Rue Montparnasse, appartement 3 with my family.

Madame Lumière: Do you want another glass of water, Bernard?

The Vampire: No. Let me finish. So, I'm walking, and then out of nowhere, I come up against a wall in the middle of the fuckin' field. Can you believe it? I lay down against it and waited. Or, maybe it came right away. Then, another chime and the Voice spoke to me in French, but over the centuries, it spoke whatever language I was speaking. It reassured me that there was nothing to be frightened of, that I had been chosen to become an Immortal.

Madame Lumière: An Immortal, not a vampire?

The Vampire: (Laughing) No, not a vampire. They understood that telling me that would scare the bejesus out of me. Their choice, Immortality, sounded good, considering I'm figuring the next shelling will likely blow me to kingdom come.

Madame Lumière: Did you feel differently when the Voice told you you were immortal, Bernard?

The Vampire: If you mean, did I walk up to the enemy and say Shoot me? (Laughing) I wasn't that foolish. Did I feel changed? I felt like I had more energy, but you have to understand there wasn't much time for me to think about things like that. When you're a soldier in battle, all you think about, all that goes through your mind, is how you can survive the next few minutes. Even when the shelling stopped, it was like, okay, I'm alive now—but how can I survive the next one?

Madame Lumière: What else did the Voice tell you?

The Vampire: The Voice instructed me to head north, where I could rejoin what was left of my battalion. I had to do this immediately before the enemy began attacking from the west. The Voice told me I'd be contacted again when I reached the battalion. Above all else, I was to act naturally and not tell anyone about my transformation. (Laughing)

Madame Lumière: What's so funny, Bernard?

The Vampire: Act naturally? You like mean constantly shaking like a leaf, afraid that at any moment I'm going to be blown up, or maybe the enemy will come over the wall and find me curled up like a baby and bayonet me before I have a chance to defend myself? You can see how that was funny, right?

Madame Lumière: I can see that, yes. I can also see being told you're now a vampire can be quite a shock to the system, and the last thing you could expect is to act as if nothing's happened.

The Vampire: Exactly. You would think there would be some getting-to-know-the-new-you, like a quiet time. Who runs before they walk? Who knows the difference between running a trap and a counter unless you have a training camp with Vince Lombardi? But that was not to be. When in Rome, do as the Romans, the Voice tells me. I didn't see any fuckin' Romans on the battlefield that day, but hey, I'm not stupid; I get the message.

Madame Lumière: I'm surprised you believed the Voice, believed you had actually become a vampire.

The Vampire: Funny, but it never occurred to me to question the Voice.

Madame Lumière: Never?

The Vampire: Never.

Madame Lumière: What about being angry?

The Vampire: As I said, I was angry that it all happened so fast, yes, that's true. (He laughs)

Madame Lumière: You find that amusing?

The Vampire: I remember the Voice telling me that just because this transformation has happened, don't become angry or vengeful, and don't go biting the neck of the first soldier you see. In fact, the Voice suggested I pass up the next ten or twenty necks I see because drawing blood is the surest way to draw attention to yourself and get the village idiots to chase you down with burning torches, and when they catch up to you, you stick a stake through your young heart.

Madame Lumière: Good advice. And did you take it, Bernard?

The Vampire: Without question. I got the message right away. The Vampire Code is into self-preservation. There was no time, then or ever, for me to deal with my emotional needs, like coming to terms with one change in the Social Register, which isn't top of mind. I doubt none of the Elders ever heard the expression, you can take the vampire out of the bourgeois, but you can never take the bourgeois outta the vampire.

Madame Lumière: Oh, Nick, I mean Bernard...

The Vampire: I was Bernard Bertrand, an ordinary twenty-something Frenchman. A country bumpkin, really, and they had no right to make me learn to be a Vampire on the job. No right at all. And for that, I can never forgive them.

Madame Lumière: Do you want to take a break, Bernard?

The Vampire. I had to get with the program and understood first and foremost that I must fit in, with the eventual goal of mixing in the highest circles, be *soigné;* for who would suspect the best dressed, most handsome man in the room to be a vampire, right, Madame Lumière?

Madame Lumière: Handsome is as handsome does.

The Vampire: *Absolutement,* but that doesn't satisfy the emotional needs of the inner you. You would think the Elders got that message during the Age of Enlightenment. Still, even when Freud wrote his eye-popping paper on how Mothers Can Be Bloodsuckers, more about Freud in my yet-to-be-written chapter, "Fathers Can Be Bloodsuckers," too, the Voice turned a deaf ear and pooh-poohed psychoanalysis. And let me tell you another thing, Madame Lumière: I have not remained silent in all my centuries. I have pitched many a bitch, but have Those In The Know taken my complaints seriously and re-vamped the Vampire Code to address the question of emotional intelligence and its importance to the well-being of a vampire, huh, huh, huh? All I get from the Voice is more lectures on the best biting angles and research on how long it takes to take blood before the recipient loses consciousness. (Clearing his throat)

Madame Lumière: Do you want some water, Bernard?

The Vampire: Madame Lumière, I've been drawing blood for over five hundred years—you think I need someone to tell me my technique sucks? Fiddle-dee! Fiddle-dee-dee!

Madame Lumière: Bernard, we should take a break, and when I count to...

The Vampire: No!

Madame Lumière:(Nervously) Of course, Bernard, I don't mean to...

The Vampire: I know W is putting pressure on Nick, so let me tell you about my 1928 visit to the Hofburg, the Austrian residence of Lord and Lady Radish of Withering, and the Habsburg Dynasty's imperial palace. I came to know Lord Radish, known to his friends as Whitey, when we met at the Sussex Historical Museum of Wax Figurines and War Armaments and discovered our mutual love of vexillology. I had a collection of multi-colored Ehrenbände ribbons and the 1792 pattern that displayed the full Habsburg coat from my days serving in the Napoleonic Wars. Whitey was especially fond of flags showing his family crests and coats of arms portraying the black Doppeladler eagle carrying a large shield that originated with his progenitor, Joseph II, the Holy Roman Emperor and sole ruler of the Habsburg monarchy. In case you don't know, Madame Lumière, Joe Two had the good fortune to be the eldest son of Empress Maria Theresa and her husband, Emperor Francis I.

Madame Lumière: Thank you for that, Bernard.

The Vampire: And, just to let you know, Joe Two was also the brother of the illustrious Marie Antoinette and the not-so-illustrious Leopold II, who was the second King of the Belgians from 1865 to 1909, and when I met him for the first time, the founder and sole owner of the Congo Free State.

Madame Lumière: Ah, hah.

The Vampire: I'll save that story for my yet-to-be-written chapter, "Jungle Vampire, The True Story."

Madame Lumière: I'm looking forward to reading it, Bernard.

The Vampire: Joe also had two famous sisters, Maria Caroline of Austria and Maria Amalia, Duchess of Parma. I met both lovely ladies frequently and knew intimately beneath their petticoats.

Madame Lumière: Could you slow down, Bernard? There is so much to take in here.

The Vampire: You wanted to hear my story, didn't you?

Madame Lumière: I'm sorry, please go on.

The Vampire: Where was I? Whitey, that's right. Well, as you can see, I had century's worth of history with Whitey's family when I first had a chance to dine with him at the Hofburg Castle and later in my role as *le détective français* to investigate the gruesome murders at Nord-Pas-de-Calais, the family residence in the north of France, just miles from the English Chanel, where I eventually caught up with the poisoner, Julio (Mad Boy Three Fingers) Tofana, slitting the villain's throat clean through and through and throwing both head and still twitching body into the choppy seas to be lost forever.

Madame Lumière: How horrible.

The Vampire: Don't ask, but when you read the yet-to-be-written chapter, "The French Shamus," you'll learn all about my crime-solving prowess that surpassed even the Great Sherlock Holmes, whose author I won't out as a vampire, no matter how hard you press me.

Madame Lumière: No, not Sir Conan Doyle.

The Vampire: You can pluck my eyes out, but I won't tell. (Laughing) Let's go back to dinner at the Hofburg. Whitey sat at the head of the table and was the most gracious and welcoming of hosts. His wife, Lady Beth Radish, affectionately known as Le Kibtizer, was, in her own right, a real Joan Rivers and had us all spitting up our food with her immense repertoire of jokes, many tres risqué, and some at the expense of her husband who took it gracefully because if he didn't, he knew, no nooky that night. As everyone knows, regular meals at Whitey's table court always began with Potage à la Wynnstay Cream of leek soup named after the Wynnstay estate in Wales where back in the day, I played hide and seek with Queen Victoria, who, as a child, spent much time with her mother.

Madame Lumière: You knew Queen Victoria? You didn't...

The Vampire: If you want to talk about looks, Mom—Marie Louise Victoria, who everyone called Victoire, the Dowager Princess of Leiningen, and the one who hired me as a Latin tutor, was one real stunner. Let me tell you, there were many a sleepless night I had, but the Code is the Code, and to satisfy my urges, I flew multiple times over hill and dale to the White Lion Hotel in Bala, where I took up with two Belgian sisters.

Madame Lumière: You turned into a bat?

The Vampire: How else, the roads were a nightmare. Anywho, the soup was a little salty to my taste, as if I, the good guest, would complain otherwise. Next comes the most delicious *Huitres d'Ostende*, fresh from Ostende on the Belgian coast, with a sly twinkle from Lady Beth. Had husband caught it, it would have caused Whitey to intuit that later that evening, his beloved Radish would pay me a sweet visit and seek proof positive that the two dozen bivalve mollusks I scoffed down would, as my pal Giacomo Casanova swore, make me *roccia dura*.

Madame Lumière: You were a very naughty vampire, weren't you, Bernard?

The Vampire: Wait, listen, you don't know the half of it. Next come *Croustades à la Victoria*. O la la! These are my favorites, don't you know! Puff pastries are filled with lobster and truffle mousse and named after Queen Victoria, *delizioso*. Lady Beth had a thing for Queen Victoria. (Lowering his voice) After too many Irish Cream Absinthe, Beth confessed that she was the famous queen's reincarnation. Naturally, I didn't tell her that she was nothing like Victoria, and she was lucky for it because Victoria was no beauty, I can tell you.

Madame Lumière: Bernard, I am amazed at how you remember these details.

The Vampire: At the time of my meeting with Whitey, I was Juan Sebastián del Mano O Mano, one of the four other explorers who sailed with Ferdinand Magellan, but you can call me *Pequeño* Sammy. (Laughing) That was the nickname Whitey had for me.

Madame Lumière: *Pequeño* Sammy—how darling.

The Vampire: Just call me Bernard, will you?

Madame Lumière: As you wish.

The Vampire. I wish. You were talking about my remarkable memory. It comes with the territory. Back in the day, when our Elders discovered they had this extraordinary talent, they didn't give it a name except to add it to the list of dark and unusual gifts. Over the centuries, neurologists, bless their pointy little heads, have assigned terms such as Eidetic memory, also known as photographic memory and total recall, and more recently, *Hyperthymesia*, a Greek term, which is a condition that allows people to be able to remember an abnormally large number of their life experiences in vivid detail. These explanations give us a clearer understanding of our unique skill set. I can see your viridescent with envy, Madame Lumière, and think how lucky I am to remember everything and not be embarrassed when you can't remember a face or the title of your favorite movie and go weak in the knees believing you've got dementia.

Madame Lumière: I envy your memory, Bernard.

The Vampire: No, no, and not on your life, Señor Wences—I love hand puppets, don't you? (Laughs) No, Madame Lumière, this so-called gift of ours is non-stop, uncontrollable, a total brain drain, and a fuckin' no-joke burden. Alas, one must make due, n'est pas, *mon cheri*?

Madame Lumière: Bernard, you may not be tired, but I'm exhausted, and I must insist on ending this session. I will count from one to three, and when I clap my hands, you will wake up, remember everything, and want a massage.

TWENTY-TWO

CONTRALTOS GOTTA SING, VAMPIRE'S GOTTA FLY

I must give Madame Lumière much kudos; the woman knows how to make your muscles sing, "You Really Gotta a Hold on Me."

Thinking back on that forty minutes of lying there naked to my skivvies while still climbing out of the nether world of Bernard's Memories, her magic-making hands pounding my torso into chop liver, I became quite the Chatty Cathy. Why this truth-telling should worry me is ironic since Madame Lumière knows as much about me as I do. I also have to give her a shout-out for keeping to her promise of having no judgments.

Judgments—shit, I have to thank my lucky Great Conjunction-Junction (Jupiter and Saturn aligning, don't you know) that Madame Lumière is not the rat fink, Dr. Turn-Me-In, aka, Rosamund Mickeltee is, and had me shipped off to Shutter Island, the first time I showed my proverbial fangs.

"Why don't I have the urge to fly?" I ask, lying flat on my stomach and at her mercy. What, you expected me to admit my lack of blood lust? Well, I'm not ready to go there.

Unexpectedly, Madame Lumière's hands fly off my back, and she calmly replies, "Well, Nick, you would first have to turn into a bat, wouldn't you?"

Then it's pound-pound, knead-knead, and dem magic-making hands melting out sweet torso punishment once again.

I welcome the beating for about fifteen seconds, then yield to the greater truth and reply, "Well, that does mean that."

As I walk up to my building from Park Avenue, I must continue to deal with the ugly scaffolding that covers all sides of the building. The work complies with a citywide ordinance that requires all buildings to maintain their facades so bricks don't fall off and bean someone walking below, a rare but fatal outcome always accompanied by the frightening NY Post headlines. (I guess, falling on the street isn't so bad.)

The roof must be closed to do the repair work, and therefore off-limits to tenants (remember my neighbor's grousing on the subject), a magnificent space filled with lush seasonal flowers, comfortable lounge chairs, and enough party-down tables to lay out spreads to feed a small battalion. The nearly 360-degree rooftop views of New York's iconic landmarks (the Empire State Building, the Chrysler Building, and the East River) are breathtaking.

I enter the lobby, wave to the desk man on duty, grab the elevator without seeing a neighbor, and return to my apartment.

I make another cup of coffee, go to the window, and stare down at Madison Avenue.

Since returning from the hospital, I have had an unrelenting and unexplainable need to violate the rules and sneak up to the roof. I go up there in the very early mornings to watch the sunrise from the west, or late in the evening when the encircling city lights form a diamond necklace sparkling in the dark from

I'm thinking about this now after my session with Madame Lumière because when I stroll the empty, wraparound terrace, the bells from the church across the street ringing in my ears, I haven't the slightest urge to turn into a bat and fly away.

I should have told Madame Lumière about last evening, for example. I remember casually leaning against the railing and staring north to 35th at the church tower across the street. The chimes at midnight ended, and there was absolute stillness.

The cooing of a pigeon unexpectedly broke the silence, and I turned and, at my elbow, sat as if he owned the ledge, the lily-white crooner. We locked eyes. We begin the Mammal vs. Aves stare down.

The distant memory of never being good at the game of who blinks first leaked into my mind, so why I thought I could now outlast the pigeon is beyond me.

Surprise, surprise, not two seconds into our orbital duel, the pigeon gave me a series of slow blinks. Was I going crazy, or did I think the bird was coming on to me?

I don't know shit from Shinola about pigeons and what gets them hot and bothered, but I'm not surprised that my appealing Robert Redford looks (I'm not tooting my own horn, but our lookalike features are what they are) haven't jumped species and made their way into the bird world.

Then, it hit me hard. If I'm a vampire, shouldn't it also hold that our frightening mythology would also leapfrog into all creatures, large and small, and scare the living crap out of them?

Suddenly, I felt a nudge. I looked down. Turn me over on the barbie and cook my ass till it's brown; the bird was at my elbow, slowly blinking at me. If it had started to sing "The Way We Were," bat or no bat, I was going to fling myself over the wall, and as I went flying, do my best Howard Beale imitation and scream, "I'm mad as hell, and I'm not going to take it anymore!"

Hold it, young fella! I didn't get the memo from The Code. Bats are passé. All vampires must now fly Pigeon Airlines. I locked eyes once again with my cooing crooner. Blink, blink-blink, blink, blink-blink-blink!

It was goddamn Morse code! One blink—dot, two blinks—dash! Fuck-all, what three blinks mean! The freakin' pigeon is a goddamn radio operator!

For a second, I considered snatching up this avian, locking him in a closet, getting a book on Morse code, and then deciphering the message. Yeah, that won't work because my fine-feathered friend flew the coup the minute I got this brainstorm. That's right, buckaroo, this bird ain't gonna be my pigeon, he's a fuckin' mind reader, that's what he is. I'm not the only one with extraordinary powers.

I turn around and walk away from the parapet. I remember that's when the strangeness last night really began. I sit and close my eyes.

"Is that you, Nick, my friend?"

I smell the unmistakable aroma of his pricy Cuban and know I'm not alone. "Ah, the mysterious José Starka Salamanca."

I turn and follow the orange tip of his glowing torpedo as he waves it in my face.

"I see, my friend, we both like to break the law a little, si?"

"Si, si."

José Starka Salamanca is my next-door neighbor, whom I rarely see. He has homes in Cuba, Santa Fe, and, I suspect, a European hideaway that he has not yet divulged, not even before I went into La-La Land.

I know this because just the other day, I overheard Angel, our daytime doorman, dishing out the dirt on JSS (as the staff calls him) to the lovely Carly Ford (in Penthouse A, don't you know).

I didn't catch it all, but there was something about Monaco and Formula 1 racing, and then on to Portugal. (Betcha it wasn't a tour, betcha, betcha.) Oh, and one more bit of trivia: Senior José has this irritating habit of calling me 'my friend' in a way that makes my skin grow cold.

"I haven't seen you lately, José. How's it going?" I want to say, 'How's it hanging?' but I don't have the balls, ha, ha, ha.

"My friend, I have just returned from two weeks in the Algarve. The sea, the sand, the food—*maravilhosa.*"

If José would stop waving his cigar and take a pull, I could see if he had a tan; then, I think how foolish of me. His swarthy complexion always gives him the appearance of one who does nothing else but bask in the sun. I think of my pasty white skin, and suddenly, the image of me flying over white sandy beaches flashes across my eyeballs.

"My friend, do you know the Algarve?"

His words snap me back into what passes for my present state of reality, and as he takes a suck on his Cuban, the glowing tip illuminates his face, and I feel his eyes bore into mine. Before I can respond, he says, in Portuguese, how his favorite place is Tavira, which is, in his mind, the most beautiful of all the towns in that region.

He lowers his cigar, and everything is dark, but then, for a moment of maddening madness, José's face suddenly becomes translucent, and I can see his facial muscles, tissues, and veins. If you've never seen someone's face light up like that, let me tell you, you haven't missed anything.

Of course, I immediately recognized the sign. It's a warning. The fucker's trying to trap me, see if I know Portuguese.

"I'm sorry, José, I don't understand Spanish."

"It's Portuguese, Nick. For some reason, I believed you spoke it. Not true, my friend?"

"No, my friend."

"I have a box of Cohiba Maduro Magicos. Are not these your favorites, si, my friend?"

I nod and smile.

"I bought them home from Havana for you, but that was the very day of your unfortunate accident. I went out of town again the following morning and haven't returned until today. Are you fully recovered, si, my friend?"

"José, that was very kind of you. Yes, I'm back to normal."

"Did you get my flowers? I know you admired my yellow roses, so I sent you a dozen. They didn't have a bed for you, but the nurses in Intensive Care said they would make sure they would be at your bedside when you did get one."

"Unfortunately, I was unconscious for a few days, and I think by the time I woke up, your flowers were thrown out, but the nurses kept your card. I'm so sorry, but I never responded—my fault."

"My friend, not to worry. All that matters is that you have regained your health and memory, si?"

"Si, si"

Off to my side, I could hear the fluttering of wings. I moved away; I didn't want to alert José. I moved away some more. Who knows, he may know Morse code.

"Looking out at the city at this time of the evening is like peering into our own private jewelry box. Is that not so, my friend? Only the lights of Paris at night from my suite at the Plaza Athénée can compare. Ah, the City of Lights! Have you been? But of course, you have, my friend. You told me of that exciting time you had attending the March 29, 1989, grand opening of the Glass Pyramid as part of the Louvre Museum's 30th Anniversary celebration."

I have no idea if what he's telling me is true or another trap, so I take the under at six points and say laughingly, "José, I guess my memory isn't totally back because I can't say I remember that conversation."

"You sat at the table of the French President, Francois Mitterrand, and you told me Daniel Balavoine, the singer, was seated next to you. I remember being so envious of you, my friend."

"You were? Envious of me?" The cooing grows louder, and I'm amazed the sounds haven't distracted José from our conversation.

"Oh, si. I've been a fan for years, and whenever I travel to Paris, I make it my business to see a Balavoine performance along with Jean-Jacques Goldman and Michel Berger. Do you remember the album *L'Aziza?*

I shake my head.

"Aziza means 'My dear' in Arabic, and in the song, Balavoine pays tribute to his Jewish Moroccan wife while denouncing racism. *Si dramatique ! Tellement dramatique*".

"*C'est vrai.*"

"*Donc tu parles français.*"

"*Oui je le fais.*" Shit, that's done me in! Even my pigeon had enough and fluttered away.

"You speak like a Frenchman, *mon amie!*"

"High school, French". How's that for a lamo comeback? I fake a shiver.

"*Tu as froid, mon ami?*"

Huh? I'm not falling for that line of Frenchie-I got-yah, again.

"Are you cold?"

"It's time I went inside."

Of course, my friend."

I jump when José takes my arm. His touch sends an unexpected and unpleasant electrical shock down my fingertips.

"Are you all right, my friend?"

"Sure, never better." Nothing like the human touch to turn my blue eyes shit brown.

I inch away and break free. Thankfully, we're at the exit. I lead the way, carefully maneuvering down the two steps into the tiny elevator foyer and pressing the down button. I get the picture. The electrical tingling in my arm is slowly ebbing. I'm thinking. (Never a good thing when you share your brain with a vampire.)

Since waking from my coma, I haven't sought the human touch except for my prurient desires for Egyptian reincarnates. Coincidence, I think not. I smile as I enter the elevator. It's a vampire thing, I betcha, I betcha.

I get up and walk back to the window. It's best I didn't tell Madame Lumière, betcha, betcha.

TWENTY-THREE

SUNDAYS IN THE PARK WITH MY VAMPIRE

Madison Square Park and Bryant Park are both a stone's throw from my apartment (okay, ten blocks, give or take, isn't exactly a stone's throw unless you just won the hammer throw at the Olympics) nevertheless, it is a pleasant, pleasure-filled sans Horn-Hocking-Sunday stroll along Madison and Fifth unless of course, your trip on a crack and break you mother's back (go fuckin' flying when your toesies gets stuck in a fuckin' subway grating and you go fuckin' face-kissing the concrete and fuckin' lose your mind). Feel me? Or do I have to keep saying 'fuckin' and bitch slap you?

The deciding factor is my taste for a Cobb salad and a side order of calamari, accompanied by a charming Chianti that the Gyro truck parked alongside Madison Square Park doesn't offer, so it's up to 40th Street and the Bryant Park Grill for this tasty brunch *du Dimanche*.

How smart am I to make my decision on Friday morning? At the time, I could still make a Sunday 1:00 p.m. reservation.

There may be fewer cars and truck traffic. Still, as soon as I hit the pavement, I quickly realize that this particular Sunday signals Neo Neanderthal Visiting Day, the time when the cruise ships dock at their Hudson River piers and unleash their unkempt hordes, setting loose the Vandals upon the Big Apple, my fair city, particularly zoning in and clogging up Mad Ad Madison and his sister avenue, Ms. She-She Fifth.

Why do these socially bereft individuals always manage to stake a claim at the street corners and make it their home, as if they're dogs sniffing and peeing up against their favorite hydrant?

Bitch, bitch, bitch! Come on, Nick, stop your kvetching and shout out; it's good to be alive!

Okay, I would shout it out to the heavens if I can find my way around a group of Greeks (not baring gifts, but iPhones) at the corner of 36th and Fifth, wheeling around like crack addicts on an out-of-control carousel, shooting off rapid-fire selfies south, toward the Empire Building and east, toward the Chrysler Building.

I'm entering Bryant Park, and no Vandals (Oh, excuse me, no *hoi polloi*). I must be politically correct and not insult the Vandals or any descendants of this proud race of Germanic people who, back in the day, built a mighty kingdom in North Africa and whose lady leaders may have provided me during the last centuries with more than a light supper, if you see where I'm going with this, Laddy.

For the moment, no one is around, so I gaze up at the sky and whisper, "It's good to be alive! Free at last, free at last!"

The restaurant is to my right, and the park and one of its main attractions, the carousel, are off to my left. I'm fifteen minutes early, so I go to my left and find a seat amongst a row of metal chairs that provide a splendid, expansive view of the green.

A man and woman occupy the first set of chairs, so I choose the next set, just feet away. As I pass the couple, I see he's a forty-something, well-built Hispanic, wearing a doorman's uniform. The chubby Anglo woman, wearing a simple shirt and blouse, is around the same age and animated.

I take a seat, and as I settle in and take in my surroundings, I overhear the woman attempting to describe the musical makeup of the New York Philharmonic.

Hold it a sec. You're wondering, aren't you, how in just seconds of passing this couple, I can pick up all those tiny details without them catching me out and thinking I'm a nosey Rosie, right?

I haven't the slightest clue except to offer up the idea that as my memory improves, so do the arrivals of new gifts from my vampire. Today, I have the capability, in a single glance, to record details that would take a normal individual minutes to perceive.

This magical ability is accompanied by very acute hearing, allowing me to detect a pin dropping feet away; as for chitchat, my power of perceiving sounds picks up and retains as much as the sensitive mikes and recording devices Gene Hackman uses in *The Conversation.*

Another of today's gifts from my vampire is my unexpected ability to hear people's thoughts and immediately understand their motives. The man sitting next to me is debating his quandary. His companion, whom he wants to bed, is a resident of his building, and it is a fireable offense for employees to have any personal relationship with a tenant.

"Do you know there are 30 violins, 12 violas, 12 cellos, eight bases, four flutes, one piccolo, four oboes, 1 English horn...."

If I tell her I'll lose my job, make her swear...

"Four clarinets, one E-flat clarinet, one bass clarinet..."

Never shit where you eat; that's what Carlos is always saying, telling me that's why Charles got the boot, and he was tight with management.

"Three bassoons, one contrabassoon, three trombones, one bass trombone..."

Dio mio, she has such big beautiful tits, and the way they rise and fall when she speaks and smiles at me.

"Five horns, four trumpets..."

And her mouth, begging for me to put my cock in it.

What is going on here? Their conversation and thoughts are drowning out my own, and I can't hear myself think! Okay, maybe their tête-à-tête is more interesting, but this switch to a channel outside my own consciousness is another disturbing, out-of-control moment.

My head ultimately clears. Gone are the dizziness and brain chatter, and I can hear my thoughts once again. Something else suddenly disturbs me even more than their chatter. I look around, and for the first time since I discovered I was a vampire, I may not be the only vampire living in New York City, and that there may be one or more sitting right here in the park.

Holy hell! My body goes cold and frigid. I concentrate on the people's faces and movements, but nothing appears unusual. Why would it? Vampires are clever. They keep under the radar. Sure, I have extraordinary detection skills, but are they sensitive enough to pick up my fellow vamps on my radar? Could I see them? Could they see me?

The thought that I may not be the only vampire in New York City is making me crazy. I don't know enough about The Code to understand how they divide up territory. I understand I can't feast here, but that doesn't mean another vampire can't live here under the same rules, or perhaps be the exception and draw blood in the Big Apple.

Who are they? Have I already met them? Are they here, in this park, right now?

I quickly reach my feet and suddenly feel the earth moving under my feet, only I ain't no Carol King. I take a few steps past the couple without falling into their lap and reach the railing. I take the three steps to the restaurant level without singing the song that made her famous or doing another face-plant on the concrete.

"Nick, Nick, is that you?"

Another vampire? I follow the voice. It's Madame Lumière, sitting by the entrance at one of the outdoor tables, a fluffy dog lying quietly at her feet.

A feeling of calm takes hold, and my entire body settles into Relax Mode. "Madame Lumière, hello."

I approach.

"Are you alone, or are you meeting someone, Nick?"

I'm alone; if you don't count the Vampire living in my head or those sitting here in the park, I tell myself. "No. I'm by myself," I reply and force a smile.

"I haven't been served yet, so why don't you join us?"

Us—right—the dog. I hesitate, thinking I won't be able to get loaded. Oh, what the hell! "If it's no trouble. Sure, I'd love to."

"Can I help you, sir?"

"Hi, I have a 1:00 p.m. reservation for Nick Cummings."

The fresh-faced James Dean lookalike at the Grill's entrance scans his reservation book. "Ah, yes, Mr. Cummings."

He turns, and he smiles at the ingénue, who has sleeve tattoos on both arms and stands at attention at his elbow. "Lulu, would you show Mr. Cummings to number eleven?"

I motion to my left. "Ah, could I join the lady over there?"

The host and Lulu the tattooed lady turn in lockstep to Madame Lumière, who deflects their brazen stare with a broad smile and a gentile hand wave. The dog doesn't move.

The host relents, and immediately, Lulu starts her engine and leads the way to the table just feet away. She expertly slides my chair out for me, and as the dog stirs, she asks, "Can I get the dog a bowl of water?"

"Paris, would you like some water?" smiles Madame Lumière.

The dog immediately stirs, looks at its master, and wags its tail.

"That would be nice," replies Madame Lumière.

I settle in, hoping the suddenly aroused Paris won't rub up against my leg and pee in excitement.

"I didn't know you had a dog?"

"I keep him in the shop when I have visitors. Don't worry, he loves everybody."

I want to say, even Vampires, but I think it's wise to keep any quips to a minimum. (I know you're curious so hold your horses, there will be more about dogs and vampires later.)

"Isn't this nice, Nick? We can have a leisurely lunch together and then walk over to my apartment for our 3:30 p.m. appointment."

Oh, dear reader, did I neglect to mention my afternoon appointment? Forgive my bad manners.

I glance over my shoulder, looking for any of my sharp-toothed brethren. If you're out there, you better not follow me, you fucker.

TWENTY-FOUR

TITS IN THE RINGER OF LIFE (PART ONE)

Recording #3/mp (English, no translation needed)

Madame Lumière: (Claps her hands three times). Bernard, good afternoon. How are you feeling?

The Vampire: Good afternoon, Madame Lumière. Give me a moment, and I'll tell you.

Madame Lumière: It's such a lovely day. It's good to be alive.

(The Vampire laughs)

Madame Lumière: What's so amusing, Bernard?

The Vampire: It's good to be alive. Nick says it all the time.

Madame Lumière: It's a recognition that we can't take being alive for granted.

The Vampire: Don't I know it, Madame Lumière. Nick and I are lucky to be alive and biting.

Madame Lumière: Alive and biting, a little vampire humor, very good.

The Vampire: So, what's on tap for today? More talk of my gastronomical experiences, or is it my sexual prowess? I bet Nick would like to know about that.

Madame Lumière: Is that what you want to discuss, Bernard?

The Vampire: (Pausing) You know, Madame Lumière, I really was a very ordinary boy, and those feelings never leave you.

Madame Lumière: Excuse me? I'm sorry, but I don't understand what you're saying.

The Vampire: I was ordinary in my origins. I was the fifth son in a family of seven children. My mother was a seamstress, and my father a stone mason, like his father before him, as were my two eldest brothers. As a child, I wasn't exceptionally good at sports and never showed any early aptitude for learning. I certainly wasn't curious. I wasn't one of the kids who looked up at the sky and wondered why it was blue. For sure, I never asked why I was born or what the meaning of life was. Religion, sure, we went to church. We were good Catholics— the whole town was. Going to church on Sunday and listening to old Père Morin was something we all did, and my brothers and I hated it. Oh, except René. He became a priest. Can you believe it? One kid becomes a priest, the other a vampire! (Laughs)

Madame Lumière: You never contacted your family after...

The Vampire: Once or twice, I flew over the village.

Madame Lumière: You did!

The Vampire: (Laughing) What—you think I'm crazy!

Madame Lumière: Oh, Bernard!

The Vampire: When I was taken, I had just completed *enseignement secondaire, but enseignement supérieur* was always out of the question, for my grades were far less than satisfactory. Unable to distinguish myself at school and showing no aptitude for anything, the only choice I had in life was to apprentice for my father. I was to join him and my brothers the following week, working for the architect Raymond du Temple, who was transforming the castle of Bernard Augustus into a primary residence and showplace for his rule. (Silence)

Madame Lumière: Bernard, are you all right?

The Vampire: Madame Lumière, you have to understand that I have come to the understanding that it was to be my destiny to be grabbed off the streets on that Sunday morning in April 1535.

Madame Lumière: Yes, yes, I see.

The Vampire: I've done well for myself, considering what I had to work with. Of course, I can't compare myself with Thomas Mann or Thomas Edison.

Madame Lumière: Thomas Mann, Thomas Edison! You don't mean to tell me that they were Vampires?

The Vampire: (Laughing) Well, no. But who knows, n'est pas?

Madame Lumière: (Laughing) You are a devil, aren't you?

The Vampire: (Laughing) When you can live forever, anything is possible.

Madame Lumière: But Thomas Mann and Thomas Edison are both dead. They didn't live forever.

The Vampire: Maybe they are, and maybe they're not. Listen, Madame Lumière, if you have nothing but centuries to live and better yourself, don't you think you could eventually write *Death in Venice* or invent the light bulb?

Madame Lumière: I don't know if that is possible, Bernard. I've never thought about it.

The Vampire: I have. Believe me, I have. Do you really believe Shakespeare could have the incredible insight into all those life experiences to understand human nature and write *Henry VI Part 1, Henry VI Part 2, Henry VI Part 3, The Two Gentlemen of Verona*, and *Titus Andronicus* all at the age of 25?

Madame Lumière: You don't believe one can accomplish great things in a single lifetime, Bernard?

The Vampire: Madame Lumière, he was only twenty-five!

Madame Lumière: I didn't mean to excite you. Please, Bernard, go on.

The Vampire: Look at me. Before I became a vampire, I couldn't read or write or know the grammar or vocabulary of *le français classique,* but spoke the local *patois* of the working classes. Once I became a vampire, I became fluent in dozens of languages, including Greek and Latin, and eventually read the works of François Villon and Pierre de Ronsard, which I had missed in my youth. Lacking any formal education, in the ensuing centuries after my transformation, I received a first in Classics at the University of Oxford, a PhD in Zoology at the University of Melbourne, and a PhD in Cosmochemistry at Caltech. (Silence)

Madame Lumière: Bernard, Bernard, are you all right?

The Vampire: The information I just provided would be but a few lines in a single-spaced, ten-page, and counting curriculum vitae. (Silence)

Madame Lumière. Bernard, do you want to take a break? Should I get you some water—Gatorade? I have Orange Zero.

The Vampire: Orange Zero? You think I'm fat, Madame Lumière?

Madame Lumière: No, I was...

The Vampire: I never thought about it, but I have never had a weight problem in all my centuries. (Laughing) Must be my metabolism? Or, could it be another side effect of Vampirism? (Laughing) Become a vampire and never have to worry about eating that third piece of strawberry shortcake! How's that for a selling proposition, Madame Lumière? You think, if at the start, The Voice sold me on that, I would have adjusted more readily to the benefits of turning into a Pteropus every time I need to nip out of town for a nip at the ole neck, so to speak, instead of being resentful that I don't have a bat mobile.

Madame Lumière: (Laughing) You're certainly not ordinary anymore, are you, Bernard?

The Vampire: Are you saying I have problems?

Madame Lumière: Bernard, I...

The Vampire: What, you think I'm not on top of my game?

Madame Lumière: No, Bernard, I never said that, but everyone has...

The Vampire: What, what does everyone have?

Madame Lumière: Unresolved...

The Vampire: Unresolved what?

Madame Lumière: Issues...

The Vampire: Everyone thinks being immortal is the be-all and end-all. That living forever makes vampires feel head and shoulders above everyone else, no matter how rich, famous, or intelligent you are, because in the end, my friend, you buy the farm while we fly over your grave, laughing our tiny wings off.

Madame Lumière: But you don't feel that way, do you, Bernard?

The Vampire: Did you know Nick has to be half in the bag before he comes here?

TWENTY-FIVE

TITS IN THE RINGER OF LIFE (PART TWO)

Recording #4/mp (English, no translation needed)

Madame Lumière: Half in the bag?

The Vampire: Two sheets to the wind, wasted, inebriated.

Madame Lumière: Drunk as Cooter Brown.

The Vampire: Right-O!

Madame Lumière: You know that expression?

The Vampire: I do, indeed, Madame Lumière.

Madame Lumière: No telling. My Aunt Cleola always said that when her husband, Carl, came banging on the front door after a night out with the boys.

The Vampire: In the '60s, I lived in Brevard, North Carolina, working for a small architectural firm. My boss, Werner, who was originally from Bern, Switzerland, loved the expression 'nervous as a cat in a room full of rocking chairs' when he was waiting for a commission.

Madame Lumière: (Laughing) Aunt Cleola had one of her own when she was at sixes and sevens, but it was a little more purple.

The Vampire: Could it be?' I'm sweatin like a whore in church?'

Madame Lumière: (Laughing) Oh, you are a naughty one, you are!

The Vampire: In the eyes of God, I made Blaise Pascal a saint.

Madame Lumière: Blaise Pascal, the mathematician? You're name-dropping again, Bernard.

The Vampire: I'm shameful, aren't I?

Madame Lumière: Just a little.

(They both laugh)

The Vampire: I'm impressed that you know the name. I've discovered that most Americans are shamefully ignorant about other countries' history.

Madame Lumière: Especially, why should a poor country girl from South Carolina know the man who invented the laws of probability?

The Vampire: My apologies for underestimating you.

Madame Lumière: His work is essential if you're to do someone's horoscope accurately.

The Vampire: I'm sure Blaise would get a kick out of that.

Madame Lumière: I detect a tone of sarcasm in your voice, Bernard. I hope you're not mocking me?

The Vampire: If you knew Blaise, you would understand.

Madame Lumière: Why don't you explain, Bernard? I understand you can't wait to tell me you invented the laws of probability.

The Vampire: No. Unfortunately, that was beyond my mathematical capabilities. But I was around when he believed he discovered the infallibility of the scriptures and developed his tragic vision of God.

(Madame Lumière nervously clears her throat)

The Vampire: In a word, Blaise held that there were no rational grounds for believing in God. Of course, I could disprove that theory in a New York Minute.

Madame Lumière: By revealing your existence as a vampire.

The Vampire: Exactly.

Madame Lumière: But you couldn't without risking your own life.

The Vampire: At first, Blaise would have attempted to convince me that I was just being argumentative, although the bizarreness of my declaration would have taken him aback. He would have said it was *stultitiam,* a folly, to believe such a wild claim without giving him any rational grounds to prove my point.

Madame Lumière: You would have had to...

The Vampire: Or, do something less extreme and turn into a bat and fly out the window.

Madame Lumière: You said nothing.

The Vampire: Either God is or is not, and Blaise believed not. I realized turning into a vampire would be an act of hubris on my part. While it would initially make him question the laws of nature, it wouldn't change his opinion on the existence of God and only risk my ultimate safety.

Madame Lumière: Is that what you believe, Bernard?

The Vampire: That he would have turned me in?

Madame Lumière: Either God is or is not.

The Vampire: I can't go there, Madame Lumière. Not if I want to keep my sanity.

(Madame Lumière clears her throat)

The Vampire: Madame Lumière...

Madame Lumière: Yes Bernard.

The Vampire: I don't want you to tell Nick what I said about his drinking.

Madame Lumière: I thought these sessions were to help him understand who he is. Who you are?

The Vampire: You can see for yourself Nick's the nervous type— no, not nervous—unsettled. And that's perfectly normal for someone in this situation. Don't you think I took a nip or two after I learned of my situation?

Madame Lumière: And what situation is that, Bernard?

The Vampire: Someone attempting to regain their memory and learning they're, ahh...

Madame Lumière: A Vampire?

The Vampire: Special.

Madame Lumière: Special?

The Vampire: Isn't that what the men with the pointy-heads call anyone different, not to make them social outcasts and feel inferior?

Madame Lumière: I'm not a medical professional; I really can't comment on that, Bernard.

The Vampire: Oh, don't be modest, now, Madame Lumière. I believe you have special gifts.

Madame Lumière: You're very kind, Bernard.

The Vampire: I also believe you to be very honest, and above all, we must be honest with each other.

Madame Lumière: I can appreciate that, Bernard, but if we are to be honest with each other, why can't we tell Nick your/his condition? It seems to me that this is precisely the information he needs to become, as you say, less unsettled.

The Vampire: Do you know what the meaning of the word trust, Madame Lumière? No—don't answer that. Allow me to provide you with my definition. 'Trust is Grow old along with me! The best is yet to be. The last of life, for which the first was made: Our times are in His hand.'

Madame Lumière: That's Robert Browning, isn't it?

The Vampire: Yes, it is. Again, I'm impressed, Madame Lumière.

Madame Lumière: I have a book of his poetry by my nightstand. I particularly love "Rabbi Ben Ezra."

The Vampire: I don't mean to name drop, Madame Lumière, but I met Mr. Robert Browning in June of 1827. Would you like to hear how?

Madame Lumière: I'm jealous, Bernard. Tell me everything.

The Vampire: I was visiting Robert Browning Sr at his home in Camberwell, and Robert was just a teen then. His father had a vast library, and I arrived hoping to purchase a first edition of *On The Ends of Good And Evil* by the great Roman orator Marcus Tullius Cicero. I could not purchase the book, but I encountered Robert in the garden while leaving. We began talking, and I mentioned my fondness for poetry. Thank goodness I didn't tell him I had written anything because it was then that he confessed he was a poet. He was shy when asked if he could recite something he had just written. I said yes. It didn't take me but a moment to recognize the boy's genius. I was correct when, several years later, he published that very same poem and was immediately hailed as such.

Madame Lumière: You were a poet, Bernard? When and where?

The Vampire: Oh, I hadn't become serious about poetry until years later. By then, I was living in Granada, going by the name Baltasar de la Cruz. I was very much influenced by the playwright Lope de Vega, but my poems weren't very good, so I won't bring that pain to your soul. I hope you understand, Madame Lumière?

Madame Lumière: Oh, I think you're being modest. I would love to hear one of your poems, Bernard.

The Vampire: That is very kind of you, Madame Lumière, but I think we must save that for another day.

Madame Lumière: Bernard, you're such a tease.

The Vampire: (Laughing) I'm the King of Tease when you think of how often I have to say, save that for another day. It's not my intention to tease you, Madame Lumière, but if I don't postpone that memory, I'll never be able to finish a thought. Think of my centuries-old memory bank as a giant beaker full of millions of water molecules. The molecules—my memories, live harmoniously ensconced in the beaker until suddenly something ignites the flame under the glass, and the molecules begin to heat, and bam—they collide uncontrollably into each other. Have you ever played with Mexican Jumping Beans, Madame Lumière?

(They both laugh)

Madame Lumière: Bernard, what can I do to make this easier for you?

The Vampire: Let's save that response for another day!

(They laugh again. A Pause.)

Madame Lumière: Bernard, you were telling me about trust.

The Vampire: When you think about it, it's hard to believe someone like me is ashamed of his parents. How many university degrees, academic honors, hobnobbing with the rich and famous, and the wealthy—oh, those offshore accounts that will make your head spin, Madame Lumière—does it take to realize it's not where you started, but where you finish that counts? And let's talk about being out of character. Absolutely, our elders have misled the great unwashed and massaged our folklore more than a bit, but one thing mythology got right: Dracula never suffered from low self-esteem. (Leaning forward) With each passing day, my presence slowly leaks into Nick's consciousness, and I want Nick to have some breathing space before he has to face his childhood insecurities. Then there is the question of reconciling his intellectual growth with a lack of native intelligence.

Madame Lumière: Nature vs. nurture.

The Vampire: What did you say?

Madame Lumière: It's the age-old question. How much of our characteristics are formed by genetics, by upbringing, or by life experience?

The Vampire: DNA vs SHFI.

Madame Lumière: SHFI?

The Vampire: Shit Happens Fuck It!

Madame Lumière: (Laughing) Très amusant monsieur Bernard. Ah, there I go backsliding into my high school French.

The Vampire: I should have warned you that vampires make you do many things you might not want to do.

Madame Lumière: I'm surprised you can understand my accent. Ah, but you did say you spent time in North Carolina. I bet you encountered many ladies who spoke French with a southern drawl, didn't you, Bernard? I know you want to save that for another day!

(They both laugh)

Madame Lumière: How do you expect to keep this from Nick when it appears to be so much a part of your/his everyday existence?

The Vampire: Well, I thought we could find him a girlfriend.

TWENTY-SIX

DEAD ROOMMATE ON THE TENTH FLOOR (PART ONE)

From the moment I left Madame Lumière's apartment, I knew she was bullshitting me. Come on, something she ate at lunch upset the spiritual energy in her body, controlling her high-alert waves, thus preventing her from entering a state of calm from which she could put me into a hypnotic trance. And I have a bridge to sell you, too.

I know the awful truth. Madame Lumière didn't want to tell me that Bernard's pissed at me for mocking his book titles and that all he did during the session was rant and rave about how insensitive I was to his feelings.

So, what was I to do? Call her a liar? Of course not! I knew she was only trying to keep me from getting upset. And let's face it, my vampire was right. I knew it the minute the words were out of my mouth, but it was too damn late, and don't you know it, I've felt guilty about it ever since.

So, I played along. I told Madame Lumière as much sincerity as I could muster that I hoped her stomach felt better, and naturally, I would get to see her the following week.

I must have called myself a fuckin' idiot a dozen times as I walked the two blocks back to my apartment. I was lucky; everybody I encountered was also yelling into thin air, only they had earplugs, and I didn't.

Have you ever wished you were a bat and could escape all your troubles by flying into someone's window and taking a bit out of their tasty neck, and sucking all the blood out of their bodies until you feel new again?

Of course, not—what am I crazy?

Had I known the man and woman talking to Kenny were cops when he and I exchanged waves as I walked through the lobby on my way to the elevators, or had I first met another resident at the elevators or up on my floor, I would have been clued in and prepared for what awaited me in my hallway.

It was the neon yellow crisscrossed tape that first caught the corner of my eye and stopped me dead in my tracks, interrupting me from concentrating all my brain power on the intriguing geometric patterns of the hallway carpet that always reminded me of another carpet that one magically flew over a white cityscape. You think I'm perhaps obsessed with flying, duh?

It takes me a moment to shift my eyes from the tape, as my mind is trying to make sense of that bird's-eye view, to my next-door neighbor (on my left as you enter).

Cora Smith is a fifty-ish blonde man-eater. I'm sure her percipient mother penned Cora on the baby's birth certificate after the infamous character of the same name played by Lana Turner in the movie *The Postman Always Rings Twice.*

Cora is a tease. She always wears high-necked blouses or sweaters, and if this isn't enough of a defense against the unwanted love bite, she always shoves her silicon mountainous twin peaks pushing out from her shrink-wrapped sweaters into my chest, backing me up and out of reach of what lies beneath the cloth.

"Why, I half expected Captain Benson to knock on my door".

When my expressionless response finally registers, Cora continues. "You know, *Law and Order Special Victims*, although I can't imagine anyone would rape Margaret, not unless they wanted to get a hernia."

Now, this is the funniest thing I've heard all day, so I give out a guffaw that would even embarrass my fellow audience members at the Gotham Comedy Club.

Had I always had this over-the-top laugh? I had to remember to ask Madame Lumière to ask Bernard.

"But no, these two flatfeet were down and dirty and right out of *Homicide Life On The Street*. Now that was a show, don't you think?" says Cora.

"You know, I don't think I ever saw it."

"Oh, silly me? You don't have a memory, do you? I can't imagine."

Every time Cora says, 'I can't imagine', her breasts heave and push me away even further.

"I was going to an art exhibit in Soho and was in my downtown black Dolce two-piece, and they thought it was because I was mourning for Margaret. I can't imagine?"

There they go, Cora's breasts heave and push me back a few extra inches. Yet again, I was overmatched by a set of tatas and sent packing toward my front door.

Over my shoulder, I hear a man's voice say, "Mr. Cummings, can we have a word?"

TWENTY-SEVEN

DEAD ROOMMATE ON THE TENTH FLOOR (PART TWO)

I don't want to bore you with a description of my apartment or venture a guess as to when, where, or how legally my vampire obtained these centuries-old pieces of furniture, priceless antiquities, and museum-quality art that covered every inch of wall space. All of this went unnoticed by the two cops, who seemed unable to get accustomed to the low-level lightning, perhaps because they refused to take off their sunglasses.

I put them on the window-facing, mid-century white French sofa while I sat on its twin, separated by an Italian glass table with fluted gold legs upon which sit several *objets d'art*.

"Mr. Cummings, when was the last time you saw Miss Havilland?" asks the forty-something male balding detective, with a broad set of eyes that threaten to run off the side of his face and a shiny green two-piece off the rack at Men's Wearhouse that threatens to make me dislike all things Irish.

"Who?" Of course, I knew who they meant, but I was in a mood.

The female officer, shaped like a pear in her black pants suit, is now interested in a small bronze statue of a man and his cock sitting on the table. Forgive me for being so crude in my description, for the piece is Mycenaean, many millennia old, and extremely elegant in design.

"Your neighbor, Mr. Cummings—Mildred Havilland," says the male cop who could also stand to lose the tire across his waist that has suddenly inflated when his ass hits the couch.

"Margaret," interrupts the thin-as-a-rail female cop without taking her eyes off the 'three-legged' Mycenaean.

"Huh?" Says her partner.

The female cop continues, "The victim's name is Margaret, not Mildred," while eying the statue.

I imagine she is not trying to guess the statue's make and model, if the tiny smile that crosses her lips indicates what she is thinking.

The male cop flips a couple of pages in his notepad. "I got it as Mildred Havilland, age fifty-one."

I guess Abbott and Costello's 'Who's on first routine' is something they practice to give the interviewee the impression they're incompetent, but Bernard's been to this movie before, and it alerts me to their game by turning my balls ice cold.

"It's Margaret, and I haven't seen her in weeks. From what my neighbors say, she suffers from agoraphobia and rarely leaves her apartment except to pick up the New York Times from the trash."

"The Times—from the trash," says the male cop.

"I guess she's too cheap to buy her own," I murmur unkindly.

"And that's when you see her? Talk to her, maybe," the male cop continues.

"No, she's always sneaking back inside if she sees me."

"Does her taking your paper upset you, Mr. Cummings?" asks the female cop.

"It's not my paper. I get the Times online."

The female cop looks deflated. Had it been my Times she grabbed, she'd have her motive, locked me up, and be hoisting a few celebratory brews at the local cop bar.

"You should be talking to Betty," I volunteer.

"Betty," says the male cop.

"You know, her cousin from Omaha who lives with Margaret."

I give this information out with a straight face, guessing they already have heard from the guys downstairs the gossip that her cousin is no more a relative than the man in the street, who, without any collaborative evidence, the Condo Board is powerless to evict.

"It's Jane, not Betty," says the female cop, finally tearing her eyes from Phallus Man and locking those baby blues on me.

I grin, and immediately, she knows I'm throwing back her Abbott and Costello dumb-as-a-stump routine.

"Jane Meadows, age fifty-one, from Le Claire, Iowa," says the male cop.

"Fifty-one, no kidding; looked much younger," says I for no other reason than to make conversation because, for the life of me, I couldn't pick her out of a police lineup.

"Margaret was sixty-three," chirps the female cop, her eyes scanning the room, probably looking for more penises.

The male cop stands, and his stomach quickly retracts like the Alien's double set of razors after unhappily missing Ripley's fleshy arm. His partner gets the message and stands, hands on hips, taking a final longing look at the Mycenaean of her dreams.

"We appreciate you talking to us, Mr. Cummings, and we're sorry for your loss. We know Ms. Havilland was a valued member of your community," says the male cop.

What the fuck is this jerk talking about? Is he expecting a Princess Diana-like pilgrimage to Margaret's front door, complete with flowers, cards, and a candlelight vigil?

And as far as calling us a community, I'd like to have him attend unarmed, a condo meeting and see how collegial we are discussing how to end the life of the Dancing Queen who insists on imitating Ginger Rodgers at three in the morning, causing her downstairs neighbor enough sleepless nights to consider suicide.

I'm happy to say that even in the dim light and with their aviator shades smugly fashioned to their faces, they didn't bump into any art on the way out, instead nimbly navigating through my living room and foyer into the safety of my hallway.

"Oh, by the way," says the female cop, making as nice a pirouette as you would see at the Bolshoi. "Do you know why Jane would say she was from Omaha when she was from Iowa?"

"Maybe she was a fan of *Wild Kingdom*."

For a painful moment, like the husband and wife from American Gothic, they stare at me, too young to get the reference to Mutual of Omaha, the show's sponsor, before they have no other choice but to pretend they get it and join me in a hee-haw or two.

TWENTY-EIGHT

DEAD ROOMMATE ON THE TENTH FLOOR (PART THREE)

When you have lived as long as I have, you learn to appreciate the importance of gossip as an antidote to the boredom of a humdrum, every day, five centuries and counting existence. Of course, gossip doesn't necessarily have to be salacious, malicious, or complete fiction; although granted, it is more colorful.

Take, for instance, my stay in Toulouse from June to July 1618. During this time, the authorities came for my fellow traveler and backgammon opponent in room 419, Lucillio Vanni.

Lucillio's fame as an Italian scientist who inspired Julien de La Mattrie to write Man a Machie was reason enough to make him a cause célèbre. Still, it was his outspoken atheism that eventually hurt him.

When I first heard from Madame Circe, the ninety-year-old owner of Hotel Le Pentateuch, that she heard from Madame George that they had cut out Lucillio's tongue before they burned him at the stake, I told her such gossip only cast aspersions on the hotel and would certainly remove it from the list of Voltaire's Guide to the best hotels in Toulouse.

Madame C certainly knew how a bad review could kill an establishment. She herself penned the anonymous letter tacked to the front door of Pension 19 Rue Gît-le-Cœur, accusing the chef of being a Fauvist.

Unfortunately, this piece of gossip that I immediately dismissed as complete bullshit turned out to be accurate and, in so doing, taught me two valuable lessons. Make sure you collect your backgammon winnings at evening's end and never doubt the authenticity of back-alley gossip or the Telephone Game, no matter how insane.

Why I'm recalling this story, what I'm leading up to, and that I must somehow communicate to Nick is this encounter—when his neighbor in 6 K, Crystal Chance, tells him that she heard from Fifi Krause up in Penthouse 15A that Margaret Havilland's body had been discovered in the tub, completely drained of blood and joked she wouldn't be at all surprised to learn she also found two tiny bites in her neck, Nick should act naturally.

I can kick myself for not revealing Madame C's story in one of my recordings, so Nick would be Ready Teddy to unveil our building's secrets that I have been keeping from Nick.

Let me back up and take you back an hour. After the cops leave Nick's apartment, I think Nick will either go to the grape or take to the bed, but never decide to unleash the beast by going down to the small gym in the basement.

So, before I can say antidisestablishmentarianism three times, Nick's into a pair of black Nike basketball shorts, a Rolling Stones t-shirt from their "Rolling Thunder Tour" (more on that in my yet-to-be-written chapter, "The Vampire Roadie"), Nike socks, and sneakers, and he's out the door without so much as a—see ya, when I see ya!

What, you didn't think vampires buff up and pump iron? Well, let me clue you into the factoid that I've become what they curiously call a gym rat over the centuries.

In my many lifetimes, I have run the Boston and Madrid Marathons; rock climbed from Freiburg to the Bernese Oberland to

Valais, and, while I'm no Simone Bowles, I once came in second in an uneven bars competition at UCLA when I was pursuing a Master's in sound engineering.

So, it stands to reason that I have a clothing collection worthy of the Sports Authority. However, because of Nick's fall, I had the mistaken impression that my boy Nick is gun-shy, avoids strenuous physical activity, and never ventures down to the basement gym, a place where residents can be busy little bees sharing rumors and starting them. And because the roof garden is unavailable, the gym has become even more popular, now second only to the lobby/front desk where the building's gossip mongers congregate.

The room is small for a gym intended to serve the entire building and appears even smaller when crammed with exercise machines. The treadmill and elliptical are taken, but the middle of the three stationary bikes is available, so Nick, after acknowledging a flurry of waves and hi-yahs, sits himself down on the Schwinn 290 Recumbent.

Before Nick can adjust the seat, Crystal Chance in 6K, who, if you look at her sideways, will disappear before your eyes but remarkably works the bike like one of the muscle-up collegians from the movie *Boys In The Boat* works the Oars, shouts over from the bike to Nick's right what Fifi Krause up in Penthouse 15A told her about how and in what condition the police found Margaret's body.

The moment Crystal mentions the tiny marks on Marjorie Havilland's neck, Barbara Banter, the ninety-seven-year-old reputed mistress of the building's owner's grandfather, seated on Nick's left and whose bowling pin legs spin the peddles faster than the croupier at a Monte Carlo roulette wheel, chimes in.

"Now, CC, will you blame this on you-know-who?"

"Me? Why, Barb, they're your best friends."

"What I told you was in confidence," whispers Barbara Banter.

"Well, Nick isn't like a stranger, is he?"

"No, I suppose not," sighs Barbara Banter, who throws Nick a phony-baloney smile.

Nick knows exactly why Barbara is unfriendly. It's because, unlike Madame L's dog, Paris, this Yorkie recoils and whimpers whenever it comes within a foot of him.

Before you blame me for not telling Nick animals can smell a vampire a mile away, that's bullshit. Nowhere in The Code does it say that, and in my centuries of living The Vampire Life, I can count on the fingers of one hand the times an animal, any animal, got crazy over me; the cause in both cases had to do with the fact I was madly waving a machete, covered with blood.

(Didn't I tell you we'd talk about dogs and vampires!)

"So go on, Barb, tell Nick what you told me, Vera's sister Eleanor told you. And don't leave out a single solitary syllable."

"Nick, I don't know how much you know about the Senator sisters," says Barbara Banter.

"Barb, Nick's just come out of the hospital, don't you know, so I'm sure he's got a lot of other things buzzing around in that handsome head of his, so why don't you fill him in? Isn't that right, Nick?" says the flirty Crystal, who never passes Nick without making a pass.

"My head's feeling fine, but thanks for your concern, Crystal," smiles Nick, trying to figure out how to respond to these two women on either side of him without throwing his neck out of joint.

"I know you are, Nick, and we're all so happy, honey. Go on, Barb, give him the lowdown," says Crystal.

"Eleanor Senator is the sister of Vera Senator, who just so happens to be the one-hundred-and-five-year-old inventor of *New Face Restorer Cream*. You know 'New Face', don't you, Nick?" Barb locks eyes with Nick and gives him that I-know-that's-why-you-look-so-damn-young wink.

The wink immediately makes Nick blush. He shouldn't be using the stuff, but it's in the medicine cabinet.

I couldn't be prouder. My boy Nick certainly has his shit together. As far as the face cream goes, I have to admit, I'm a fool for anything

146

that smells like coconut, but as far as slowing down the aging process, coal to Newcastle, I'm afraid.

Barbara Banter basks in the glow of uncovering Nick's fountain of youth secret and continues, "Now you have to understand that Eleanor is the businessperson, the one who keeps the company books, while Vera is the creative one and invents the products; by the way, Vera just celebrated her ninety-fifth birthday and tells anyone she meets that people think she looks seventy-five."

"I wouldn't go that far, but I should look so good when I get to be ninety-five," interrupts Crystal.

"Amen to that, sister, Crystal." Barbara Banter continues. "Eleanor tells it, when she and her sister Vera first moved into this building, there were rumors that a vampire couple lived in 2C and D."

Nick flinches and stops pedaling.

And there it is! The secret I should have revealed to Nick the first time he went under. Why he didn't, it was that bitch Dr. Mickeltee; she was already becoming suspicious. Too late for that now.

Steady boy, steady. And don't get pissed off at me because I never told you about Carolyn and Florien.

"You know, Barb, back when our building was built, all the C and D apartments were joined," interrupts Crystal.

"Some still are," says Barbara Banter.

"No, they're not," argues Crystal.

"I'm on the Board, Crystal, so I know 12C and D and 14C and D have their original configuration," argues Barbara Banter."

"They must pay a fortune," says Crystal

These women talking past Nick as if he isn't there provide him with a momentary respite, although his head is beginning to ache from all the swiveling.

He begins to pedal again.

That's a boy. Find your A-game, Nick, find your A-game!

"Crystal, do you want me to tell Nick the story or not?" scowls Barbara Banter.

Crystal nods.

Barbara Banter nods and begins. "As Eleanor tells it when she and her sister, Vera, first laid eyes on the couple they suspect are vampires, whose skin, by the way, Eleanor describes as the color of porcelain and wrinkle-free, and who didn't look a day over thirty even though rumor had it they had been living in the building sixty years."

"Why are some people so lucky?" asks Crystal.

"You're asking me who spends a king's ransom with Dr. Silvertone," says Barbara Banter.

Nick tries to keep a straight face as he increases his pedaling.

Don't you dare make a wisecrack, boy, don't you dare.

"Anyway, as I said, Nick—I'm not being too confusing. What with Crystal always interrupting."

"I am not," says Crystal.

"Nope, I'm fine. Go ahead with your story," says Nick, who has settled on a decent pedaling speed.

"Where was I? Oh, I remember. Naturally, when Vera became obsessed with their neighbor's youthfulness, she wrangled a dinner invitation to their apartment, hoping to discover the couple's secret. According to Elenore, they spent a delightful couple of hours. Still, when they return to their apartment after dinner, Elenore tells me Vera goes into their kitchen and begins concocting what eventually turns out to be *New Face Restorer Cream*."

"Barb, I can see Nick's confusion all over his handsome face. Please fill in Vera's background," says Crystal.

Crystal puts a more-than-friendly hand on Nick's hand. Bernard fights the impulse to pull Crystal over his body and bite her neck, while Nick fights the impulse to pull his hand away.

Barbara nods. "All right, if you think so. Vera had just graduated from college with a degree in chemistry and was interested in getting into the cosmetic business and, to that end, was trying to make lipstick. According to Eleanor, Vera had been experimenting for the last few months, mixing up batches of deer tallow, castor oil, beeswax, and red root dye and stinking up the kitchen."

"But no face cream, right, Barb?"

"Will you let me finish, will you, Crystal?"

"Sorry."

"I was going to say no face cream. However, that changed when Vera mixed up an entirely new brew of—guess what, face cream immediately after they returned home from dinner. So, I asked Eleanor if she thought her sister somehow got the formula from the vampires, I mean, neighbors. Eleanor says Vera's always been a Nosey Rosey, and whenever she visited someone's house, she would sneak away and go through their medicine cabinets."

Whether it was Crystal's hand on his or it was the story, Nick's becoming progressively agitated.

As I said, nowhere in my recording have I given Nick a heads-up on how to deal with vampires, in the building or otherwise— or told him this isn't the first time His Vampire has stepped into shit like that.

For instance, I should have told him the story of the Freud Affair. Let me think, yes—it's the year of our Lord, nineteen hundred and seventy-two, and I'm living in Palo Alto, California, on Lincoln Avenue when the body of my next-door neighbor is found murdered.

I've just returned from two years in Hawaii (See my yet-to-be-written chapter, "The Best Places for R&R"), and I'm out buying a new wardrobe (wide lapels and flared pants are in), so I'm fortunate to have an alibi at the time Dr. Hartmann buys the farm.

The cops interview me, but when they notice my Lightning Bolt surfboard, shaped by Gerry Lopez, lying up against a corner wall, they become more interested in learning where the best place to catch a wave is on the Big Island and neglect to ask me to provide clothing receipts and prove my alibi. (Yes, vampires surf!).

Two days later, my world turned upside down when two neighbor ladies accosted me by the mailboxes and demanded to know what the cops wanted.

When I told them we only talked about surfing in Hawaii, they were amazed because when they questioned me, the main topics were Freud's books *Totem and Taboo, Moses and Monotheism,* and the unpublished *Vampires Make Good Fathers.*

Now, Freud and his work have come into my life several times. The first time was when I was a pupil of Professor J. Z. Young and studying zoology at Magdalen College, Oxford, in 1928, four years before Sir Peter Medawar took a seat in the same classroom and two months before my Marienbad adventure.

I bring up Sir Peter because he's one of the leading scholars who helped discredit the yet-to-be-published *Vampires Make Good Fathers,* causing such outrage among patients, leading several to even murder their Freudian shrinks in the most gruesome ways. If you guessed castration, you wouldn't be wrong.

So, it was entirely reasonable to believe the same motive, and possibly cause of death, led to Dr. Hartmann's premature demise because, as anyone who knew him knew, the good doctor went to the extreme of erecting a giant size marble statue of Freud's nemesis Carl Jung on the lawn in front of his house—and completely expected when Sue (the other is Nancy) whispers that she heard from someone in authority, the good doctor had been murdered by a vampire who took issues with Jung's belief that all vampires had mommy issues.

At that moment, I experience what Nick must be feeling now in the basement gym, the heat of the torches on our backs as villagers try to thrust the stake through the heart of the vampire.

However, I keep my cool and don't bite anyone's neck off. Instead, I'm ready, willing, and hell—able to show the appropriate horror and accompany the two old maids back to Sue's apartment for some afternoon refreshments, quickly realizing these gals have wooden legs and magical livers and can drink me and any ten longshoremen under the table.

"Robert Redford's in the house," shouts Vera, her name stitched in red against the black satin jacket, as she motors toward Nick.

The old woman's shouts bring me back to the moment's reality. As the Sister's Senator enters, the gym becomes deathly still, dressed in identical black Prada warm-ups with enough bling to make Lil' Kim jealous.

They each push matching red Drive Medical Nitro Aluminum Lightweight Foldable Rollators through the narrow door as if vying for the pole position at the Indy 500. They scan the room before setting their sights on Nick.

"Look, Barb, I'm not the only one who thinks Nick looks like Robert Redford," squeals Crystal!

The Robert Redford reference always makes me uneasy because it pigeonholes me as the actor in The Way We Were. Now, fifty-one years later, it sets me up for a very uncomfortable meeting with anyone from 1973.

Nick increases his pedal speed until his thighs burn.

I love it. In the face of danger, Nick runs headlong into it!

Nick's move is exactly the kind I made back in Moravia in 1865 when I jumped into the Olympic-sized pool at the monastery in Brno for my first practice run just days before I was threatened with exposure and certain death.

Let me provide a little context. At the time, I worked as an administrative assistant to Auguste Wiseman. When the monk Gregor Mendel challenged Auguste to the 100-meter freestyle and 200-meter backstroke, Auguste immediately begged me to join his team.

As I mentioned, I felt energized when I jumped into the Olympic-sized pool at the monastery in Brno for my first practice run. I would be practicing the backstroke that morning and was easing into my second fifty meters when, out of the corner of my right eye, I caught sight of Marie-François Xavier Bichat, who was studying me through a miniature telescope the biologist received from his bible study partner, Zacharias Janssen with whom he spent his last summer holiday in Holland.

I knew that Bichat had been collecting blood plasma samples from everyone in Wiseman's department at the University of Freiburg in Freiburg im Breisgau. It was only a matter of time before the biologist discovered some irregularities in my protoplasm, leading Bichat to examine the rod-like structures in my nucleus, which he named chromosomes, which were stained differently.

Bichat would then make the connection between my abnormalities and the survival of the fitness mechanism behind Darwinism. I would be exposed and murdered by nightfall.

Let me tell you, I didn't lose a stroke and proceeded to finish the two hundred meters. When I got out of the pool and toweled off, I made it a point to walk right up to Bichat on his way out and ask the man who would become the father of modern histology if he would attend the meeting the following day.

When he said yes, I offered to pick him up and drive him to the meeting. What happened the following morning is up for conjecture. We'll never know whether it was indigestion or a mysterious bug that caused him to become indisposed that morning, but by that evening, he was returning to Heidelberg. He never continued with that particular line of inquiry. Instead, he began a lifelong study of longevity in the paramecium vs. amoeba.

I'm forced back to the moment when Nick's muscles begin to ache, so he slows his pedaling.

"It's so lovely to have a man around the gym," smiles Vera Senator as she rolls up in front of the bike.

Nick looks up from his recumbent position and locks eyes with the one-hundred-and-five-year-old inventor of *New Face Restorer Cream.*

Oh shit, here it comes, and there is nothing I can do!

Suddenly—wham-bam—thank you, Ma'am; just as it was when Nick was pulled into the Sherlock Holmes movie and experienced the reality of being in London, Nick's now drawn into a 24-per-second moving image of Vera, viscerally connecting him with every pixel of this twenty-something standing in a kitchen, mixing ingredients into a beaker.

The mind meld lasts only seconds, but he requires a second to experience the same sensation of bodily transportation.

For me, Nick's trip down memory lane is a say hello again to two vampire frenemies, Florien and Joanna—the fucking bloodsuckers that stabbed me in the back and nearly cost me my life. But that misadventure is another story and one definitely not for publication.

Nick blinks and focuses. Behind Vera stand two figures in the shadows. The man speaks. "We had two choices, my darling. We could take her blood."

The woman interrupts. "Both their bloods."

"That's right, Honey Bun, both sisters," smiles the man.

"Certainly not enough to make them one of us," laughs the woman.

"Certainly not, Dear Heart," agrees the man. "And even though they wouldn't remember the incident, we couldn't have the nosey one..."

"Vera," says the woman, "Her name is Vera."

"Yes, Love of my Life—her name is Vera. We couldn't allow Vera to start poking around—be a matter of time before she caused us real trouble," says the man.

"Then I came up with the perfect solution, didn't I?"

"You did, Sweetums," smiles the man.

"I led her to believe the secret to our youthfulness was in the face cream we used, and made sure I left a jar of it in our bathroom cabinet for Vera to see and from which she could take a small sample," laughs the woman."

"You see, we knew she was a chemist, and that's all she would require to discover the ingredients," says the man, staring right at Nick.

Nick's blood turns to ice, as does Bernard's.

"I'm so smart, aren't I?" smiles the woman.

"I didn't marry no dummy, My Precious," replies the man

"*A* dummy, not *no* dummy! For heaven's sake, can't you stop using double negatives after nearly a thousand years, Florien?"

To Nick, the sound and the fury of the images go puff as quickly as they appeared, and he's back in the gym wondering how the fuck do they know my name?

I'm sorry, Nick, my son. If I had been a good host, I should have seen this coming a mile away. I can't entirely bury the past, and I certainly can't prevent it from coming back into Nick's consciousness and scaring the living daylights out of him.

"My sister tells me you're a mystery writer. Is that true, Nick?"

"I did not, Vera. I heard he was a writer, but I never said a mystery writer," shouts her sister, Elenore."

"So, Mr. Mystery Writer, do you think the tiny marks on Margaret Havilland's neck came from the bite of a vampire?" Vera giggles.

"That's not funny, Vera. Margaret was a very kind, sweet young lady. It was that dreadful woman pretending to be her cousin who we wanted to kill, Jane Meadows, or whatever her real name was; she's the person who spread that ridiculous story of the bite marks to throw blame elsewhere before she conveniently disappeared. If that vanishing act is not a sign of someone guilty, I don't know what is," says Eleanor.

Nick's muscles feel better now that he has reduced his pedaling speed, so he's now better able to concentrate and figure out his next response.

"If it takes a murder in the building to get Nick down here, I say it was worth it. Now we must figure out how to make him a regular," chirps Crystal.

"Crystal, that's a horrible thing to say," says Barbara Banter.

"Oh, Barb, take that stick out of your ass and admit you've been eating up Nick's lovely body ever since he came down here like the rest of us. Just look at those calf muscles—as if you haven't taken your eyes off them."

"You do have the body of a much younger man, Nick. You must tell us all your secrets," smiles Vera as if she already knows the answer.

"My neighbor, Bruce, said he saw you having coffee with Jane Meadows at the wine bar next door," says Eleanor.

"Have you been? Their prices are insane," says Barbara Banter.

"And you didn't invite me," meows Crystal.

"It was last Friday, wasn't it, Nick?" asks Eleanor.

"And no one has seen her since; that's what I heard," says Crystal.

"Friday, do you think that's when she killed Margaret?" asks Barbara Banter.

"Don't be silly. They discovered the body on Monday," says Crystal.

"If it were Friday, someone would have..."

"Smelled the body. Oh, Barb, that's terrible," says Crystal, holding her nose.

I want to strangle the lot of them, the bitch with the big tits first, but Nick appears to find the entire scene amusing. My god, he laughs, remembering this was his exact response when caught up in the disappearance of Judge Crater back in August of 1930.

At the time, he worked at the New York Sun as a gossip reporter named Vince Aleto. Several days later, after the Judge's disappearance, he was having his customary Wednesday tea at Delmonico's with his three 'nobs and swells' (members of New York's Four Hundred, the society of the only people who mattered), with whom he relied on for rumors, tittle-tattle, and brewing scandals.

These ladies of the smart set were one hundred percent certain the missing Judge, who was suspected of being involved in some Tammany Hall Hanky Panky, had been bumped off by mobsters, just like their notorious beer baron pal, recently massacred by a Chicago gunman at a summer resort south of the Windy City.

"Oh, Agatha, the poor, naïve wife is always the last to know," says Julia of the 'marrying Greens' of Park Avenue and Palm Beach.

"So, there is no truth to the rumor he's run off with his mistress," says I, looking for details on that sordid affair.

"Flo the floozy, ha! She's still prancing at the Central in the back of the chorus of "Always You" and always off-key, don't you know," snickers Beebee Margot of Fifth Avenue and the Hudson Valley.

"I'm telling you, Vincent, my sweet boy, they filled him full of holes and buried his body under the boardwalk at Coney Island," laughs Agatha Emerald FitzRoyce of Fifth Avenue and the North Coast of Long Island.

"Wait a minute! Wasn't it you who ambushed the Judge outside the Criterion last week?" declares Beebee Margot of Fifth Avenue and the Hudson Valley. She slaps him on his wrist. "Why, you devil, it was you that Lillian Davidson Owens saw!"

"Did you confront him with proof he paid off the political bosses in Tammany for his appointment to the New York Supreme Court? Or was it the Liberty Hotel affair? That was it; you got to somebody in the know to give you the tip," exclaims Julia of the 'marrying Greens' of Park Avenue and Palm Beach.

"Nobody saw him after he went into the movie house, isn't that right, Vincent?" voices Agatha Emerald FitzRoyce of Fifth Avenue and the North Coast of Long Island.

"Maybe Nosferatu got him," offers Julia of the 'marrying Greens' of Park Avenue and Palm Beach.

"That's it, the vampire jumped out of the movie and into the audience, sucked out all the judge's blood, and made him one of the walking dead, and then they hop back onto the screen and disappear into the movie," laughs Beebee Margot of Fifth Avenue and the Hudson Valley.

"I bet you followed him into the movie house and saw it all," laughs Agatha Emerald FitzRoyce of Fifth Avenue and the North Coast of Long Island.

"You know, don't you? Confess, now! Tell us everything, Vincent," demands Beebee Margot of Fifth Avenue and the Hudson Valley!

Nick continues to pedal while Bernard, the vampire, unspools his remembrance of unnerving things past, when suddenly Crystal looks up from her buzzing phone and shouts, "Margaret installed Nanny Cams in the apartment!"

"That means..." utters Barbara Banter, recognizing the awful truth.

"The murderer is on film," cries the group in a single terrifying voice!

TWENTY-NINE

HE'S TRYING TO KILL ME

You would think that my head would be exploding, or I'd be bouncing off the walls, or better still, be safely away on a flight to Tangiers under an assumed name. Still, for some unexplainable reason, I'm right here in 6J, calm as a cucumber and not a bit concerned that the murderer captured on film is me, or more precisely, Benard, my vampire.

More to the point, he would not have been able to survive these last two-hundred years plus had he been careless, and don't forget the 'Don't shit where you live' axiom that's written in stone in the Code.

Well, calm as a cucumber might not be entirely accurate because last night, I had a bizarre, if not disturbing, dream (like many I've had since I've awoken from my amnesia). I'm that's not entirely copasetic.

Last night's dream was about Kirsten Hayward, who first appeared as a seven-year-old girl trying out for the role of Annie in the musical. I knew the child was Kirsten because she wore the same Christian Louboutin Mimiflirt Leather Red Sole Ballerina Mules when I met her at Carly Ford's party.

When Child Kirsten refuses to take direction and instead sticks her fist into her mouth when the director asks her what she thinks of the lines, the director throws up his arms in frustration. Child Kirsten shrugs, turns, and walks off the stage.

The scene jumps to a full-grown Kirsten and me entering a Synagogue. We are attending a funeral. As we were late, we had to walk all the way down the center aisle to the third pew to find a seat. In my clutches, I have a white skullcap the size of a teacup, and when I attach it to my head, Kirsten quickly snatches it off.

"Nick, you look like a trained monkey with that thing on your head; she snickers."

It's a yarmulke and not a thing to mock, but you don't show disgust or the slightest bit of upset to the lassie at the moment in your dream, you're slo-licking your way into her Treasure Island of Delight. Oh, sweet mystery of make-believe.

We enter the row, and grunts and groans meet our efforts as we brush by mourners and take our seats. Immediately, the middle-aged woman in a paisley summer dress sitting in the pew directly behind me leans over and whispers, *"When are you going to get me my drugs?"*

Another jump cut, and I'm looking to meet my man who hangs out on Canal Street and Broadway next to the fake designer handbag stand.

My Paisley Pal, now accompanied by a hairless miniature dog of an unknown breed, and my sweet Kirsten, still in her funereal black Dolce & Gabbana Men's Martini Two-Piece Solid Suit, lean against a light pole on the other side of the stand, eying a Louis Vuitton grey and white checkered Tote lying on a blanket amongst the items for sale. It is a knock-off of the bags slung over their shoulders.

The African selling the merchandise looks me in the eyes and, without moving his mouth, says, *"....I'm thrilled to be transmitting to you my secret instructions for today's timely Psycho-Cranial-Telepathic session at this decisive moment in your life so you may discover the unlimited potential that lies dormant inside you. Buy one of these bargain Louis Vuitton's so you can impress your girlfriend, and I can send money back to Ghana."*

Now, what can you make of that? One thing I can tell you is that I'm never going down to Canal Street. You can bet on that.

The only thing I need now is a hot shower to clear my head and get me ready like Mick for another night of 'Rolling Thunder.'

Big fuckin' deal, Nick, you can never go back to Canal Street. You'd have a coronary if I told you all the streets I can't return to.

While Nick yearns for carnal pleasures, how pathetically human, and has these pedestrian dreams about trading handbags for sex, I yearn for eternal sustenance, a flyaway to Dorchester up in Boston, for instance, where memories of a particularly succulent Recipient, a Miss Bertha Von Halloran, still stir my blood to boil,

Ah, Berti Halloran, what a hell-raiser she was. It was an early April 19 morning, in the year of our Lord 1897, and the sun had yet to rise over the sleepy Boston neighborhood.

Had I read the newspapers in the days leading up to his fly-in, I would have postponed my visit, for that day happened to be the first running of the Boston Marathon, though back in 1897, it was called the American Marathon and was the final event of the B.A.A. Games.

I had just worn out his welcome in Halifax, Nova Scotia. I was considering returning to England, particularly Dorchester and Hardy's Cottage, where Mary Elizabeth Wilkinson could always be relied upon to provide the ten minutes of nourishment required to read Tess of the d'Urbervilles.

What made me spin the globe and land my finger on another Dorchester, this destination, an up-and-coming Boston, Massachusetts neighborhood, can only be a matter of choosing one from column A: Fate, Destiny, Luck. Or, from column B: Shit happens, Shit Outta Luck, May The Bird of Paradise Fly Up Your Nose.

The first running of the Boston Marathon began at the entrance to Metcalf's Mill in Ashland and finished up at the Irvington Street Oval near Copley Square. A John J. McDermott of New York came out of the pack of fifteen starters to win the inaugural Boston Marathon.

I had long since left the area for New York City after spending twenty delightful minutes with Berti, who had injured her calf in a riding accident two days previously, causing her to be left home alone.

At the same time, I began my feast; Berti's husband and their four children joined the crowd in a VIP viewing stand near Copley Square (Mr. Caleb McCarthy Halloran being the District Court judge from Dorchester, don't you know).

All right, the fact that Nick has fantasies of oral sex with a progeny of Queen Nefertiti illustrates a tiny vampire leakage, and for that, I should be grateful, but I'm still troubled. No, I'm more than troubled for my boy, Nick.

Readers—yes—you know, don't you? It's the question you've been asking since Nick returned home from the hospital. The question I've been asking myself. Why the fuck, doesn't Nick need blood, the precious icon that sustains our life and provides life everlasting?

Oh, I get it! He had a little ka knock to his brain and temporarily lost his memory. So what? Football players get their brains scrambled every Sunday, but by Monday, they're back on the practice field. Am I right, or am I not watching the NFL on Fox?

Okay, so you may temporarily forget what day it is, but after a while, you get over it and remember what's really important. You remember your ATM password, and you go on with your life.

Can you see why I'm freakin'? It's been over a month, and Nick still doesn't want to bite the neck that feeds him! How fucked is that?

Another thing? Why isn't Nick physically ill? I can assure you if I miss a meal for more than a month, all sorts of nasty shit happen to my body: Heartburn, irregularity, sinusitis, backache, rapid heartbeat; I even had a case of vertigo back in 1865 that nearly did me in.

At the time, I was living in Liverpool and between jobs when the opportunity presented itself to enter the blockade-busting business. Now, one of the rules of the Code is to stay out of politics. Still, since Britain was split right down the political fifty-yard line regarding the war (liberals anti-Confederate, Tories pro-Confederate), I didn't think it mattered much what side I joined if the right opportunity fell into my lap, which it did when a banker pal did me a solid and told me there was serious money to be made from supplying guns, uniforms, medicines, textiles, and even food to the south.

I got so caught up in the deal that I forgot that I hadn't gone hunting in over a week, so things went south when I was about to set sail for America on the Lellia.

I began to suffer such an extreme case of vertigo from lack of nourishment that the ship's medical officer, upon examining me, had me immediately taken ashore for fear I would fall over the side.

It was a stormy night, and the ship was heaving up and down and threatening to break free of its moorings before they could load all the cargo, so while it was embarrassing to be called a landlubber, my sudden vertigo didn't arouse suspicion.

I was at my lodgings preparing a trip to Dordogne with the American Ex Pat, Lady Eve Monckton Hoffe, who was always available for a weekend nibble, when news reached me that the Lellia had gone down in a squall off the coast of Liverpool, causing the loss of forty-seven of my shipmates.

Had I been aboard that doomed vessel and been unable to reach the safety of a lifeboat, I would have been forced to transform into a Winged One, the very act instantaneously outing me and forcing me to leave Liverpool immediately and not return to England for who knows how long, or risk capture and certain death.

But Nick doesn't suffer from vertigo or exhibit any of my other debilitating symptoms. Nor, why should he, for apparently, Nick doesn't need precious ichor.

Is my boy trying to kill me—is that what's going down?

This dreadful suspicion fires up my synapses like crazy, spraying electrical impulses of mistrust all over my centuries-old cerebral cortex, making me doubt my own mortality.

Oh, yes, can we not be a doubting Thomas? Do we not suffer the same pangs of paranoia?

Why does he injure me so, I wonder? It's not my doing; I was in the wrong foxhole at the wrong time.

I've for eternity played by the rules of the Code. I've continually lived The Vampire Life with impunity, rigor, and gusto without patting myself on the back too much. I've never shirked my responsibilities as written in the Code.

I have always seized the opportunity to better myself (put a little dinero in my pocket), and I have never sullied the myth of the Vampire by going on the dole.

You can look it up in the Big Book Of Feasting, but more times than not, I flew miles out of my way so I would keep the time-honored rule of never supping at another vampire's table.

I have in no way, no how, done a walkabout for a century or two, as rumored others of my clan, succumbing to the promises of turning their life around by Tony Roberts or another smooth-talking, self-help guru.

And another thing, Ladies and Gentlemen of the jury, I don't believe I should be treated in this unjust manner by anyone, let alone someone with the emotional intelligence of a one-month-old. Sorry, Nick, I call 'em as I see 'em.

And, don't give me that old shibboleth—what is, is.

I'll fuckin' tell you what is, is!

I've given food, shelter, and emotional intelligence to this Nick fella, and hundreds like him, since I've become what I am—that's what is, is—mister!

If I sound like Rodney Dangerfield, he must know what it's like to be a member of my tribe, which is suddenly forsaken and turned out from within; when Rodney complains, he gets no respect.

THIRTY

A SINGULAR SENSATION (PART 1)

Recording #5/mp (English, no translation needed)

Madame Lumière: How are you today, Nick?

Nick: Fine, perfect, ready for your voodoo, Madame L.

Madame Lumière: Now you're starting to talk like my ex-husband.

Nick: He didn't get what you're doing here?

Madame Lumière: No, he didn't. That's why he's my ex.

(They laugh)

Madame Lumière: Anything on your mind before we start?

Nick: I need to go higher, to the Moons Of Jupiter, perhaps?

Madame Lumière: Go higher than the Moons of Jupiter? What do you mean, Nick?

Nick: I have no idea. It just came into my head.

Madame Lumière: What do you know of astrology, Nick?

Nick: Me? Not much. I know there are twelve signs in the Zodiac, but I'd be hard-pressed to name them in the correct order. I'm not even sure of my sign. Wait; let me look at my driver's license. (Laughs) How stupid. I have no idea when I, I mean Bernard, was actually born.

Madame Lumière: Look any way. Perhaps Bernard kept the actual day and month but changed the year.

Nick: Okay, it reads September 9/30/82.

Madame Lumière: That makes you...

Nick: Forty.

Madame Lumière: Forty.

Nick: I don't feel forty.

Madame Lumière: You don't look it, either.

Nick: Thirty-five.

Madame Lumière: At the most.

(They laugh)

Madame Lumière: September 30th. That indicates that you're a Libra.

Nick: If Bernard's not lying.

Madame Lumière: Would you like me to ask him?

Nick: Sure, why not?

Madame Lumière: (As if memorized) Libra, September 23 - October 22, is an air sign represented by the scales and the only inanimate object of the Zodiac, an association that reflects Libra's fixation on balance and harmony. Libra is obsessed with symmetry and strives to create equilibrium in all areas of life.

Nick: (Laughing) Well, obviously, that's not me, is it, Madame L?

Madame Lumière: Why do you say that, Nick? In what way are you not well-balanced?

Nick: In every which way and back up to those Moons of Jupiter, Madame L. In case you haven't noticed, I'm drowning. I'm not sleeping, and my appetite—let's just say I'm not ordering steak and potatoes with a large slice of apple pie a la mode with dinner every night.

Madame Lumière: Anything else?

Nick: Isn't that enough, Madame L?

Madame Lumière: How about your drinking?

Nick: Oh, he's told you about that, has he?

Madame Lumière: He's worried about you, Nick.

Nick: If he were so worried about me, he'd get out of my head and leave me be.

Madame Lumière: Weren't you going to try to meditate?

Nick: Surround myself with the yellow light and eliminate the white noise, huh? Very colorful, Madame L.

Madame Lumière: Did you try the Candle Meditation?

Nick: Haven't you seen the films? Don't you know that vampires are a bit shy around a flame? That's why you never see us toasting marshmallows or sitting around a campfire telling scary stories about vampires. Now, that's funny, don't you think? (He laughs)

Madame Lumière: What about chanting? Did you try that, Nick?

Nick: Chanting Om sounds like I'm calling for Uma Thurman, and that only makes me...

Madame Lumière: I get it, Nick—I get it.

Nick: I'm trying to press on, Madame L. I really am trying, but you've got to help me out. That's why I'm here. You put me under, and I find out what's what.

Madame Lumière: And the tape I gave you of ocean sounds?

Nick: Boring, dull, and more boring.

Madame Lumière: Nick, will you hold on a second? I want to look something up.

As Nick nods off, I watch Madame Lumière walk across the room to the floor-to-ceiling mahogany bookshelves that line the far wall. For the first time, I examine the room and, without even thinking, I can identify every decorative element reminiscent of the furnishing at the Château de Chantilly, a remembrance of a weekend in the distant past that suddenly washes across his memory banks, sending hot flashes of hot, hot assignations down to his phallus.

The floor is covered with an antique rug, Aubusson, with its intricate details and floral and architectural-inspired designs. The desk, chairs, tables, and chest are 19th-century French mahogany and rosewood with clean lines, classical motifs, and a sense of symmetry.

Sevres Louis XV Style Bronze Mounted Porcelain Table Lamps and a couple of marble statues of Roman gods and goddesses, probably stolen from Nero's home on the Palatine; how he can suddenly visualize that visit is unexplainable and disturbing, for such a visit would have had to have taken place centuries before Bernard was born.

Madame Lumière returns and sits: (Reading) Jupiter is a functional malefic, being Libra as the ascendant sign. But Jupiter in its own house of the third sign from Libra will give good longevity, and you...

Nick: Longevity!

Madame Lumière: (Reading) Jupiter in Libra's 12th and 9th house and located in the 7th house of the Kalpurush, an individual may be drawn towards foreign countries. There is the possibility of his going abroad or his tendency to go overseas. He could be making money from foreign places. (Stops reading) Of course, we can only know for sure once we know the exact time and place of your birth, Nick.

Nick: *Do* you think you should call me Bernard?

Madame Lumière: If you think that will help, Bernard.

Nick: (Laughing) Don't be absurd! I'm only joking! I'm Nick. Calling me Bernard will make me more confused than I am.

Madame Lumière: I shouldn't be surprised that you like to make a joke. Humor is another characteristic of Libras.

Nick: I'm a regular Billy Crystal, right?

Madame Lumière: More to the point, Nick, the additional problem facing us is that, besides knowing the year, I will need the exact time and place of your birth so I can accurately prepare your chart.

Nick: You'll have to put me under for that and ask Bernard. I can't tell you what I don't know, can I?

Madame Lumière: Is there anything else you want to ask Bernard today?

Nick: Besides his stories, can I write this book and become famous? Oh, you're talking about my drinking, aren't you?

Madame Lumière: Libras are usually well-balanced. Overindulgence in any aspect of their lives is typically not an issue.

Nick chuckles.

Madame Lumière: Did I say something funny, Nick? Let me in on it.

Nick: You don't often hear well-balanced and vampire in the same sentence. Ghoulish motherfucker, blood-sucking fiend, get away from my neck, maybe, but not a vampire just sucked my blood, and he was so well-balanced, so, so emotionally stable.

Madame Lumière: You don't believe you must be emotionally stable to live forever, Nick?

(Nick thinks about that for a moment)

Madame Lumière: I've done numerous astrological charts and studied and seen hundreds of relationships, and I have discovered that two people might experience striking disagreement, discord, disenchantment, tyranny, mistrust, or manipulation...

Nick: Whoa there, Madame L. I might have trouble calling Bernard well-balanced but striking disagreement, discord, and...

Madame Lumière: Disenchantment, tyranny, mistrust, or manipulation.

Nick: No way, no how, Madame L. Okay, I've temporarily misplaced my memory. (Starts singing) 'But I'm working my way back to you. Girl'.

Madame Lumière: Nick!

Nick: (Singing) 'Give me a little bit more time, and our love will surely grow.'

Madame Lumière: Nick!

Nick: (Singing) 'Love will bring us together.'

Madame Lumière: Nick, Nick!

Nick: (Stops singing) Yes, Madame L?

Madame Lumière: That's quite an enlightened analysis of your relationship with Bernard.

Nick: I've been listening to the 70s on 7 on Sirius XM.

THIRTY-ONE

A SINGULAR SENSATION (PART 2)

Recording #6/mp (English, no translation needed)

Madame Lumière: How are you feeling this morning, Bernard?

The Vampire: Madame L, now, is it?

Madame Lumière: (Laughing) I thought Nick was rather charming.

The Vampire: You liked it, did you, Madame Lumière?

Madame Lumière: I did, actually.

The Vampire: I thought you didn't cozy up to your clients? Doesn't that type of intimacy ruin your objectivity?

Madame Lumière: I'm for anything that makes my clients comfortable.

The Vampire: He didn't admit that he had a drinking problem, did he? No. He blamed me for it, didn't he? He wants me to get out of his head, isn't that what he said? Now, that's really funny, don't you think? *Trop amusant, trop drôle.*

Madame Lumière: Funny, how so, Bernard?

The Vampire: He just doesn't get it.

Madame Lumière: What doesn't he get, Bernard?

The Vampire: (Laughing) I'm not in his head. He's in mine.

Madame Lumière: Ah, I see.

The Vampire: Do you?

(Madame Lumière remains silent)

The Vampire:' Oho! said the pot to the kettle. You are dirty and ugly and black! Sure no one would think you were metal. Except when you're given a crack. Not so! not so! kettle said to the pot; Tis your own dirty image you see; For I am so clean – without blemish or blot – That your blackness is mirrored in me'.

Madame Lumière: I had not heard that, Bernard. It's very good. Is it yours?

The Vampire: It was published in 1876 in the St. Nicholas Magazine, anonymously, of course. I wrote it in response to a Catholic scholar friend who had referred to Mathew 7:3-5. 'Why do you look at the speck of sawdust in your brother's eye and pay no attention to the plank in your own eye?' I just wanted to make the same point, but poetically.

Madame Lumière: Very impressive. You certainly are a man of many talents, Bernard.

The Vampire: Nick doesn't see it that way, does he, Madame Lumière?

Madame Lumière: Why do you think Nick feels this way, Bernard?

The Vampire: You're the professional, Madame Lumière. You tell me?

Madame Lumière: Perhaps it's because Nick doesn't feel a true and meaningful connection to you, Bernard.

The Vampire: We share the same body, the same cells.

Madame Lumière: I don't mean a physical connection, Bernard.

The Vampire: Oh, you're not going to go spiritual on me, are you, Madame L. (He laughs)

Madame Lumière: (Laughing) Not quite. I'm speaking more of a mental connection. Some constant, conscious memory, event, person, place, or thing that both of you share to the point that you, Nick, come to believe he is one with you, Bernard?

The Vampire: You've listened to the recordings and interviewed us, and nothing like that comes to mind?

Madame Lumière: He remembered living in England brought on by viewing the Sherlock Holmes movie, but you never mention that particular incident.

The Vampire: Did he mention that he's being followed?

Madame Lumière: What? Who, when, and where?

The Vampire: Someone was waiting for him that first day he got out of the hospital. Then, every day since, they have been waiting outside and ready to follow his every move discreetly, of course.

Madame Lumière: Nick never mentioned it.

The Vampire: He's very good, but I spotted him immediately. But of course, he knew I would. Recently, there has been another set of watchers. Police, I believe. They haven't been as careful. I spot them in the morning, waiting in a car, a black Dodge with several conspicuous antennas, and other times, watching the house at night from the northwest corner of Madison and Thirty-Fifth, again in the ubiquitous Dodge. I'm guessing Nick is one of many suspects they're watching.

Madame Lumière: If the second group is the police, who is the first?

The Vampire: Who do you think, Madame L?

Madame Lumière: I can't imagine. I've never heard you speak of enemies to Dr. Mickeltee or me while under hypnosis. Nick certainly hasn't. Do they mean you harm? Should I warn Nick?

(Silence)

Madame Lumière : Bernard!

(Silence)

Madame Lumière: Can you hear me? Should I warn Nick? Bernard?

The Vampire: You're shouting; of course, I can hear you.

Madame Lumière: I don't understand you, Bernard? You tell me you're being followed, but you appear calm and unconcerned. Don't you think this is serious, Bernard?

The Vampire: Through the years, I learned to play the piano quite well, if I say so myself. The *Bach Partitas*, of course, but there is something else, *Liszt's Piano Transcriptions of Famous Operas*: *Lucia Di Lammermoor, Il Travatore, Norma, and Oberon*. If you had a piano, I could play it for you. Perhaps that could be our connection?

THIRTY-TWO

AMANDA WOODS
(PART 1)

Recording #7/mp (English, no translation needed)

Nick: Very lovely. Is this what you want me to listen to? I'll try if it puts me in the right mood to meditate, Madame L.

Madame Lumière: No, I wanted you to listen to it to see if it brought back any memories.

Nick: Memories of what, hearing it being played?

Madame Lumière: Do you play the piano, Nick?

Nick. I think I've always wanted to play the piano.

Madame Lumière: You have?

Nick: I just said, so I guess I have. Do you have a piano?

Madame Lumière: No.

Nick: Not even in the shop?

Madame Lumière: No, no antique pianos.

Nick: I could ask one of my neighbors. Better, I will ask one of the doormen. I need to talk to Angel, anyway. I hear the police have located Jane Meadows. She's been living in Park City, Utah, and she's being extradited back to New York and charged with the murder of Margaret Havilland.

Madame Lumière: That must be a relief.

Nick: I knew I didn't have anything to do with it.

Madame Lumière: And, Bernard?

Nick: What do you mean, and Bernard? Are you saying he does things—makes me do things I'm unaware of? No-no-no—absolutely no! I'm not attacking women and draining their bodies of blood until they're dead. How can you think that?

Madame Lumière: Nick—Nick, I didn't mean to upset you. Please, take a moment and take a breath.

Nick: What, you think I'm not in control of my actions? I somehow lost consciousness and murdered one of my neighbors. Is that what you're telling me, Madame Lumière?

Madame Lumière: Nick, Nick, sit down.

Nick: You know what, I think this whole thing is bullshit.

Madame Lumière: Thanks better. Now, take a moment.

Nick: Sure, I fell in the street and knocked myself out. Okay, I've lost my memory, but I'm no fuckin' killer. I'm just an ordinary Joe whose brain is a bit scrambled-up, and when he's hypnotized, he speaks a whole bunch of foreign languages and tells stories of being a freakin' vampire. How do you know it's not all made up? That it comes from dreams.

Madame Lumière: What do you mean, it comes from dreams, Nick?

Nick: Look, we all know dreams have no place in reality. I had a dream just last night where I was in command of a group of soldiers, but I suddenly lost track of them just when a group of angry townspeople attacked an encampment of homeless people. I couldn't help the encampment until, fortunately, my soldiers came back on the scene, and together, we overpowered the townies and saved the encampment.

Madame Lumière: That sounds like quite an exciting dream.

Nick: That's not all. Right after that dream, a voice introduced me to Amanda Woods.

Madame Lumière: Amanda Woods?

Nick: I'm hearing it now, actually.

Madame Lumière: What is this voice saying, Nick?

Nick: Nick is having a meltdown, refusing to believe he's a blood-sucking vampire killer monster like Bernard.

Madame Lumière: Bernard has never admitted he's ever killed anyone, Nick.

Nick: He wouldn't, would he?

Madame Lumière: This is a grave accusation, Nick. Do you have any proof? Just because you're hearing this voice...

Nick: He's stopped talking to me.

Madame Lumière: Could this person be...

Nick: The murder in the building isn't proof enough, Madame L?

Madame Lumière: I thought the police determined it was the cousin.

(Silence)

Madame Lumière: Nick, has this voice-over person returned?

(Silence)

Madame Lumière: With your permission, I want to talk to Bernard now. Is that all right with you, Nick?

Nick: Ask him about Amanda Woods.

Madame Lumière: Nick, what are you doing? Where are you going?

(Nick stands, sings "One" from *A Chorus Line* ,but changes the lines to describe Bernard.)

"One singular sensation, every little step he takes
One thrilling combination, every move that he makes
One smile and suddenly, nobody else will do
You know you'll never be lonely with you-know-who
One moment in his presence and you can forget the rest
For the guy is second best to none, son

Ooh! Sigh! Give him your attention
Do I really have to mention that he is the one
He walks into a room, and you know he's
uncommonly rare, very unique
peripatetic, poetic, and chic
He walks into a room, and you know from him
maddening poise, effortless whirl
One thrilling combination, every move that he makes
He's a special guy strolling
Can't help all of his qualities extolling
Loaded with charisma is he
jauntily, sauntering, ambling, shambler
One, and you know you must
Shuffle along, join the parade
He's the quintessence of making the grade
This is whatcha call trav'ling!
Oh, strut your stuff!
Can't get enough!
Ooh! Sigh! Give him your attention
Do I really have to mention
He's the one!"

Nick: (Taking a bow) I thank you, my father thanks you, and my entire family thanks you! Now go on, wave your magic wand, Madame Lumière!

THIRTY-THREE

AMANDA WOODS
(PART 2)

Recording #7/mp (Continued. English, no translation needed)

The Vampire: Bet you didn't know I could kick up my feet like that, did you, Madame L?

Madame Lumière: Nothing you do surprises me, Bernard. I suppose you had a part in Chorus Line?

The Vampire: (Laughing) Nope. However, back in 1931, I did audition for *Away We Go*, but at the last minute, I came to my senses and realized I would be violating the Code by setting foot on a Broadway stage.

Madame Lumière: *Away We Go*—I don't think I know that one, Bernard.

The Vampire: I never cared for the title, and I was happy that the producer changed it to *Oklahoma* for the 1943 revival.

Madame Lumière: *Oklahoma*, what a wonderful play! Oh, and I enjoyed the movie, as well.

The Vampire: It was November of 1931, and I just concluded a very successful gold mining adventure in South Dakota's Black Hills when I decided to find a place to live in New York City. I had been back and forth to the city many times but had yet to live in Greenwich Village, so I said, Let's try it. I found a delightful second-floor, two-bedroom apartment in a charming brownstone on Perry Street and West Fourth. My apartment faced the street, and across the way was a church. One day, I noticed on the church announcement board a call to join an amateur theater group looking for members. I always had a nice singing voice, and for a lark, I would give it a go. I never imagined that a theater producer would see my group audition and immediately ask me to try out for a Broadway play he was producing. I must admit, the smell of grease paint and the allure of the Great White Way almost threw me off my game and put me in jeopardy with the Ancients, but thank god, I came to my senses before the show opened. Otherwise, I would have risked certain exposure as I had been cast in the part of Curly.

Madame Lumière: You speak of exposure, but you're writing a book about your adventures? I've always thought that odd and something you would avoid.

The Vampire: You're right, Madame L. I cannot explain this self-destructive behavior. It was a foolish mistake, an act of hubris that was never to go further than an outline, but that would be a lie. Truthfully, had I not injured myself, I'm not sure how far I would have gone with the project.

Madame Lumière: Wouldn't you be breaking one of the rules of the Code?

The Vampire: Ah, the Code. You're certainly right about that, but there are ways around it. I would use a pseudonym or a pen name. V—for instance. (He laughs). I can see that might be inviting trouble. K, C—or perhaps Robert L Stevenson are some other choices.

Madame Lumière: Nick mentioned Robert Louis Stevenson and a woman named Amanda Woods? He was hearing voices. What do you know about that, Bernard?

The Vampire: (He laughs) I knew him, of course.

Madame Lumière: Whom did you know, Bernard?

The Vampire: Robert Lewis Stevenson.

Madame Lumière: The famous author who wrote...

The Vampire: *Treasure Island, The Strange Case of Dr. Jekyll and Mr. Hyde.*

Madame Lumière: It's been a long time since I read them.

The Vampire: The movie version starring Spenser Tracy scared the bejesus out of me. You can imagine, though, that I loved it!

Madame Lumière: I don't go to scary movies, Bernard.

The Vampire: A shame. They're chock-full of imaginary adventures, hair-raising twists and turns, and deeply fascinating characters that keep you on the edge of your seat. Of course, the Jekyll and Hyde characters are based on my double life.

Madame Lumière: It's a book about vampires?

The Vampire: Oh, no. That I would never allow.

Madame Lumière: Was Mr. Stevenson one of your...

The Vampire: (Laughing, then in a deep, announcer voice-over) Amanda Woods! It's an important time in Amanda's life when she meets Robert Louis Stevenson, and they both smoke hashish and visit the same brothels while exploring the dark side of Edinburgh's nightlife.

Madame Lumière: Very good Bernard. You do an excellent imitation, or have you heard the same voice?

The Vampire laughs.

Madame Lumière: Did this Amanda Woods... she wasn't a vampire, was she, Bernard?

The Vampire: (Laughing) No. She's a movie star.

Madame Lumière: A movie star?

The Vampire: Actually, a character in the film *The Holiday*. The woman who plays her part, Cameron Diaz, is the movie star. It's on Prime if you want to watch it.

Madame Lumière: I just have HBO.

The Vampire: Throughout the film, there is an announcer voice-over describing Amanda's predicament, but this second Voice is using that same technique to frighten me—tell me Nick's having a meltdown because he's finally refusing to believe he's a blood-sucking vampire killer monster like me.

Madame Lumière: What do you mean, this second Voice?

(Silence)

Madame Lumière: Of course, now I remember! On the tape with Dr. Mickeltee, you mention hearing a voice giving you directions upon leaving the trench. A bell, not a chime, always accompanied it.

The Vampire: At first, it was bizarre and very frightening to hear a strange voice give you directions in your head and never know when it would come or what it would say. And I hated those chimes; because of them, the sound of church bells drives me up a wall. Over the centuries, I got used to the Voice and depended on its guidance. During that time, the Voice has changed languages to speak to me in my current language. In the 1920s, I realized that the Voice mimicked famous announcers. First, it was the BBC's Leslie Mitchell, then in the 30s, the *Movietone* voice of Terence Gallacher. In the 40s, the Voice sounded like Lowell Thomas, who had done all the war newsreels. Since then, most voice-over guys have been doing car commercials like Alan Blevis for Mitsubishi.

Madame Lumière: What do Amanda Woods and Robert Louis Stevenson have to do with you?

The Vampire: Just switch out 'Amanda Woods' for Bernard Bertrand, and that's what I heard the second Voice say.

Madame Lumière: What?

The Vampire: It's an important time in Bernard's life when he meets Robert Louis Stevenson. They both smoke hashish and visit the same brothels while exploring the dark side of Edinburgh's nightlife. And the Voice it was Robert's voice, the one he used when he read *The Strange Case of Dr. Jekyll and Mr. Hyde* at its first public reading. Can you see now, this second Voice is mocking me!

Madame Lumière: Where is it coming from, Bernard? Can you guess?

The Vampire: My guess—it's leaking out from the conscience of the young Bernard Bertrand before he became a vampire and into Nick's head.

(Silence)

The Vampire: Is there anything we can do to hurry the process along, Madame L?

Madame Lumière: The Process?

The Vampire: Returning Nick's memory, full stop, and end this leakage.

Madame Lumière: I'm not a doctor, Bernard. I'm certainly not the person to ask.

The Vampire: It's almost a month since the accident.

Madame Lumière: I'd like to do your astrological chart, Bernard. Perhaps that would provide me with some answers.

(Silence)

Madame Lumière: Has anyone ever done your chart, Bernard?

The Vampire: You're not the first astrologer I've gone to, Madame L. Have you ever heard of Robert Cross Smith, who wrote under the pseudonym of 'Raphael'?

Madame Lumière: No, I never have. Does he live here in New York? I don't recognize his name.

The Vampire: (Laughing) I met him along with G.W. Graham in London in January 1822 and helped them put together one of the first and most important books on geomancy. But I really did him a greater service by supplying him with material for an essay on Merlin the Magician. In turn, he did my chart.

Madame Lumière: So, you must have given him the exact time and place of your birth.

(Silence)

Madame Lumière: You wouldn't have the chart lying around, would you?

The Vampire: You mean, have I stashed papers, diaries, anything of importance, say, in a vault, starting back, say, in the 16th century?

Madame Lumière: I'd settle for the 18th century.

The Vampire: (Laughing) I bet you would. And so would Nick. That would save him and you from asking me a lot of questions. Of course, you'd have to get it translated.

Madame Lumière: Naturally.

The Vampire: There were times I wrote articles and, of course, poetry, but I never kept any for any length of time. Moving around as much as I did made that impossible. Most importantly, putting anything down on paper is against the Code.

Madame Lumière: You can see how it could help.

The Vampire: Helena Blavatsky. She wrote books and quoted me. They're still in print. And her live-in, what the heck was his name? She called him the Astral Tramp. (Silence) This is driving me crazy. Before the accident, not the slightest event over the last five hundred years escaped me.

Madame Lumière: It could be stress. The reason you haven't...

The Vampire: I'll tell you what it is—it's Nick's problem.

Madame Lumière: Nick's problem?

The Vampire: Oh, sure, once or twice, he's given a second look at a neck, but has he ever gotten on his wings and taken off for even a nosh? No—no, and no! Has he even looked at a map to locate an area accessible for hunting should the time present itself? And—and, Madame L, it's easier now than ever with our app and Google Maps.

Madame Lumière: You have an app—a Vampire App?

The Vampire: Being an Immortal doesn't make you a Luditte, Madame L. Do you think vampires could survive all these centuries if we didn't change with the times, ride the wave, and keep up with the Kardashians?

Madame Lumière: You told me you become physically ill when you don't...

The Vampire: Drink the blood of an innocent, unsuspecting Recipient and possibly turn them into a vampire?

Madame Lumière: Feast—I was going to say feast.

The Vampire: As, yes, let's continue to use euphemisms and stay away from the vulgarities of the curdling cruelties of blood-sucking vampirism.

Madame Lumière: Are you deliberately avoiding my question regarding your health, Bernard?

The Vampire: All right—all right, Madame L. If you want to know the truth, I haven't felt myself these last few days. I'm feeling fatigued and run down, and just yesterday, I didn't want to get out of bed.

Madame Lumière: What about vertigo and some other symptoms you mentioned you've had over the centuries when you've missed...

The Vampire: Yes, Madame L?

Madame Lumière: Draining the blood out of an innocent victim.

The Vampire: Excellent, Madame L, and very decent of you.

Madame Lumière: A vampire's got to do what a vampire got to do.

The Vampire: Survival of the Fittest.

Madame Lumière: I suppose you knew Darwin, too, Bernard?

The Vampire: Almost. I missed him by a few days in July of 1881 when he was surveying Tierra del Fuego and the approaches to the harbors on the Falkland Islands, where I had just spent a week as part of a delegation deciding on the Island's request for sovereignty, ultimately denied. Sir Woodbine Parish brought me over from London after meeting me at the Royal Society and discovering our mutual admiration for the king of Naples, whom he met when he was King Edward VII's minister, whom I grew to know when Napoleon asked me to help spirit his brother out of Corsica and get him to Naples so Joseph could assume the throne.

Madame Lumière: Is there anyone of historical relevance you haven't met, Bernard?

The Vampire: I think it's time you looked into your crystal ball, Madame L.

Madame Lumière: I don't understand.

The Vampire: Look.

(Silence)

The Vampire: Don't be afraid. Look.

(Silence)

Madame Lumière: All right, I'll look.

(Silence)

The Vampire: Do you see? Do you see?

THIRTY-FOUR

TO BE OR NOT TO BE

Madame Lumière stares harder into the glowing orb. Minutes pass as she appears to be drawn into the ball. Finally, she pulls away as if she has broken a mesmerizing spell. Madame Lumière locks eyes with Bernard. Her healthy complexion is now ghostly white, as if the experience of entering the globe drained her of all her blood.

THIRTY-FIVE

PORTION CONTROL

Recording #8/mp (Continued. English, no translation needed

Madame Lumière: I'm glad you could come this evening, Nick. How are you feeling?

Nick: I listened to yesterday's recording when I got home and again this morning. How do you think I'm feeling?

Madame Lumière: Do you want to tell me, Nick?

Nick: He thinks I want to kill him. I'm no murderer, Madame L.

Madame Lumière: You can understand where he's coming from, can't you, Nick?

Nick: What about where I'm coming from, huh, Madame L? You believe I'm someone who wants to hunt down women, drain them of their blood, maybe even kill them, or turn them into vampires so that I can go on living forever? That's crazy insane! This whole thing is insane!

Madame Lumière: Nick, Nick, sit down, please.

Nick: I came to you to learn about who I am after that crazy bitch doctor; Mickeltee hypnotized me and diagnosed me as delusional because I think I'm a five-hundred-year-old vampire. And what, you're no help. You're telling me the same insane story?

Madame Lumière: Nick, where are you going?

Nick: I'm leaving. I've had enough of this bullshit. And let me tell you another thing, Madame L, I'll never let anyone hypnotize me again. And, I'm going to destroy those goddamn tapes, and then, I'm going to take a nice long vacation, to the Italian Coast maybe, and put this nightmare all behind me.

Madame Lumière: Don't you want me to tell you what I saw when I looked into my crystal ball, Nick?

Nick: Oh, nice try, Madame L or whatever your real name is?

Madame Lumière: Ann Asbill. My real name is Ann Asbill. Now, will you please sit, Nick?

Nick: Ann Asbill, huh?

Madame Lumière: That's correct. Now, please, sit down for a moment, take a breath, and hear me out.

Nick: Okay, okay, Ann.

Madame Lumière: I asked you how you felt this morning.

Nick: Yeah?

Madame Lumière: You never answered me, Nick.

Nick: For your information, I couldn't sleep until I took something; then I got maybe an hour or two. I wonder why?

Madame Lumière: Have you eaten at all?

Nick: Are you trying to be funny, Ann?

Madame Lumière: Nick.

Madame Lumière: Tell me what you have been eating.

Nick: Just some Saltine crackers and coffee, plenty of coffee.

Madame Lumière: Have you weighed yourself recently?

Nick: I don't have a scale.

Madame Lumière: You've lost weight, haven't you?

Nick: I see where this is going, Madame L.

Madame Lumière: What about fatigue, feelings of anxiety, and depression?

(Silence)

Madame Lumière: Vertigo? No dizziness when you get up in the morning?

Nick: Maybe, occasionally.

Madame Lumière: And you spoke of nightmares, didn't you, Nick?

Nick: I never said I had nightmares. Dreams, I told you I had some weird dreams.

Madame Lumière: Yes, you were a soldier in one of them. And then, there was a voice-over you heard calling your name. The Voice that Bernard said was mocking him.

Nick: Hold it! Where are you going with this?

Madame Lumière: What do you mean?

Nick: It's fucking bizarre, impossible to wrap my head around the fact that you're providing emotional support to a mythological monster. That—get this for weirdness—you're actually having conversations with a vampire, talking to him as if he's a regular Joe about why he doesn't feel like eating his veggies. So, who is crazier, you or me? Tell me that, Madame L, aka Ann Asbill?

Madame Lumière: I believe there's another way to look at it.

Nick: Don't be shy, do tell.

Madame Lumière: Let's, for a moment, suppose that you and Bernard are two different people inside of a third person's body. And let's call this third person John.

Nick: Why the hell would we do that, Madame L? And, why, John?

Madame Lumière: You don't like the name, John?

Nick: It's so common. How about Cameron or Drew? I like Drew, don't you, Madame L?

Madame Lumière: Drew it is

Nick: Nah! When I think Drew, you're probably thinking about Nancy Drew. I'm no Girly Boy—forget, Drew.

Madame Lumière: Cameron, then.

Nick: What am I thinking? Too close to Cameron Diaz.

Madame Lumière: Cameron Diaz?

Nick: You know, the movie star playing the role of Amanda Woods!

Madame Lumière: Then John...

Nick: Frederick! As in Frederick the Great, I bet Bernard knew him. Frederick! I like the sound of that, don't you, Madame L?

Madame Lumière: Frederick it is. The third time is a charm.

Nick: I suppose you want to play zither music, too?

Madame Lumière: Zither music? I don't understand?

Nick: Frederick—our 'Third Man'—zither music—the movie—*The Third Man*? Oh, forget it.

Madame Lumière: Where are you going?

Nick: (standing) I don't look like I've lost weight, do I, Madame Lumière? See, no belly and no big tush! I've been weighing myself every morning and am a constant 160. I looked it up on the Internet, and it's a perfect weight for my height, 5'11. And my appetite's been good; don't deprive myself. I'm a fool for Dim Sum and tacos, fish sticks, chicken fingers, and pizza.

Madame Lumière: You just told me you didn't have a scale and that you just eat saltines?

Nick: I didn't want you to think I was so vain, Madame L.

Madame Lumière: It's Bernard I'm worrying about.

Nick: The secret's portion control.

Madame Lumière: Portion control?

Nick. Madame L, have you ever looked at how much food they give you in a restaurant, or a frozen food package for one serving? You have to leave half of it on your plate if you want to keep the weight off. That's what I mean by portion control. Of course, there are certain foods that all I have to do is look at, and I gain weight—bread, for instance, rye, pumpernickel, and whole wheat, are killer dillers. And red meat—won't touch it.

Madame Lumière: Red meat?

Nick: But that's a different kettle of fish, so to speak. (He laughs) Don't get me wrong, Madame L, I miss my Big Mac with cheese, and if restaurants didn't charge an arm and a leg for a steak, I'd be champing at the bit for a rib eye, you know what I mean, Madame?

Madame Lumière: So, why do you avoid red meat, Nick?

Nick: My present condition?

Madame Lumière: Ahh, you mean you're worried about Bernard?

Nick: Suppose it comes out rare when I say well-done? The meat could be pink, but what if it's—god-forbid—bloody? (Low voice) If it's bloody, I'm shit out of luck—like blood turns my stomach, and I become physically ill. What do you say to that, Madame L?

Madame Lumière: Nick—calm down and relax.

Nick: Are you joking? Don't you see what I'm doing, Madame L? I'm slowly starving, my vampire.

Madame Lumière: Take a breath and breathe, Nick, breathe. Let's talk about the 'Third Man'.

Nick: I'm committing suicide, Madame L, f-ing hari-kari, but without the knife. (He laughs) And, fork—get it, without the knife and fork?

THIRTY-SIX

YOU LOOK GOOD FOR YOUR AGE

Recording #9/mp (English, no translation needed)

The Vampire: You asked me to give you an exact time and place of my birth, but when I go back over my life, I discover that's impossible. The best I can do is September 30, 1524, in the Saint-Marcel quarter of Paris. As for the time, early morning is also the best I can do. I remember *Mamon* talking about my birth as being extremely painful and long, and that she finally gave life to me sometime in the early morning, and how surprised she was that my older brothers never took nearly as long.

Madame Lumière: Well, that is a start and something I can work with.

The Vampire: Wait!

Madame Lumière: What's the matter, Bernard? I thought we agreed that doing your natal chart might help you discover your future. Perhaps try to understand why Nick, in his words, doesn't have a taste for blood and, therefore, thinks you think he's trying to kill you.

The Vampire: I didn't see that coming.

Madame Lumière: So, what's your problem?

The Vampire: I don't have a problem with you doing my chart, Madame L. As I told you, I've had many favorable interactions with astrologers.

Madame Lumière: Then what is it?

The Vampire: I've not been truthful about my actual age.

Madame Lumière: Bernard, I understand you can't tell me the exact time, but as I just said, I can work with that as long as I have the other required information. I'm sure astrologers you've seen in the past have said the same thing when they worked up your chart.

The Vampire: Nostradamus told me I was born in Egypt in the 14th century BC, around 1370.

Madame Lumière: The 14th century BC!

The Vampire: I look good for my age, don't you think?

Madame Lumière: You say it was Nostradamus—*the* Nostradamus—the infamous French fortune teller of the Renaissance?

The Vampire: *Seer*—not a fortune teller—he never likes to be called a fortune teller—but yes, the very same. (He laughs) I told you, I got around. Nostradamus wrote about doing my horoscope in *Les Prophéties* but referred to me as Monsieur V. The V was his amusing shout-out to me being a vampire, but of course, he shared that revelation with no one. He died days after, so he took that secret with him to the grave.

Madame Lumière: You were in *Les Prophéties!* I have copies in both French and English.

The Vampire. I know; I saw them on your shelf over there.

Madame Lumière: Every astrologer worth their crystal ball has read *Les Prophéties!*

The Vampire: And it was more than a paragraph.

Madame Lumière: He knew you were a vampire?

The Vampire: The moment he drew up my horoscope.

Madame Lumière: You didn't...

The Vampire: What? (He Laughs) Kill him? No, he died of heart failure in his sleep.

Madame Lumière: Incredible.

The Vampire: Consult your crystal ball if you don't believe me.

Madame Lumière: (Muttering) Nostradamus, the famous French fortune teller of the Renaissance...

The Vampire: French *seer*—French *seer*.

Madame Lumière: How did you meet him?

The Vampire: Katie introduced me.

Madame Lumière: Katie?

The Vampire: Catherine De Medici, the daughter of Lorenzo De' Medici, Duke of Urbino, who had to be the most handsome man in all of Italy, besides me, of course, and his wife, the lovely and gifted Madeleine De La Tour d'Auvergne, who had the most enchanting singing voice. By the way, I knew them long before Katie married King Henry II and became the Queen of France.

Madame Lumière. Of course you did. Is there anyone you didn't know? I know—I know, you got around.

(They both laugh)

Madame Lumière: It's remarkable that you actually had your horoscope done by one of the most respected astrologers of his day, in all of history.

The Vampire: I also know you are fond of his other major work, *Countdown to Apocalypse.*

Madame Lumière: Of course, it's on the shelf over there. You've been a busy boy, Bernard. Or, perhaps, should I call you by your Egyptian name—now, who could you be? Tutankhamun? You had to be one of the pharaohs, am I right?

The Vampire: I'm glad to see you're up on your who's who of 1370 BC.

Madame Lumière: So, let me get this straight in my mind. Are you telling me you may have been born in the 14th century BC and that you were once a famous what—Egyptian Pharaoh?

The Vampire: According to Michel, I was Akhenaten, who reigned from 1351–1334 BC. I was the tenth ruler of the Eighteenth

Dynasty, and to set the record straight, before my fifth year of reign, I was also known as Amenhotep IV. Pretty impressive, *n'est pas*?

Madame Lumière: Michel?

The Vampire: Nostradamus was born Michel de Nostredame, but it was Latinized to Nostradamus somewhere along the line.

Madame Lumière: Naturally, you're fluent in Latin.

The Vampire: *Sed utique.*

Madame Lumière: Were you always such a wisenheimer, Bernard? Don't answer that because I'm sure your response will be in Sanskrit or some other dead scroll language. You know, nobody likes a smart aleck, Bernard, even if he's a vampire from the 14 century BC.

The Vampire: Maybe that's why I don't have any friends—you think, Madame L?

Madame Lumière: I think it's the other thing.

The Vampire: The other thing?

Madame Lumière: Changing into a bat and taking off at the drop of...

The Vampire: Blood, Madame L?

Madame Lumière: I would say a hat, Bernard—a drop of a hat.

The Vampire: (Laughing) You kill me, Madame L., you kill me.

Madame Lumière: Then I'd be losing a paying customer, and I wouldn't like that. You are going to pay me, aren't you, Bernard?

The Vampire: Talk to Nick, he's write the checks, I just cash them.

THIRTY-SEVEN

VANITY, THY NAME IS VAMPIRE

Recording #9/mp continued (English, no translation needed)

Nick: So, you're telling me he wasn't angry with me?

Madame Lumière: You can play and hear the recording when you get home.

Nick: I don't understand why he doesn't want to wring my neck until I come to my senses and get on board his bloodmobile.

Madame Lumière: He doesn't.

Nick: And, you say he's not suffering from lack of blood?

Madame Lumière: How about you, Nick? No health issues you're not telling me about?

Nick: You mean, am I suddenly feeling my age? (Laughs)

Madame Lumière: That was quite a shock.

Nick: I was just getting used to being a two hundred and fifty-nine-year-old fuddy-duddy vampire, but fuck me, Madame L, you can't tack on another three thousand years and think I'm not going to feel a little fatigued.

Madame Lumière: That's what he believes.

Nick: And he's kept this fact from me all this time.

Madame Lumière: I'm just as surprised as you.

Nick: You'd think the extra two thousand seven hundred years would be something he's proud of? Goddamn, he was an Egyptian Pharaoh!

Madame Lumière: That's pretty amazing, isn't it, Nick?

Nick: And he kept it from me, damn his eyes.

Madame Lumière: Perhaps he believed it was too much to spring on you and...

Nick: Who else has he been in those extra two thousand, seven hundred years, Madame L? Who else did he meet? What other parts in history did he play?

Madame Lumière: It's your history, too. You do understand that, don't you, Nick?

Nick: I thought it was Fredrick's history?

Madame Lumière: Who?

Nick: (Laughing) The Third Man? Remember, you would spit us up into threes: me, Bernard, and this third person you wanted to call John, but I wanted to call Fredrick after Fredrick the Great.

Madame Lumière: I got the feeling you didn't like that idea, and you were mocking me, Nick.

Nick: Yeah, well, sorry for that. Look, you've got to put me under, again, right away, Madame L.

Madame Lumière: What do you want to know? Why did he lie to you about his age? I don't think that will serve any meaningful purpose,

Nick: I don't want to piss him off, Madame L. I want to know what being this Akhenaten fellow is like. Who else did he know? He must have met Cleopatra, Mark Anthony, and maybe even Julius Caesar. For chrissakes, f-ing Julius Caesar, Madame L!

Madame Lumière: That's quite a trio, isn't it, Nick?

Nick: Can you believe an Egyptian Pharaoh was a vampire?

Madame Lumière: Quite a revelation, isn't it? Nick?

Nick: Is that when it all started? Is that when somebody turned into a vampire? Maybe he was a normal Egyptian Pharaoh when someone in his court...

Madame Lumière: Or family...

Nick: Sure, it could have been anybody. Oh, man, that's something, isn't it, Madame L?

Madame Lumière: I'll ask him.

Nick: You think he's suddenly worried about his age?

Madame Lumière: What do you mean?

Nick: You said he looks good, right, Madame L?

Madame Lumière: He looks like you, Nick.

Nick: People in my building say I look like a young Robert Redford.

Madame Lumière: I know, you said.

Nick: In *The Way We Were.* I just played it the other day.

Madame Lumière: Can't tell you apart, for sure.

Nick: Maybe he sees wrinkles that we don't? That's nuts. Vampires don't age. I bet the boy looks as good now as he did three thousand years ago. Look, my face is as smooth as a baby's bum.

(Madame Lumière smiles)

Nick: And what was that crack about him not having friends?

Madame Lumière: He's got an acerbic wit, our vampire.

Nick: You called him a Wisenheimer.

(Madame Lumière laughs)

Madame Lumière: You're staring at me? Is something bothering you, Nick?

Nick: No—Nothing.

Madame Lumière: I know you now well enough to know that's not true, Nick.

Nick: I know we have already talked about this, but isn't it sad— all the famous people he's met—Beethoven, Nostradamus, Napoleon, not one has ever become a friend?

Madame Lumière: The price you pay for being a vampire.

Nick: That would make Bernard one lonely guy, don't you think, Madame L?

Madame Lumière: It would, wouldn't it.

Nick: You never told him what you saw in your crystal ball, did you?

Madame Lumière: No, I didn't.

Nick: What did you see? He's hiding something from us, isn't he?

Madame Lumière: At the very least, not being entirely open and honest.

Nick: You think he's made the entire thing up, don't you?

Madame Lumière: I'm not entirely certain.

Nick: So, what—he's trying to impress us with these stories?

Madame Lumière: That's a possibility.

Nick: Why would he do that?

Madame Lumière: It may be his personality.

Nick: His personality? Exactly, what does that mean, Madame L?

Madame Lumière: He may be prone to...

Nick: Delusions of grandeur?

Madame Lumière: Telling tall tales.

Nick: So, he's not a vampire?

Madame Lumière: We all have an image of ourselves we like to project to the outside world, and our vanity might cause us to embellish, even misrepresent events, so to speak.

Nick: We're all grown-ups here, Madame L. Let's call a spade a spade. Why don't we? You think he's been lying to us—plain and simple. He's never met any of those people because he isn't a three-thousand-year-old vampire?

Madame Lumière: Let's not be too quick to throw the baby out with the bathwater.

Nick: So, he's never met anyone famous? Sweet Jesus, Madame L, if that's true, the poor son of a bitch must be the most boring and provincial vainglorious three-thousand-year-old ever to walk the face of this earth.

Madame Lumière: *Vampire*, three-thousand-year-old *vampire* to ever walk the face of this earth, Nick.

Nick: Vampire—fuck, yeah. No wonder Bernard's making this shit up! He's embarrassed as all hell. Who wouldn't be in their afraid-to-fly-high-bat wings? When every other vampire worth his fangs is living the life of a monster without being a myth, our poor, pathetic Bernard shirks the role of a party animal. He is a stain on his fellow blood-sucking dandies, preferring instead to lurk in the shadows of history, preying on the *hoi polloi*, the great unwashed, the near-do-well, instead of tasting the breakfast of champions.

Madame Lumière: Nick, don't you think you're being too hard on Bernard? After all...

Nick: After all—what? Say it, Madame L! He's me-I 'm him 're one!

Madame Lumière: I was going to say—after three thousand years, we should cut him a break.

THIRTY-EIGHT

THE TRUTH, YOU CAN'T HANDLE THE TRUTH (PART 1)

Recording #10/mp (English, no translation needed)

The Vampire: What, you think Jack Nicholson was the first to say those words?

Madame Lumière: My apologies, Bernard.

The Vampire: Call me Mr. Amenhotep IV, Akhenaten, or if you prefer, the Greek Amenophis IV. I also answer to the Sun God, Your Kingship, Majesty, Divinity, and Ruler of all Egypt, Babylonia, Assyria, Mitanni, and the Hittites.

Madame Lumière: Enough, Bernard—I get it. You used to be somebody.

The Vampire: Not used to be, *I still am* somebody.

Madame Lumière: How many times must I apologize, Bernard? I mean, your majesty.

The Vampire: All right, you can continue to call me Bernard. Madame L.

Madame Lumière: You can understand our confusion, can't you, Bernard?

The Vampire: Our recovering amnesiac maybe, Nick, the poor sod, but not you, Madame L. I know, you know, what I know.

Madame Lumière: I don't know what you mean, Bernard.

The Vampire: Nonsense, Madame L. Stop pretending. I know what you saw in your crystal ball. I've told you I've met your kind before.

Madame Lumière: My kind, Bernard?

The Vampire: The High Priest of Ra, Cassandra, Boudicca, the Druid queen, and, of course, Nostradamus. Prophets, diviners, oracles, seers, Madame L, People of the Sight, as the Ancients call them. Go on, do it again, gaze into your crystal ball, and I will describe what you see for Nick when he plays the tape later. (Mimicking the voice-over announcer from *The Holiday*) Madame L is slowly placing her hands on the globe. Nothing, nothing—no, wait—her body is suddenly radiating a yellowish glow that jumps from her hand onto the globe. The sphere is turning bright orange, then bluish, and now crystal clear. I can see the image of two Egyptians dressed in ceremonial white robes filling the globe. That's me on the right, and the other is the High Priest of Ra. He's the one who turned me into a vampire. Madame L is now removing her hand from the globe. The two images fade, and the globe returns to its crystal-clear appearance. The glow radiating from Madame L is also disappearing.

Madame Lumière: Are you happy now, Bernard?

The Vampire: (Regular voice) You knew the truth, yet you allowed Nick to think me the most boring and provincial vainglorious three-thousand-year-old ever to walk the face of this earth.

Madame Lumière: *Vampire*, three-thousand-year-old *vampire* to ever walk the face of this earth, Bernard.

The Vampire: You had to remind him because he even had doubts in his mind that I'm really a vampire.

Madame Lumière: I wasn't going to let that happen, Bernard.

The Vampire: No.

Madame Lumière: The truth always comes to light, but it's how it's revealed that's important, don't you think, Bernard?

The Vampire: With kid gloves, huh? Is that how you see this playing out? After all, you can see the future.

Madame Lumière: Not consistently and not always clearly.

The Vampire: Which is it now?

Madame Lumière: Not so clearly.

The Vampire: But you know what's on his mind, don't you?

Madame Lumière: I have my suspicions.

The Vampire: I think it's best to get it all out in the open if we're to get Nick's memory back.

Madame Lumière: Nick. How should I handle it, Bernard?

The Vampire: With kid gloves. (He laughs)

THIRTY-NINE

THE TRUTH, YOU CAN'T HANDLE THE TRUTH (PART 2)

Recording #11/mp (English, no translation needed)

Nick: You made me look like a fool to him.

Madame Lumière: I'm sorry, Nick. That was not my intention.

Nick: Were you ever going to tell me?

Madame Lumière: I'm not sure. I was trying to make sense of it myself.

Nick: What—that Bernard is a three-thousand-year-old Pharaoh.

Madame Lumière: I was as surprised as you are, Nick.

Nick: So, he's really a vampire?

Madame Lumière: I don't know what he is, Nick.

Nick: What about Napoleon, Beethoven, everyone he says he knew, came in contact with?

Madame Lumière What about them?

Nick: Did he turn them into fiendish ghouls or leave them alone? That's hard to believe, knowing what we know about vampires.

Madame Lumière: He says he didn't.

Nick: I don't believe it. Somebody would have known and written about it if he had. All those biographies and movies made

about Napoleon and Beethoven! Gary Oldman playing Beethoven—
oh, God!

Madame Lumière: What, what is it, Nick?

Nick: Gary Oldman—he played Dracula! Coincidence, I think
not!

Madame Lumière: I told you...

Nick: You're not a fan of horror movies.

Madame Lumière: I much prefer Gilbert and Sullivan.

Nick: *The Mikado*, huh?

(Madame Lumière stands, begins to sing, expertly mimicking
one of the maidens from the *Mikado*.)

> "Three little maids from school, are we
> Pert, as a school-girl well can be
> Filled to the brim with girlish glee
> Three little maids from school!"

Nick: Impressive, Madame L, or shall I call you Yum-Yum?

Madame Lumière: (bows, sits) I dreamed of acting and singing
in musical comedies, but, alas...

Nick: The road not taken, heh, Madame L?

Madame Lumière: I was going to say, many a slip from the cup
to the lip.

Nick: You, Madame L? You who can divine the future, missing
your mark?

Madame Lumière: The Spirit in the Sky divides, Nick. He giveth
me the sight to see others, and He taketh away my ability to see my
image.

Nick: We're all taken to the wall, aren't we, Madame L?

Madame Lumière: Not at all, Nick. The true meaning of that
phrase is that He removes the stuff that we don't really need and
provides us with things we do require.

Nick: In what universe do I want to be a vampire, Madame L? Give me the pluses for me needing to suck the blood out of my fellow man. Not something a little boy dreams about doing instead of—I don't know—wanting to play centerfield for the Yankees? Or, how about being the next Mick Jagger or Eric Clapton?

Madame Lumière: I think you're being unfair to Bernard, Nick. After all, it wasn't his choice. No, it wasn't. And considering he has no choice, he's to be commended for how Bernard has come to terms with his fate, and, from what Bernard tells me, he has gone on to do many wonderful things.

Nick: You mean to turn Napoleon and Beethoven into vampires?

Madame Lumière: You don't know that. I don't know that, Nick.

Nick: Say he turned them all into vampires; they would be immortal, too. They'd be alive this very moment, walking around, maybe here in the city, just like Bernard?

Madame Lumière: Nick, how many times must I repeat myself? Bernard never said he attacked any of them, and you know by now, not every victim becomes a vampire.

Nick: Recipients—he doesn't like to call his victims, victims— they're Recipients. What's the matter, Madame L? You look pale. Would you like me to get you a glass of water or something stronger— Vodka, straight up?

Madame Lumière: I think you're taking Bernard's words out of context and twisting them around.

Nick: You don't think he's a monster? He's just a guy who goes around doing nice things for people? A good neighbor, Sam, so to speak? (Laughing) In my building, for instance, do you think he's been a good neighbor to Mildred Havilland?

Madame Lumière: Mildred Havilland?

Nick: Oh, don't be coy, Madame L. Mildred Havilland, the murdered neighbor lady. Surely, you remember Bernard mentioning her?

Madame Lumière: Didn't her cousin do it?

Nick: (Laughing) Yeah—with a candlestick in the living room.

Madame Lumière: Oh, that's awful!

Nick: Nah, just jiving you, Madame L. That was Colonel Mustard in the library.

Madame Lumière: Bernard?

Nick: Yes, Madame L?

Madame Lumière: You've been snooping, haven't you?

Nick: It wasn't exactly hidden.

Madame Lumière: I have a weekly game of CLUE with Tony Troy, another dealer who lives at the Beekman. You know what happened to the cat, don't you—curiosity killed him?

Nick: I also know what brought him back—the satisfaction of knowing it might be worth it.

Madame Lumière: Have you ever thought about meditation?

Nick: If it didn't work for Bernard, what makes you think it will work for me?

FORTY

AUM... DO WAH DIDDY DIDDY

Recording #12/mp (English, no translation needed)

The Vampire: Let me get this straight. You want me to meditate?

Madame Lumière: Yes. Is that going to be a problem, Bernard?

The Vampire: Is the Pope catholic?

Madame Lumière: I'm glad you cleaned that up.

The Vampire: Nick's become a bit undone with his language, hasn't he?

Madame Lumière: I wonder where he gets it from? (Laughing) Have you ever been a sailor, Bernard?

The Vampire: I can't blame him, can I?

Madame Lumière: Funny what his memory has uncovered, Bernard.

The Vampire: To your question—I've never been a sailor, but when the occasion arose, I've used salty language.

Madame Lumière: Always keeping up with the latest slang, too, Imagine. The Code doesn't miss much, does it?

The Vampire: Survival of the fittest dictates when in Rome...

Madame Lumière: Never met a stranger, I bet.

The Vampire: We're getting into troubled waters again, Madame L.

Madame Lumière: What do you mean, Bernard?

The Vampire: You and Nick were putting me down for not having lasting friendships, remember?

Madame Lumière: It wasn't our intention to make you uncomfortable, Bernard.

The Vampire: Pish posh! In order to survive, vampires must blend in, which translates into making acquaintances. I can't call them friends because, as you correctly guessed, we can never create a friendship that lasts long enough for the friend to question why they are aging and we're not. On the flip side, we can never give them the impression that we're cold, without feeling, and incapable of having a lasting and meaningful friendship.

Madame Lumière: I can see how that can create a stressful situation. How do you manage, Bernard?

The Vampire: (He laughs) Come on, Madame L.

Madame Lumière: I don't understand, Bernard?

The Vampire: Stop treating me as if I were one of your normal clients and come clean—admit you've been peering into your crystal ball for years now, just waiting for someone like me to come knocking at your door.

Madame Lumière: I'm not able to see the future as clearly as you think, Bernard, but I admit, I did expect someone like you...

The Vampire: Someone like me? You mean, a vampire, don't you?

Madame Lumière: At first, I wasn't entirely sure.

The Vampire: Were you frightened by what you saw, Madame L?

Madame Lumière: I wouldn't use that term, Bernard.

The Vampire: What term would you use?

Madame Lumière: At first, intrigued and a little apprehensive.

The Vampire: And then, Madame L?

Madame Lumière: I began to see your image more clearly and knew that you would eventually pay me a visit and ask for my help.

The Vampire: And that didn't frighten you, Madame Lumière?

Madame Lumière: Surprisingly not.

The Vampire: I don't have your gift of sight, although I have my own gateway into the future. But it's limited, so I can't be certain you're telling me the truth.

Madame Lumière: Why would I lie, Bernard?

The Vampire: (Laughing) Can I count the ways, Madame L.

Madame Lumière: What can you see, Bernard?

The Vampire: My abilities only allow me to glimpse what lies ahead. Believe me, those glimpses have saved my bacon numerous times over the past three millennia. And to your next question, yes—I use the process of meditation as my gateway.

Madame Lumière: As I said, I could see your image when I looked into my crystal ball and meditated.

The Vampire: I was shown the way by the great Sun God, Aten, who himself created the Glorious Light Meditation.

Madame Lumière: You never cease to amaze, Bernard. Naturally, I've heard of the Sun God, Aten. Glorious Light Meditation is one of the oldest forms of meditation, but I've never seen or known anyone who practices it. Isn't it when you employ visualizations and chants of words of power until you are One with the ABSOLUTE?

The Vampire: The words of power are called *Hekau*, Madame L.

Madame Lumière: Yes, of course. Would you teach me how Bernard? I don't mean right now, but after...

The Vampire: If you want, of course, Madame L. But first...

Madame Lumière: But first...?

The Vampire: *Sillage...*

Madame Lumière: *Sillage...?*

FORTY-ONE

A DISAPPEARING ACT

Recording #12/mp continued (English, no translation needed)

Nick: *Stillage!* I've never heard of the word before. Not that I'm a wordsmith. Maybe I was before the accident, but not now. I was reading a Phillip Kerr novel the other day, and I had to go onto the Internet to look up the meaning of a word.

Madame Lumière: I don't know him. What does he write?

Nick: Detective books, but he's something special. He's the second coming of Raymond Chandler.

Madame Lumière: Raymond Chandler, the author of the Phillip Marlow books?

Nick: Not many writers come close to Chandler's wit and style, but Kerr does. And for me, there's something especially intriguing about cops who worked in Berlin before and during the Second World War.

Madame Lumière: I've been a fan of Agatha Christie since my teenage years and, more recently, Louise Penny and her Inspector Gamache books, but I'm always willing to read someone new.

Nick: Bernard has all of Kerr's books. I'll bring in his first one, *Berlin Noir*.

Madame Lumière: This is the first time you referred to your possessions as belonging to Bernard.

Nick: Ah, must be a Freudian slip. (Laughing) Tell me, does that mean I'm jealous of my father's love for my brother over me, Madame L?

Madame Lumière: Nick!

Nick: Oh, skip it, Madame L. *Sillage*—what the hell does it mean when Bernard says he's lost his *sillage*?

Madame Lumière: *Sillage*—it's a French word. It refers to the scent trail a perfume leaves behind as it evaporates. Heavier scents will have more noticeable sillage, while lighter scents will have less.

Nick: I know what the dictionary says. I looked the word up, too, Madame L. I'm wondering what Bernard means when he says he's lost his *sillage*.

Madame Lumière: (Pauses) I'm not sure, Nick.

Nick: I thought we would be honest with each other, Madame L?

Madame Lumière: If I were to guess, he was referring to one of the side effects he's experiencing from going without blood for a specific time.

Nick: That's what I was afraid of.

Madame Lumière: I don't believe Bernard was trying to frighten you, Nick.

Nick: Maybe not. So, what's next?

Madame Lumière: What do you mean, what's next?

Nick: Come on—Madame L. Look—stop lying to me.

Madame Lumière: I've never lied to you, Nick.

Nick: Ahh, fuck it! I was going to bring this up later.

Madame Lumière: Nick, what...

Nick: Do you think I'm stupid? I heard the last recording. You can see the future.

Madame Lumière: Nick, let me explain.

Nick: Look, I'm just about ready to walk out on you and drop all this craziness in the nearest sewer where it belongs so that I can get on with my life.

Madame Lumière: If you would just let me...

Nick: This *sillage*—suppose he doesn't get blood next week? What else does he lose— his sense of smell, taste...

Madame Lumière: We don't know if he will lose anything else, Nick.

Nick: How about his hearing or his sight?

Madame Lumière: Nick, will you stop?

Nick: Or—or—am I just going to disappear? Is that what you see in your goddamn crystal ball?

FORTY-TWO

LET THERE BE LIGHT

Recording #12/mp continued (English, no translation needed)

Nick: This isn't going to work.

Madame Lumière: Nick, just relax. Focus on the photo, and when you think you're ready, close your eyes and picture Paris in your mind's eye.

Nick: I can't keep my eyes closed for a few seconds. I'm trying—you can see I'm trying. I'm sorry, Madame L.

Madame Lumière: A couple of seconds is a good start. This isn't a test, Nick.

Nick: No shit, Sherlock! I'm about to disappear, be gone—Nick, gone forever—and you want me to picture your stupid Pekingese dog in my head?

Madame Lumière: We talked about trust, haven't we, Nick?

Nick: I don't remember. You may be confusing me with Bernard.

Madame Lumière: You both have to trust me.

Nick: With your record?

Madame Lumière: If Bernard can get over that, you can.

Nick: I don't know how Bernard can sit for hours doing this.

Madame Lumière: He's had practice.

Nick: (Laughing) That's an understatement. Unfortunately, I don't have much time.

Madame Lumière: Nick—Nick, please, just try to relax.

Nick: You keep telling me meditation lowers your blood pressure? It's doing the opposite of mine.

Madame Lumière: Everybody has difficulties at first, but you just have to have patience, stay with it, and give it some time.

Jesus Christ, on a peppermint stick! When the fuck will you get it through your spiritual self that I don't have time?

Madame Lumière: What are you saying, Nick?

Nick: Sorry, Madame L, but I keep getting distracted. Voices in my head, terrible thoughts keep flying in—horrible, frightening thoughts. I don't want to disappear, Madame L. I don't want to die!

Madame Lumière: That is why you need this. Meditation will erase those distractions, or what we call the white noise. Once that happens, your mind will be clear, and your blood pressure will drop. I promise you'll feel totally at ease, Nick.

Nick: Can we use something else? The picture of your dog just isn't working for me.

Madame L: Let me think. How about that apple over there?

Nick: No! Don't get up! I'll get it!

That's it, young son. Go to the beautiful 18th-century Italian side table by the window that I remember the Duchess of Amalfi, bless her plumb delicious neck, loved so much, pluck up an apple from that lovely crystal bowl full of wooden fruit, come back and place it here, in front of Madame L's crystal ball, then grab your French side chair and belly-up to this magnificent 18th-century Bouillotte card table just like the one. Oh, never mind.

Madame Lumière: Remember—no pressure. Focus on the apple momentarily, then close your eyes and picture it in your mind's eye. Keep the image of the apple in your head for as long as possible. Don't worry, Nick, if you open your eyes or if other thoughts get into your mind and make the apple disappear.

Nick: What do I do, then?

Madame Lumière: Repeat the process. Even now, it may take me two attempts to focus on the image for minutes on end.

Oh, that's bull Madame L!

Young Son, cool it

Nick: That's it. I'm seeing an apple in my head for five minutes. What's that going to do for me?

Madame Lumière: At the very least, shut out the white noise while lowering your blood pressure, which should relax your entire body.

Nick: I want to know my future, Madame L.

That's it, my Nick, don't hold back!

Madame Lumière: Amnesia is a tricky thing, Nick. You know what Dr. Mickeltee said. Some patients regain their memories quickly, while others may need more time for full recovery.

Nick: Damn that bitch! That's not what I mean; you know it, Madame L.

Whoa, there, Boyo, watch your language. Now's not the time to go Full Potty Mouth.

Nick: Sorry, Madame L, sorry.

Madame Lumière: Nick, please try to relax and calm down.

Nick: Blood—Madame L—just look into your damn crystal ball and tell me why I don't need blood.

I'm feeling wobbly. Don't get up, Young Son.

Nick: If I'm a vampire, why don't I crave blood, turn into a bat, and go find a neck to bite and drain it?

Fuck, fuck, fuck, I can't believe I just said that!

Just don't get up, Laddie Boy, don't get up!

Madame Lumière: You heard Bernard, Nick. There were times he could go for long periods without...

Nick: Bull! I heard what you let me hear. That vertigo and nausea crap, sure—but I think you left out the other stuff. I want to listen to what you edited out.

Don't tell him, not yet anyway. Damn, I can't be sick now.

Madame Lumière: Nick, I assure you, I didn't edit these recordings.

Nick: Then Bernard's lying.

And there you have it!

Madame Lumière: Why would he do that, Nick? Bernard wants you to regain your memory and resume living an everyday life.

Nick: He may not be lying, but he's hiding something from me; I know it—you know it, too! You've seen his lies in your crystal ball, haven't you? I don't know how, but you've seen my future, too. What, you stare into it? Let me stare into it; I want to see what you see!

Oh, that won't work, Madame L.

Nick: Fuck the apple! I don't want a piece of your fruit! Gimme the crystal ball, lemme look—lemme look!

FORTY-THREE

TALKING TO MYSELF

It was like learning to ride a bike, algebra, a foreign language, or anything new when it suddenly clicks, and you get it. I mean, get it!

Damn, if I knew it would happen, but there I was, staring, while my eyeballs hurt like hell into that crystal ball until Madame L commanded me to close my eyes and keep them closed until I could finally see the crystal ball in my mind's eye.

So, I see the crystal ball; I mean really seeing it in its minutest details when all my pent-up nervous tension, wham, bam, thank you, ma'am, shoots right out of my body like when non-union workers screw up and hit a gas main and boom, concrete blows apart into a thousand pieces and gas explodes right up into the sky.

An intense white light hits me right between my baby blues, and again, wham, bam, thank you, ma'am, I'm suddenly in another dimension, rushing down a long tunnel.

I'm swallowed up in an ocean of love. No kidding, an ocean of love. Yes, siree, that's my happy feet feeling as I'm propelling back into what— the womb. The womb, baby, the womb! That's how sweet it is.

Naturally, Bernard is waiting for me, not in the womb, but in our living room at 31 East Thirty-fifth Street. He's enounced (vampires don't just sit like ordinary folks, you know) on one of our matching Naugahyde sofas.

He motions me to sit across from him on the tan sofa separated by the glass table as he admires the assorted museum-quality pieces, smiling as he eyes the Mycenaean couple fucking (that our nosey police gal couldn't wait to caress); a collection of pieces he's picked up and somehow managed to keep—a remarkable achievement, considering his moving around from place to place over his three-millennium journey.

The music playing in the background is one of Bach's three-part inventions. It is a favorite of mine and one I enjoy listening to first thing in the morning, as its soothing contrapuntal motif sets the tone for a calming and tranquil day.

Sit—sit, make yourself comfy, Nick. How are you feeling?

Bernard is wearing my favorite light blue slim jeans, a black turtleneck sweater, and black Adidas sneakers with pink socks. I wonder what I'm wearing, but that question evaporates into thin air when I see my image in an 18th-century Venetian mirror facing me from across the room. Our eyes lock, and our mouths close.

Okay, I guess.

Madame L is something— a real bad motorcycle.

Where did you find her, Bernard?

You found her, Nick, remember?

So, we're going to play that game, are we?

We're not going to play any game, Nick. Facts are facts.

Oh, damn, he can read my mind!

Great minds and all.

You're right; I found her in the phone book.

It was the right move. I've invited her over later.

.I want to show her the art. As someone in the antiques business, I think she will appreciate it, don't you think, Nick?

I'm sure she'll love to hear your stories regarding each piece, where you found it, and how you purchased it.

And how I've managed to keep them all these years.

Don't you get tired of reading my mind?

(Nick laughs)

Okay, since you know what I'm thinking, answer this..

Why must I take drugs to sleep?

I don't like taking stuff. It makes me feel strange in the morning. And I have some really bizarre dreams, like the one where I'm kissing a strange woman while she's watering her roses in an apartment I've never been in before.

A little NyQuil and half an Ambien never hurt anyone. On the other hand, perhaps you shouldn't be watching the Hallmark Channel before you go to sleep.

So, I should watch the news? That's even worse than seeing a woman watering roses. With all the murder and mayhem in the city, god knows what that crap will do to your head.

You have to know what's going on, Nick. I didn't survive all these centuries by living like an ostrich.

I shouldn't eat anything before sleeping, especially something heavy.

What? And give up those meatballs. They're so easy to defrost and taste just as good as fresh.

Why did I fall, Bernard?

You tripped.

I know, over a subway grating.

There you go.

How many times have you fallen in your three thousand years?

Bernard stares into space, thinking. Once, twice, perhaps. Are you implying I'm clumsy, my Son?

And amnesia— how often have you lost your memory, Bernard?

If you must know, I've never fallen—and I certainly have never lost my memory, not that I can remember. (Bernard laughs.)

Stop! Just stop! (Nick's head begins to ache)

Okay, I fell because I wasn't paying attention. (Smiling) It was a lovely derrière, and you know I'm, what they call, an ass man.

Why so crass, Bernard? For someone who was a Pharaoh, that's beneath you, don't you think?

Look who the pot is calling the kettle crass, Mr. Potty Mouth.

Touché, mon ami.

That's better, Boyo.

I've got another question.

Ask away, Young Son.

I'm not your Young Son, Laddie Boy, or Boyo. I'm Nick Cummings. That is the name you gave me.

Okay, I'm simply trying to be sociable, Nick.

You've told Madame L you've lived three thousand years and had—who knows how many occupations—how is it you were never a doctor, perhaps even treated someone with amnesia.

I never said I wasn't a doctor, Nick.

I knew it!

Have you ever heard of Galen of Pergamum, considered one of the most renowned physicians of the Roman Empire?

You were that guy?

No, I worked in his laboratory. My name was Asclepius, and I was the living embodiment of the demi-god son of Apollo.

The what?

The reincarnation of the son of Apollo.

Holy shit! Now you're telling me!

And as the son of Apollo, I was endowed with unbelievable curative powers, so commanding that Zeus, the almighty, was so jealous of me that he even believed I might achieve immortality for humanity.

Vampires aren't that charitable, are they?

(Bernard laughs)

Go on, what happened next, Doctor Vampire?

As Apollo instructed me in the ways of healing when I went to assist Galen, and of course, without him knowing, I could use my knowledge to help him formulate the theory and practice of what we now call modern-day medicine.

Always keeping in the shadows, huh, Bernard?

Keeping in the shadows has helped to keep me alive all these millennium; You'll be wise to keep that in mind, Nick.

You can bet I won't be writing my biography.

Again, Touché, mon ami. Vanity caught up with me on that one, young Son. You can bet that will never happen again.

So what else happened when you worked for this Galen character?

You'd be interested to know that we personally treated Marcus Aurelius and his notoriously evil son, Commodus, whom you may know from the film Gladiator.

I just read there's a *Gladiator 2* coming out.

Well, let's see if another evil bastard, the emperor Septimius Severus, is in the remake.

Who?

Septimius Severus, who proclaimed himself the adoptive son of Marcus Aurelius, allowed that conniving SOB to eventually gain military power, and by 193 BC, Septimius Severus turned Rome into a military monarchy. What a bad boy he was.

How could you stomach working for these guys, Bernard? With all your vampire ways, why didn't you turn into a bat and fly the heck away? Or better still, drain him of all his blood and kill the bastard?

I couldn't leave Galen to certain death, so I bided my time until 194 BC when we finally escaped and made our way to Arabia. But therein lies another story for another time.

And the other alternative.

We don't drain anyone's blood and kill them, Nick. It's against the Code.

You're telling me you were an Egyptian God, and before that, the reincarnation of the son of a Greek God, holy hell—I bet you're one of the Ancients who wrote the Code, aren't you?

Now, who's trying to read whose mind, Nick?

You're no ordinary vampire, are you, Bernard?

(Bernard laughs) *Ordinary's not a word usually found in the same sentence as a vampire.*

Come on, out with it. And don't spare the details, I can take it. No—I deserve to know the entire story.

All vampires are bound by our sworn oath never to reveal who the Five are who wrote the Code Of The Vampire. That's not to say my oath to The Brethren of Ancients does not preclude allowing you to regain The Full Awakening?

Bernard reaches across the table, touches my hand resting on the glass, and says, Full Awakening, my brother will free you to follow your destiny and meet the fate foretold.

You mean us, not me. Come on, let's be real here, Bernard. If I don't regain total memory load, you, my Brother, will stay in a continued state of not-so-splendid isolation, unable to fly freely and bite necks.

In other words, I'm toast.

Now we're cooking with gas.

You know, I wrote that slogan.

In late September of 1931, after you finished your stint on Broadway, you went to work writing marketing slogans for the American Gas Association.

I don't remember telling Madame L that.

You didn't.

Your memories are returning, aren't they? (Smiling) So, there are still certain things you can't see, am I right, Bernard?

What else do you remember? Tell me, Nick!

You first, Bernard.

No, you.

You!

YOU!

FORTY-FOUR

THE VAMPIRE'S LAST BITE (PART 1)

So, now you know what I know. We've been an Egyptian pharaoh, played second fiddle to Beethoven, been buddy-buddy with Napoleon, had our horoscope done by Nostradamus, oh yeah, not to forget played a demi-god and pissed off Zeus (there goes any thoughts of visiting Mount Olympus during Spring Break).

We haven't killed anyone or turned anyone into a vampire (as if sucking a little blood out of their veins isn't bad enough). Still, and that's a big still until my memory totally returns, I can't be entirely sure there isn't a darker side of a life half spent as a man, a half-vampire that our Bernard's been hiding from me.

In the previous chapter that ended with a screaming match, Madame L had planned to put me under and talk mano a vampire to Bernard in the cozy confines of the apartment, reasoning Bernard would be more willing to answer the remaining questions (will there be blood or no blood) regarding my future (and his) sitting comfortably cocooned amongst his treasures.

Unfortunately, as you just witnessed, the best-laid plans of men and vampires always seem to go sideways. (If you need to hear the sound of four hands clapping, what a great talk, don't carry on a conversation in your head.)

It was a little after 2:00 p.m. this afternoon when Carlos at the desk called me. Still feeling the effects of the NyQuil and half an Ambien (and more crazy dreams, this time flying jet planes), I managed to get my mouth to say, in my best Arnold impersonation, "Send her up."

Carlos knows his *Terminator* movies, so he knows whom he's dealing with and smartly directs Madame L to the elevators—that's when things really go kaput.

As Madame L tells it, she's about to press the Up Button when who should show up after grabbing her mail a few steps down the corridor but the gorgeous CEO of Nefertiti, Kirsten Hayward,

Don't you just know it; they embrace like long-lost sisters, and why not? Kristen Hayward is a long-time client! Not only does Kirsten shop there for antiques, but Madame L also does her horoscope—and get this, my readers—every month!

Does Kirsten discuss my relationship with Madame L, or does she even have to if it's all in the stars for Madame L to see, like reading the chyron running down the bottom third of your television screen?

More to the ugly truth, has Madame L discovered in Kirsten's chart the young woman's ancestral relationship to Nefertiti and, by six degrees of nookie, the incestuous link to Bernard by way of Akhenaten? Has she seen this all in her crystal ball? Oh, what a tangled web we weave in three millennia.

Not to get too crazy, because the first words out of Madame L's mouth when I open the door to her ring are: "Did you hear Margaret Havilland's cousin was murdered in Red Hook?"

I want to ask if anyone calls Olivia Benson. But I don't know that she's been sexually attacked as well as murdered, and besides, that's cold, so I smile and say, instead, "So nice to see you, Madame L., please come in."

I lead Madame L through the winding hallway until we enter the dining room. "May I take your coat?"

"Thank you, Nick."

I take her coat.

Madame L gives me no sign of what she thought of yesterday's drama, saying nothing other than she would see me today after bringing me out of my last trance.

"She had all her blood drained from her body. Imagine that"

says Madame L as if she's playing the dispassionate Quincy M.E on the tube.

"I try not to," I say.

Madame L looks at me, but I turn away as if she expects me to get down on my knees and confess to the murder and beg for forgiveness. I want to admit, but my secret has to do with always wanting to visit Red Hook because there's an IKEA there, and I've heard they serve delicious Swedish meatballs; and now that I can conveniently walk down the street to the pier on East 35th and the FDR, there's a ferry there that will take you right to the door, it sounds doable. I fluff up her coat.

"And listen to this: not a drop was found near the body or anywhere in the apartment; imagine that," continues Quincy, AKI, Madame L.

"I try not to, but it's getting harder," I mumble, sure that Madame L can't hear me.

I point toward the living room and say, "Madame L, why don't you sit down and make yourself comfortable while I hang up your coat? Do you want anything to drink, coffee, tea, or something stronger?"

"It's two in the afternoon, but it must be five someplace in the world," she says laughingly, then continues, "I ran into Kirsten Hayward by the elevators. She told me all the gory details. I swear, if a pin drops in Chicago, that girl hears it."

Drawing Nick closer, Madame L whispers, "This you won't believe. Even though the body was drained of all its blood, it hadn't decayed. In fact, she looked better than ever, and there was no wrinkle on her."

Nick and Madame L together, "Imagine that!"

"Apparently, the murderer opened all the windows, and the cold air preserved the body. I get chills thinking about it, don't you, Nick?" says Madame L, leaving her no-nonsense Quincy imitation and going more for the neighbor-with-a-heart character.

"I would if I could, but I can't. Apparently, it's a vampire thing." I whisper, but Madame L doesn't hear me, or does and doesn't want to engage in any whippy repartee.

"Oh, by the way, when I told her I was visiting you, Kirsten wanted me to tell you that she's back from her European trip and hopes to see you soon."

I also know this from the messages of love I've been getting on WhatsApp after our cute meet and the glorious lovemaking with whom I thought was the reincarnation of Nefertiti's daughter, Meketaten, that was cooler than the other side of the pillow but that was before Bernard confesses, we're actually the reincarnation of the Pharaoh Akhenaton and Nefertiti's my wife, and Kirsten— hold your horses, Masked Man! It would be written all over Madame L's face if she knew that Kirsten was my daughter!

I play that last sentence back in my mind and want to shoot myself. How I have been able to correspond with Kirsten and parry her admissions of love has been a nightmare.

I trot into the bedroom and tenderly lay Madame L's Chanel coat on the bed, but first, I admire the artistry and caress the silk material. I do this without fully understanding what I'm admiring, and I only wish Bernard could guide me. I'm certain that sometime during his illustrious three millennia, he couldn't pass up the opportunity to bite someone's neck at Fashion Week.

On the night table is a Chinese doll, reminding me of another of my anxieties (blood/no blood, immortal/dead man walking).

Oh, how they plague me, these constant drip, drip, drip of revelations, but no definitive answers; not as painful as the infamous Chinese water torture (something Bernard probably witnessed, or god forbid, ordered during his visits to the Orient), nevertheless as agonizing.

Now, my hypothalamus, for no good reason, fucks with the temperature of these revelatory drippings, pouring cold water on any hope that I'm on the verge of complete memory retrieval and the answers to the enigma of my existence.

I return to the living room, and Madame L is perusing the treasure trove of antiquities, especially intrigued by a bronze statue of a lover's embrace of the Mycenaean Civilization.

"Who are the two lovers?"

"You never said coffee, tea, or something stronger."

"Imagining the story of this couple almost made me forget about poor Margaret Havilland. Vodka, if you have, Nick."

"I have Belvedere if that's okay."

"If it's good enough for Daniel Craig, it's good enough for me." Madame L does a little shake, rattle, and roll and giggles.

I have no clue what's going on and can only guess Madame L already had a few to fortify herself before she came here. In that case, I'm in for a bumpy ride as Miss Betty drolly drawled in *All About Eve*.

"So, Nick, did you do as I asked and write up a series of questions you want me to ask Bernard today?"

"Yep, just like you wanted. I have them right here." I touch my pocket.

Now, this is a great big fat Greek Wedding, lie. They are not in my pocket. I don't know where the hell they are. I know I wrote them out last night, but I can't find them this morning.

"Oops, they must be in another pocket. I'll be right back."

"Take your time. If you don't mind, I'll continue to browse. Your place is like a museum, Nick, but I bet everybody says so."

If you're counting the pieces plundered and stolen outright from their home countries, you're right on, Madame L.

I'm tempted to go to the bottle for some Dance-Like-Daniel-Craig or maybe a taste of the grape, but I'm not sure that would mix so well with the NyQuil as mentioned above and the half-an-Ambien I took early this morning so I could finally get some sleep.

I go to the kitchen for the Belvedere that I keep in the freezer, plus the Wheat Thins in the pantry that my local wine merchant sold me. It's the perfect complement in Russia when drinking Vodka because it brings out the potato flavor.

I still have half a pot of coffee and the remnants of a melted cheese and tomato sandwich I picked up this morning. I was hoping it might start me up, but instead, it just made me a little queasy.

I warm up the coffee and the sandwich in the microwave by putting the sandwich on top of the coffee and zapping them both for one minute.

I open the fridge for some almond milk and then the pantry for a new jar of mayo, and I discover my list of questions wedged between a bag of almond nuts and the box of wheat thins.

I look around to see if Madame L's crept up behind me. She's still where she's supposed to be, examining all the pilfered loot in the living room.

I'm safe from 'dem prying eyes, so I deftly pluck the folded sheet of yellow legal and open it just to be sure it's my list.

I nearly shit in my pants. Beneath each of my blue pen questions are red ink answers.

FORTY-FIVE

THE VAMPIRE'S LAST BITE (PART 2)

You swear you are going to tell me the truth?

I swear, cross my heart and hope to continue to live forever.

Did you have anything to do with my fall?

No. That was unplanned.

And, my amnesia is real?

That was also unforeseen.

How is it that I remember movies from the forties, but I can't remember you?

I'm not a mind reader.

But you're a vampire?

Yes.

And you're three millennia old?

But I don't look a day over two millennia. Forgive me, but I've always wanted to say that.

Did you meet all those famous people you told us about?

Vampires never lie.

You never exaggerated or embellished your stories?

Oh, pish posh, pish posh!

Which person did you find most interesting?

Nick, you're trying to get to the truth, not emceeing an episode of This Is Your Life. Ask the big one.

If you're a vampire, what does that make me?

I am you.

Then I'm a vampire?

Yes.

This isn't a dream?

No.

This isn't all in my head?

What a place to be.

Will I live forever?

One has to follow the rules of the Code, and only then if you're lucky.

Why don't I crave blood, turn into a bat, and hunt down a victim?

What makes you think you haven't, my brother?

FORTY-SIX

PT BARNUM SHOWS ME THE WAY

The first thing I do is defrost the rest of the meatballs. The last thing I need is for the cops to go through my freezer and find evidence that immediately places me in Red Hook. Not that meatballs are the only thing that will do me in, not with cameras on the ferry and all over IKEA, but hey, there's nothing I can do about that.

The next order of business is to look for a moving company. No problem; there it is, the Delicate Deliveries business card, on my fridge door, staring me right in the face, along with the magnetized cards of a local wine merchant and sushi restaurant.

I dialed the number and swear the guy, Logan Nebbs, awaited my call. He told me straight away, "Say the word, Mr. Cummings, and he can be there in two hours and have the apartment cleaned out and taken to Mayflower Storage straightaway, no problem."

How Logan Nebbs knows me, how much I need to move out of my apartment, and where to store it are questions (and answers) that only occur later that evening.

Let's backtrack a little. Actually, the first thing I do after I read Bernard's reply is not to defrost the meatballs but to grab onto the side of the fridge to steady myself and prevent myself from falling. (It crosses my mind to grab a paper bag from the pantry, but I surprise myself by not hyperventilating.)

Next, I go to the bottle and take a long pull of Dancing-With-Daniel-Craig Belvedere. The liquid sets my throat, gasping for a piece of ice, but real men don't yell fire when doing shots of vodka, so I gulp down another in silence.

Then, it occurred to me to get rid of the evidence. I quickly defrost the meatballs, and when they are ready, I place them on one plate, the Wheat Thins on another, and put them both on a serving tray along with the Belvedere and two gimlet glasses. I then bring it out to Madame L.

Never forget your manners, and look on the bright side: As long as you have a complete set of Limoges dinner, tea, and coffee sets, yada, yada, yada, you're good to go.

Madame L is so enamored with the Mycenaean couple that she doesn't see my future until she smells the meatballs. She immediately seizes the moment, grabs the vodka, fills her glass, and downs the contents in one gulp.

"Nick, we have to have a serious talk."

As if all our talks aren't *serioso*. "You got it, Madame L."

"Sit."

I sit.

"Have you made your calls?"

"Calls?"

She points to the kitchen. "Delicate Deliveries."

How the fuck...

"Of course, you have." She smiles. "I'm going to miss you, Nick—this place." Looking around. "It's been a marvelous home these last ten years, hasn't it? Ah, but we knew it would have to end. It always does for us."

"Us?"

"Have a meatball," I say for the hell of it."

Madame L stares at the meatballs.

233

"Oh, damn, I forgot utensils and napkins." No—I see napkins from last night on the table, so I say, 'I'll just get us some forks."

"No, sit, don't bother." (She uses a napkin to pick up a meatball.) "It's delicious."

Madame L licks her lips, then gazes out the window. "The weather's good for flying, don't you think?"

Is this some joke?

Madame L laughs at my pained expression and says, "By plane—silly, boy."

It's incredible how you can be such an idiot in times of enormous stress.

"I'll just finish these meatballs and have another drink. She waves her hand. "No, I'll pour it myself. You just sit there, Nick."

I fish out the paper with my questions and Bernard's answers and hand it over to Madame L. She smiles, downs another glass of vodka in one gulp, and casually peruses the paper. Her hands are as steady as a rock, and this mild-mannered Southern Belle could drink a roomful of sailors under the table.

I make a command decision and pour myself two fingers of Vodka.

"I had hoped we could have put you under for all this." She waves the paper, then looks at the last meatball, plucks it up, and eats it.

I wait.

"Well, that's the last of it." (Laughing) "Oh, if you're worrying about the cameras, don't."

"No?"

"It's a vampire thing."

I look toward a mirror and see my image. Madame L follows my gaze.

"You know, Nick, we're not Luddites; we try to stay technologically relevant. Since the invention of the camera, which you were intimately involved in, you can imagine having our image captured on celluloid raises all sorts of problems. So far, our kind has been lucky, but it would have been only a matter of time and bad luck before someone got hold of pictures that showed one of us over the centuries not aging a single day. Fortunately, we have recently developed a solution that prevents our image from being replicated when applied to our faces."

I should have picked up 'our' kind' and 'our' faces, but confusion overcame me, and instead, I shouted, "A solution: I don't know about any solution."

"Not to worry—it's in your cologne—all your colognes." She laughs. "Bernard liked his fragrances, as you can tell from his huge collection."

"So, I shouldn't worry about anyone noticing I took the ferry to IKEA in Red Hook. Is that what you're telling me?"

"That piece of paper changes everything."

"What do you mean?"

"As I said, Nick, we had hoped your memory would have returned to you in a..."

"Less threatening way." I want to say, fucked-up, but hold back.

"That's what we've been hoping for," she says.

I can't resist. "Like waking up in the middle of the night and I'm a bat, flying high around the city and taking in all the lovely young necks."

"That's one way of looking at it." (She picks up the Mycenaean statue) "You don't mind if I keep this for you, Nick?" (Smiling) "Until the next time?"

Then it hits me, and the truth that she's a vampire comes by the way she knows how to pack for a quick getaway. Just the essentials, no two of anything, and all to fit comfortably in my SwissGear 7366 Expandable Hardside Spinner Luggage, which I never knew I had, but Madame L sure did.

Great Balls Of Fire, she's been doing this for what—centuries, getting out of Dodge a few steps ahead of the angry mob, the law, even a fellow vampire whose territory she's violated. I imagine how strong she is in carrying her all-seeing crystal ball, which weighs a ton, safe from breaking as she, figuratively or literally, flies the coup.

As Madame L flits around the house like a spring chicken, a smile on her face, and I swear, humming "Blue Berry Hill" by Fats Domino, I wonder if she's one of the ancients or a recent model.

Nah, no one is as old as Bernard. Something about her age gnaws at me, but I must leave that for now.

Realizing that Madame L is a vampire and has hidden that alarming news in plain sight from the first day we meet for some unexplainable reason doesn't send me into anaphylactic shock. I accept it as coolly and rationally as I do when I see I'm charged three percent if I use my credit card to pay for a meal at my local Greek diner.

Speaking of Greek diners like the one I frequent, I only wish I knew of Bernard's exalted lineage when I showed up for my weekly breakfast. Whether or not I'm treated to a free meal is up for discussion, but hey, it's not every day that the adopted son of Zeus the Almighty sits in a window booth and orders a grilled cheese and tomato sandwich on rye toast and a cup of joe.

Funny, when I hear the Greek owners (brothers?) squabbling (every Greek discussion sounds like a squabble), no Greek words, phrases, not even an image of the Acropolis, let alone ones with me dancing arm and arm with Zorba doing the Sirtaki, fill my mind with memories of wild nights in the hills of Athens or any other Greek city or village.

The plane tickets and passport appear as if by magic. Does Madame L have a side gig at Expedia and the US Department of State passport office? Of course not, silly! She doesn't have to. Don't you know it's *de rigueu* for all vampires in the game to have at the ready a suitcase full of travel documents, including those valuable Letters of Transit that would make Rick or anyone else trying to get out of Casablanca hoodwink the gorgeous Ingrid Bergman, jealous?

"Nick, would you like me to go through your suitcase before I close it to ensure I didn't miss anything for your stay in Punta Ala?

Like that would ever happen. "Nope, I trust you," I say, trying to believe my own words. I wonder why she chose a beach resort in Italy instead of a big city, like Rome, Paris, or London. I remember it's the place I'm always fantasizing about.

Madame L senses my puzzlement but, oddly, reads me the wrong way

"Oh, and don't worry about reserving the service elevator."

"Oh, right, sure, yeah!"

"I reserved it weeks ago when I made arrangements with Delicate Deliveries. Tomorrow, the Board will get a letter informing them that you're leaving for a year and that your cousin will be coming from Las Vegas and bringing his own furniture. I provided them with a postal box if they wish to contact you. Other than that, you will be incommunicado. In two weeks, the Board will receive another letter stating that your cousin won't be coming and that the apartment is up for sale."

"How did you know two weeks ago that I would be moving out today?"

"You've been here over ten years, and you know our ten-year rule. This business with Margaret Havilland just made a move more..."

"Urgent."

"Timely."

The most amazing sensation overcomes me. I feel calm, cool, and collected, very much in control. I realize I'm getting my vampire mojo going, and everything will work out just fine and dandy.

"I think I'm going to take a shower."

"What a good idea. While you are there, I'll make a fresh pot of coffee."

"Sounds good to me."

I take in the room and all its treasures as if it's the last time, and of course, it is. I feel like a transient without a connection to the pieces or the apartment. It's funny, but I've never realized that's always been how I've felt since returning from the hospital.

"I've laid out your clothes for today. I hope you don't mind, but I thought the fewer choices you had to make, the easier it would be for you. "

"Thanks, Madame L".

I wonder how much more vodka the vampire in me will allow before he cuts me off? More to the point, how do I get to swig even a drop down the ole gullet before Madame L grabs the bottle out of my hands?

"I like you in the boot-cut black Levis and the light blue Frank Stella Sport Shirt I bought for Bernard last Christmas. Everybody says it goes with your baby blues, but you know that, don't you, Nick?"

I may be in my vampire mojo, but that doesn't stop me from blushing and stammering out, "Ahh, thanks, Madame L."

When I get where I'm going, I have to make it a point to watch some of Robert Redford's early movies. I get up. Head for the bathroom. I'm sorry now that I didn't ask Bernard about those strange out-of body-experiences like being sucked into the TV and going back in time or hearing people's thoughts when I'm in a crowd.

"If anyone calls, let it go to voicemail. It's better not to talk to anyone today unless it's someone down in the lobby."

I strip and get into the shower. I must suffer from short-term memory loss because I always forget which hot and cold faucets are hot and cold. I have to ask Bernard if he's had the same problem. Hold on. Now that I'm leaving Madame L, how will I get to him? Who will put me under?

When I'm dressed and Ready Teddy, I find Madame L in the living room. She smiles at me and then asks Alexa to play Erik Satie's "Gymnopédie No.1."

"Do you remember this, Nick?"

I listen, but nothing comes to mind or that part of my brain that I can actually access.

"Sorry, no. Should I?"

"When you brought me to Arcueil, where Erik lived, you and I were the only people he allowed in. In those days, Erik was very eccentric. Still, you and he were pals from your student years at the Paris Conservatory, and later, you became even closer when you got Erik caught up in mysticism and had him join the Rosicrucian movement."

"The what?"

"Oh, Nick, I'm sorry, you don't remember that yet, do you? Actually, when I first wanted to know, you told me Rosicrucians were this wondrous brotherhood claiming to possess mysterious wisdom handed down from the Ancients, combining occultism, Jewish mysticism, and Christian Gnosticism."

"The Ancients, you mean vampires?"

Madame L laughs. "No, my *corazón,* there were the Ancients and then there were *the Ancients.*"

Ahh, so she speaks like a Spaniard, *muy interes-ante,* says I to myself, enjoying that I have no ear for correct pronunciation, including, I'm ashamed to say, English unless it's potty talk and gutter slang.

Madame L begins swaying to the music; I've never seen anyone sway to classical piano music.

"But these Rosicrucian characters were right down Vampire Alley, right?" I say, and she stops swaying.

"There were similarities, yes, I'm sure, and that's why you and other vampires through the ages joined the Brotherhood."

Pointing to Alexa, whose existence is weirder and more ominous than that of any band of religious fruitcakes, I say, "This music—did the Rosicrucians or the vampires inspire it?"

Madame L laughs. "Good question. Erik was never one of us, but his music was surreal and had more than hints of mysticism. If you could characterize music as inspired by the occult, his would be it."

There she goes again, referring to her being a vampire. How could that be? She's got to be in her forties, maybe fifties. For some reason, I have it in my head that all vampires look young.

Ah, that discrepancy was gnawing at me when I first suspected her of being a vampire. Then again, what do I know about the age requirements for being a vampire? That's right, fuckin' nothing!

I attempt to read Madame L, but I've lost her to the music again. Not me, my heart's not beating to the beat. And apparently not Bernard, who continues hiding somewhere in the darkest recesses of my mind.

I concentrate on the music, and you know what? It's starting to speak to me. Do you know what it's saying? Maybe Nick is Nick, and there is no Bernard?

Yeah, baby! Maybe that voice on the tape is a phony baloney, wholly made up by that dodgy Dr. Rosamund Mickeltee and kept alive by an even dodgier fortune-telling antique dealer?

I scan the room. Then why the fuck should I get out of Dodge? Leave all these beautiful things? My life as I know it isn't such a bad one if I x out the nutcase in my head, who any real shrink would certainly tell me is only a figment of some imaginary nightmare I had as a child; I'm just a regular guy, right?

Madame L's is moving even closer to Alexa.

Or, how about this for a book idea? Getting me to believe I'm a vampire is simply a devious plan to either rent this place out as an Airbnb and make some pocket change for Madame L, or the charlatan plans to sell it and make some real dough re mi?

What does PT Barnum say? 'There's a sucker born every day and two to take him?' Well, I'm the sucker, and Madame L and this Bernard character are the ones to take me.

I leave Madame L to her dancing, go into the kitchen, and dial Delicate Deliveries. The Nebbs character isn't there, but there's a Sally T with a thick Italian accent right out of *The Godfather*, who takes my call and gruffly agrees to cancel the move.

What's my plan now? That's an excellent question. Do I stay? There's the murder of Margaret Havilland and her faux cousin, Jane Meadows, to deal with. Hold the phone there, Charlie! There's not a single shred of evidence linking me to Margaret's murder, and as far as me going to Red Hook, sure, I went, but I went to IKEA, not to murder the fake cousin. Damn, I shouldn't have destroyed the meatballs.

Not to worry—I have the credit card receipt. I'm staying put; even wild horses couldn't drag me away.

FORTY-SEVEN

THE VAMPIRE DOESN'T LIVE HERE ANYMORE, A CAUTIONARY TALE

Hey, hey, don't spite your nose to save your baby blues. Staying in my apartment certainly proves I'm not running away from anyone or anything. On the other hand, if I'm innocent, there's no reason not to take a little trip to Puta Ala for a week.

Seven days in the sun ought to be good for me. Clear my head and really bake Bernard, the SOB, out of my noggin for good. And I'll be back. I'll make sure I tell the front desk to hold my mail and any Amazon packages until I return. I'll even leave the name and number of my hotel in case the building needs to reach me. If the boys in blue come by and ask, but I'm sure they won't, they'll see I'm not skipping town, just going on a bit of vacay.

What do I do about Madame L? Well, for one thing, make sure she doesn't have access to my apartment so she can't try anything funny while I'm away. When I get back, well, I'll figure it out. Whatever I do, I'll also make sure she never tries to hypnotize my ass or feed me any bullshit about Bernard or me being a vampire.

For a moment, I consider killing Madame L, but I can't think of a way to get away with it. And boy, if anyone deserves to be sliced and diced, it's a person who tries to get you to believe you're the second coming of a real-life living dead vampire just to get ownership of your apartment.

Damn, their eyes, not even the most double-dealing real estate agent would sink that low, and that's saying some from what the doormen tell me.

A temp at the front desk doesn't even glance at Madame L or me when I stroll through the lobby and head onto the street. The black Cadillac Escalade is waiting at the door. The driver hops out, grabs my wheelie, and puts it on the row of seats behind me.

I help Madame L into the back seat. "Hold it a second; I forgot to do something," I say, turning and heading back into the building, almost running into a woman with her white Terrier that I nearly kick upwards through the scaffolding and into the air.

I walk up to the desk and hand the temp an envelope containing my trip information and instructions not to let Madame L or anyone else into my apartment.

"I'm Nick Cummings in 6J. I'm going to Italy for a week to get some sun. Please make sure Carlos gets this, okay?"

"Yes, sir, Mr. Cummings. Have a nice trip."

I hop into the Escalade, which is almost as big as my bathroom. The driver turns on his GPS, and I hear a woman's voice. "In ten feet, make a right onto Madison Avenue."

"Driver, do we have to hear that all the way to the airport?"

"Company rules, but I'll make it lower, Miss."

"Thank you, Driver."

We settle back in our seats.

"I love airports, and just give me an excuse: I'm at JFK or Newark. I even like La Guardia, with all its new construction, if you must know." She squeezes my arm. "Besides, I'd never let you go off by yourself."

"Thanks, I appreciate that, Madame L."

When Madame L touches me on the hand, I feel Bernard's memory bank riding the train out of town as it travels down through my arm out through the glass window to be gobbled up by the strobing lights of the Midtown tunnel.

I'm glad to be rid of Bernard. He's such a loser. How messed up to believe you're the reincarnation of the all-powerful Pharaoh Akhenaten, ruler of the greatest empire on earth, and all you do is beat yourself up because you don't know whether it's nature or nurture that made you that way.

But, but, but—to be told you're a vampire. I admit, that disrupting piece of WakeUpAndSmellTheNightmareThatThisIsNowYourLife, threw me for a gigantic loop de loop and put my Hollywood Handsome face out of whack; okay, fucked seriously with my brain to the point I actually believed I had on an odd evening, turned into a bat and flew out of my zip code to suck out some beautiful babe's blood!

Look here, Johnny, don't give me that holier-than-thou stare. You don't believe you'll ever come 'under the evil influence'? Go to the dark side of your brain where rationality doesn't live: buy a 'can't miss' stock with your kid's tuition, bet your 401K on the 'Over' on Fan Duel, or never imagine you'll get a splash of blood lust served up with your next morning cup of joe that will make you believe you're going to live forever.

Don't believe me, do you? Then you had better watch your step while walking down these city streets. Do you feel me, Reader?

www.ingramcontent.com/pod-product-compliance
Lightning Source LLC
Chambersburg PA
CBHW071306250626
47159CB00004B/1328